The Dream Vessel

The Dream Vessel

Jeff Bredenberg

INTEGRATED MEDIA

NEW YORK

This is a work of fiction. Names, characters, places, events, and incidents either are the product of the author's imagination or are used fictitiously. Any resemblance to actual persons, living or dead, businesses, companies, events, or locales is entirely coincidental.

ISBN 978-1-4976-3726-9

This edition published in 2014 by Open Road Integrated Media, Inc.
345 Hudson Street
New York, NY 10014
www.openroadmedia.com

Prologue

HUNDREDS of years after the nuclear destruction known as Big Bang Day, humankind had crawled out of the rubble sufficiently to revive a few traditions of the ancients. Among them: dictatorship.

Interspersed among the radiation fields of the land called Merqua grew a new myriad of cities and work camps under the servitude of a secretive ruler known as the Monitor. Rumors about the Monitor were many: that he was mutant—large and bull faced; that he was centuries old; that he hoarded certain technological secrets of the ancients for his own vile purposes. These particular whisperings, as it turned out, were true.

Such a civilization has its doubters and reprobates, of course. The Revolutionaries hunkered in their remote eastern outpost, buried under a mountain in the range once known as the Blue Ridge. From there they launched their largely ineffective assaults against the repressive regime of the Monitor. Ineffective, that is, until they struck an odd alliance with the rogue magic man named Pec-Pec.

Pec-Pec was many things to many people. To the dark-skinned outcasts called Rafers, he was a god. To the common people of the work camps, he was a master of cheap theatrics and a thief. Finally, to the Monitor in his remote canyon hideout, Pec-Pec meant death.

So it was that the marginally competent Revolutionaries learned the lesson that had been surprising their counterparts for millennia: It is one thing to overthrow a despot; it is quite another to create a satisfactory Government in his place.

1

The Human Harvest

HOO! To a human's nose, it's other humans that make the worst smells. Little Tom leaned into the rail on the aft deck, as far upwind as a body could get without being trolling bait.

His eyes were red rimmed and his face dark from lack of sleep. Below deck, even with the superior ventilation of the master's cabin, the stench was just too close. For the last four nights he had slung a hammock topside and threatened the crew with a de-balling if he were disturbed. Still he slept fitfully in the cool nights, the hammock swinging in its exaggerated arc up here. His neck and shoulders were stiff.

Ach. Human reek was a haunting booger.

Now in the bright of morning, a strong breeze at his back and sipping coffee, Little Tom could at least admire his new sailing yacht, the Lucia, named after the mother he had never known. The Lucia was a handsome and odd sea beast. For a 140-footer, it was unusually broad beamed, thirty feet, and had a draft of nothing but six feet with the centerboard up. She was a bitch for any man to helm—was only for the sharpest of captains—but there was nothing afloat that could escape her hit-and-runs or catch her after the fact.

The Lucia was full sail now, 20,000 square feet of blinding white canvas bulging like the throat of an albino bullfrog. They would be home quickly, praise God, within two days. Father, Big Tom, would be at ease again with his skimming new creation in harbor. And he would be pig-grin pleased at the cargo of three-dozen red-leggers.

Little Tom sipped at the coffee and did the math in his head…nearly 325,000 centimes! Why, after a few more runs, in a year maybe, Big Tom might entrust him with the entire fleet. Commander, trade master of the Caribbean, twenty vessels harvesting the troublesome red-leggers off the Blue Islands. He would be powerful, one day, even more feared than Big Tom himself.

Oh. He had almost forgotten: Had the one red-legger died in the night—the one with the head injury, the one that went to fever the other night? He would have to ask. He refigured the bounty—still a nice haul. Too bad about the injured one, strong and handsome, might have brought a bonus. The first mate Bark had joked that the dying pig-poker looked a lot like Little Tom. Ha, there but for the grace of God….

The sea was rough enough that Little Tom had to roll out of the hammock before he was tossed out. His bare feet squeaked in the damp of the polished deck wood, and he sniffed the impossibly moist morning air. The low sun was hardly penetrating a blustery sky, an overcast like Little Tom had not seen in months.

Damn. Half a day out of home and we're going to storm.

In the master's cabin, he folded and drawered his nightclothes. Down here the lolling of the Lucia was more tolerable. Still…he padded naked to the horseshoe-shaped desk, which arced in a grandiose sweep across the forward end of the cabin. He slid open a brass latch, pulled out the top drawer, and flipped open a black-enameled cigarette box bearing his name in gold paint. He selected a fat one, fired it, and sucked the smoke into his lungs as he rubbed his neck.

It was powerful ganja, and within moments he felt the cooling ease seep through his limbs. He felt better.

Little Tom had left the cabin door open for better ventilation, and there was Bark—staring in disapprovingly.

"Helps with the nausea," Little Tom said, holding the cigarette aloft. As he spoke he exhaled a fragrant cloud.

"Storm's blowin' up," Bark grumbled. "Ya'd best tell yer tum-tum it'll be getting nothin' but worse."

Little Tom drew off the cigarette again and choked out his words as he held the smoke in: "I can swing-swang with the best of 'em. It's the red-leggers. That reek."

Bark twitched his nose, shrugged, and looked quizzically at the ceiling, as if to say, What reek?

"I tell ya, I nearly can taste it, a scum in my gut," Little Tom said. In his blooming euphoria, he had nearly forgotten his nakedness. He glared down at himself in mock surprise, then pulled on a pair of full-length khakis in anticipation of a cool day. The cigarette smoldering between his lips was developing a precarious ash.

The first mate turned to go, but Little Tom stopped him with "Ho, up!"

"Yeah?"

"There's a red-legger, down ta slot twenty or so. A girl, slender, shaved head. In the slot right beside the guy with the gawdawful tattoo, the man with the head crack. She's pretty...."

"Ya, so?" Bark felt an ill mood descending like a shroud. He had mated for Big Tom since he was this age, and the old man had always insisted: No ganja by day, and no sampling the merchandise. Bark was stalling. He wiped his nostrils with thumb and forefinger, then ran them through his graying beard. He would wait, make the boy say it.

Little Tom sucked the diminishing cigarette again. "Bring her here. Please. In ankle irons, so she won't try much."

Bark spat—an offense that would earn him a flogging had Big Tom witnessed it. But this little whip wouldn't dare. "Okay," he said. "But the injured one. One with the crack—weren't you wondering?"

"Oh. Yes, how is he?"

"If we can get underway today, I figure he'll make it to port. But not by much."

"Ah, good," Little Tom replied. "We'll be underway soon, then. I'd be skinny to make port with a vacant slot, no?"

Bark turned away toward the slot holds, but scowled back over his shoulder, not so sure about getting underway in this weather.

Little Tom was sprawled on the master's bunk, his hairless chest bare as he stared at the ceiling. He heard her enter, the sound of chain dragging against flooring. "Hmn," he said, rolling his head to the side, and then he considered how her looks had changed since she was captured ten days ago. Shackles never did much for human beauty—the eyes grew dark circles, the skin drained pale. The longer a red-legger stayed in the hold the worse the damage—and the lower the price at market. Longer expeditions were impractical, a matter of diminishing returns. Not unlike shipping vegetables, he mused.

"You gully English?" he asked. "Ya don' look to be a Northland runner."

The woman said nothing. Her hair had grown to a quarter inch of stubble, and she squinted now into the glare of the cabin's lavish portholes.

He tried again. "Bark. Big man, Bark, the mate, where is he?"

This she seemed to understand—they all knew the big one with the easy name, Bark. She gestured vaguely toward the door and then upward.

Little Tom swung his feet over the bunk's side and stood. His chest felt full and invigorated. In his pants there was a stirring of anticipation he would soon satisfy, but first...he bounded to the door and up the ladder and thrust his torso through the hatch.

"Ho, mate! Bark!"

"Ya, captain?" Bark had been in conversation with the navigator, a palsied old crust, apparently about the rising weather—they were in very familiar seas now, and charting would not be a concern.

"Are ya ready to set sail, mate?" Little Tom asked.

A snarl twisted Bark's bushy upper lip and then vanished just as quickly. He motioned for the navigator to follow him from the backboard rail to the hatch—to hear their young leader's foolishness. A witness.

"Captain..." Bark let the word fall somewhere between respect and sarcasm. "Captain, I say we stay at anchor for the blow-over. We'll lose not but half a day, sir."

Little Tom felt his gut tighten and his face harden. Slowly he placed his left fist on the deck in front of him, near the sailors' knotty bare feet. "Bark," he said evenly, calculated to sound near-bursting with fury, "I want all sails set now, all sails. Anchor up inside of fifteen."

"Ya, Little Tom," the creaky navigator said. "Full sail inside of fifteen." The old man pulled at Bark's elbow and they strode away to bellow their orders into the rising wind.

Little Tom backed down the ladder and returned to his cabin. The young woman was hunched over the wash basin, timidly admiring a round porcelain water jug mounted on the wall with a teeter hinge. She ran a forefinger over its pearl-like smoothness and studied the hinge and clamp around the jug's stem neck. She seemed unsure how the mechanism worked, but certain the vessel contained that most precious of substances, fresh water.

A floorboard creaked under Little Tom's feet, and the bristle-haired woman leapt back, gasping, "Oh, gawd!"

Little Tom laughed. "Now we do have some English there, don' we?" She didn't answer, but backed away from him until she stumbled into the bunk. She gasped again, seeming to fear her hands might have soiled the sheets.

"It's okay," Little Tom said, murmuring in the tone he would use to soothe a jittery horse. "It's a water jug, and we'll have a sip here, wash your face. Here."

He walked calmly to the basin and grabbed the jug by its neck. "You don't have to take it off the wall at all. Just tilt it up, like this...." He cupped his left palm and splashed it full, then held the dripping hand up for her to see. "Here. C'mon. Here."

Her eyes widened and her dried lips parted to emit a sticky clucking sound. Instinctively she stepped forward, then stopped, suspicious. Her yellow-glazed eyes met Little Tom's, then she shrugged—what the hell. Nervously, she tipped the jug, threw the water at her face and open mouth, and returned her hand again and again in a series of splashes. Her T-shirt and cutoff trousers were blotched dark now, and rivulets of water cut clean, pink lines down her grimy legs and pooled at her feet.

Little Tom grinned broadly as he watched the impromptu shower. All around them the yacht was creaking alive as the sails were hoisted, and that, too, lifted his spirits. A sailboat lolling at anchor had a groaning lethargy about it. But now... ah, now with the sails filling, the sheets grown taut, the mast empowered, the timbers shifting into the tension they were designed for—it was not unlike a sexual awakening.

The pig-pokin' runt. Shouldn'ta be allowed in a bathtub alone, nary less captain a sea skimmer like this 'un. Huhn. Smoke-head. Dancin' on his willie below decks while we put sail into a storm. Hoo. Pig-pokin' runt....

Bark had worked through his anger enough to be functional, and now he was carrying out the orders to the letter. The low, dark hump of Dunkin Island nearby appeared and vanished again in the mists. Here and there the roiling clouds parted to show whisps of dull blue sky—maybe it wouldn't be so bad after all. And home soon. He softened more. Home soon—Ma and the little ruggers, a good sousin' tonight.

"Har, ya there, up anchor," he shouted to the two decksmen that weren't manning the sheets. At once they were abreast of the aft winch, cranking the metal muscle furiously. The sails were cracking in the bluster and the Lucia's entire structure murmured. The deck shifted with abrupt jolts.

Bark cursed and looked to the sky again, then southwest out to sea. And he froze, first not comprehending, then disbelieving. Fear gripped an icy claw around his heart. He about-faced, filled his lungs to the bursting point, and screamed, “Drop sail! Drop saaaail!”

The ancient navigator, mid-deck by the wheel, whipped around thinking he could not have heard right. He looked beyond the wild-eyed, howling first mate and saw for himself. His toothless jaw dropped open.

A gust of wind may be fairly invisible, but it colors the water with fine, dark rippling. It tears across the sea looking like a giant school of fish, dotting the surface the way an impressionist painter stipples a canvas. An alert sailor can easily adjust to meet such a burst of wind with the proper angling or sailset.

But this was not a normal gust. It was a killer squall blown from the gut of Satan himself. It was upon them, dragging the sea like Death’s coattail.

Later, Bark would remember the next two seconds with slow-motion clarity. One of the main sheets, a hemp rope the thickness of a man’s wrist, snapped like twine. The freed sail corner whipped that halyard across the deck, neatly slicing through the navigator’s midsection. Still agape, the old navigator fell in two, torso splashing to the deck and legs and pelvis standing, then wobbling onto the knees, then sliding into the backboard rail as the yacht careened onto its side.

The hollow-center, steel-reinforced mast snapped without protest, and the sails, some of them one-eighth inch thick, fluttered onto the water like tissue paper.

Bark was airborne, catapulted by the Lucia’s twisting deck. Then he was under water, his back wrenched by the impact. He clawed at the foam and murk, inhaled in pain and gagged on the salt water. Bark flailed again, broke surface this time and bit the air. Coughed, spat. Breathed.

The Lucia was still listing perilously. As Bark watched he heard, amid the wind blast and human cries, a dark rumbling in the yacht’s hull. He knew—he could almost see it. Her ballast, a slender mound of lead bars, had shifted and broken out of their bins. Now, even with the wind dying, the Lucia could not right herself again. Most likely, the lead bars had pounded a hole in her hull, and she would be taking on water now.

Bark peeled off his trousers slowly, mindful of a newly pulled muscle throbbing in the small of his back. He tied a knot at each cuff, blew several lungsful of air into the waist end of the pants, and tied it shut with his rope belt. The makeshift float would help for a few minutes, anyway.

The first mate looked again. Yes, the Lucia was sinking, her backboard rail mostly under water. He wondered what it would be like to be below deck right now, wearing leg irons.

2

A Meeting

"WHAT we really need is a very large ship."

Rosenthal Webb's words boomed over the chatter in the Revolutionary Council meeting room. The other conversations withered. Surprised faces turned toward the old warrior. Virginia Quale was standing at the front of the room where she had tacked up a map of Merqua's eastern sectors (from New Chicago to the coast, for the most part). Her hand dropped away from the map, and her lips pressed into an impatient corrugated circle.

"I was attempting a discussion of rail lines, Mr. Webb," she said. "The tracks what you and your boys were detonating just a year ago must be laid new now if we're to have sufficient supply lines."

As was his habit, Webb drummed the four finger nubs of his right hand against the dark polish of the conference table. He repeated himself: "But what we really need is a large ship. Ta cross the Big Ocean. It's been our policy long-standing that we would assess what has become of the other continents if we ever came free of the Monitor."

Winston Weet thrust his round face out over the table to interject. He waved a hand toward the map. "The Monitor's nay dead but a few months," he said, jowls waggling.

"There's a mountain of arrangements to be made before we dare announce our new...uh, proprietorship of Merqua."

"And priorities," said Eliot Kohrn, the dark-eyed man to Webb's left. Kohrn rarely spoke up in the large council meetings, but felt more comfortable as long as he did not have to compete with the babble of three or four people at a time. "Shouldn't we repair our homeland afore we off an' tip-toe through some foreign radiation fields? There are the work camps to set to voluntary, no? The timber camps, hmm? The farm camps? Slavers to scuttle?"

Webb fell back against his chair impatiently, pushing a long sigh out his nostrils. His skin flushed red, giving an odd glow to the tendril of a fresh tattoo that wound around his neck. He said no more.

Quale looked uneasy. "Um, Winston, I gully you have a report on our infiltration of management in New Chicago? Would you give the briefing now, please?"

Winston Weet obediently rattled open a folder of papers as Quale strode to the hatch leading into the hallway. Before disappearing through the small door, she stared in Webb's direction, arching her eyebrows. The aging Revolutionary caught the signal, pushed away from the conference table, and limped out after her.

The black-lacquered piping against the hallway ceiling gave just enough clearance to allow Webb to stand erect. But he hunched down anyway, looking like a schoolboy about to be punished.

Knowing the direction that the conversation would take, Webb started in himself: "Well, I never did pretend to be a detail man—sit there an' plant railroad ties or whatever."

Quale did not look perturbed now, just concerned. "Rose, there is much to do yet," she said. "How can we justify the expense of commissioning an ocean craft—even if there were a builder what knew how? There are boat builders here and there, ya, but none that's made a ship like that. Not since the ancients self-destructed."

Her words echoed away down the dark corridor. The two Revolutionaries, the tired bomber and the graceful administrator of headquarter operations, could hear Winston Weet droning on in the conference room about Revolutionaries taking on responsible positions in New Chicago.

It was not like Webb to be without a quick response, and Quale read mischief in his eyes.

"Okay," she demanded, "what is it?"

Webb shrugged.

"What is it? You've done something, no?"

Webb nodded. "I sent Gregory out. Sent 'im to find a boat builder in the Out Islands."

Quale's eyes widened. "Any boat builder out there is a pirate, most likely. Or a slaver. Either one would deserve ta hang, but you would like to keep one in business?"

Webb nodded again. "You're worried about spending money on a ship? Well, I gully a slaver would hammer us a fine one free of charge—juss to keep his balls swinging where they ought."

Quale frowned. "Gregory's gone. Hoo. I guess there's no surprise that you'd proceed without council approval. But we're going to stop with this, Rose. When Gregory returns to report, nothing more happens until a full council vote. Understood? Ya?"

Webb nodded his head in unenthusiastic consent. Quale kissed him quickly on the chin and thrust herself back through the hatch into the meeting room. Webb almost followed, but decided against it. Instead, he followed the corridor until he came to the metal ladder disappearing into holes in the floor and ceiling.

He climbed down two floors to Level Five, hand over hand on the steel that gleamed from decades of wear. It occurred to him that its usefulness was coming to an end—the whole smothering under-the-mountain complex would no longer be needed for hiding once it was announced that the Monitor had been killed. A month, maybe—four or five at most. The bunker smelled dank to him now, rotting.

On Level Five, he paced wearily down the circular hall past the identical plank doors until he came to his small, private warren. He pushed it open, slammed the door after him, and tore off his shirt furiously, letting the buttons clatter to the floor. Webb turned up the dim bulb over his dresser—overtaxed generator be damned—and checked himself out in the spotty mirror.

His new tattoo was 100 percent now—all of the scabbing had fallen away to reveal a large swirl of red, yellow and black. Its core was an intricate cross-hatching of color three inches wide on his lower chest. Four tendrils spiraled away from the center to wind around his neck, under each arm and into his crotch.

He turned to the side and squinted, admiring the artistry—damned Rafer artistry. The tattoo was a souvenir of his last mission, the killing of the Monitor. They had given him no more choice about having it needled into his skin than he'd had in losing four fingers years before. He recalled the dark-skinned fighter Tha 'Enton returning to his Rafer encampment victoriously, a partner in the killing of the foul Monitor. Naively, Webb and Gregory had followed the strutting Rafer, anticipating a celebration. The entire night was a druggy blur, but Webb was thankful to have left the village alive, albeit decorated.

The lightbulb dimmed abruptly, then returned to full power. In a pang of guilt, Webb set the lamp's switch back to its lowest setting and flopped onto his bunk. He stared at the ceiling and wondered how Gregory was faring—a young man set adrift so quickly into yet another strange land. A young man with so much life ahead of him. A long life to live as a walking Rafer tapestry.

3

The Tempting Twins

BIG Tom was daydreaming. Pinned to one of the oversized drafting tables in his office was a schematic of his latest creation, the Lucia. He could take in everything from here: this penciled beaut tacked down before him, and the shipyard outside where she was actually built—the past, present and future.

He leaned his large belly into his walking stick and again and again savored every detail of sailing perfection. A shipbuilder may father hundreds of handsome and servicable craft in his good years, but rarely does he experience the sweet satisfaction of having spared nothing—time, materials and design—to build a skimmer absolutely right. The Lucia, he told himself, was the perfect blending of the forces of nature and the needs of man.

Just below there in the shipyard, over the veranda rail and down near the bay, were the drydocks where she painstakingly took shape. It was the ideal, linear shipbuilding layout: From the offload dock, into the yard of lumberstock, into the millhouse, and out to the construction yard, the long and awkward timbers never needed to be turned, not even at a right angle, on their path to becoming a sea skimmer.

It was from this office that Big Tom watched the Lucia's

delicate skeleton rise and her graceful body fill in over the months. Meticulous craftsmen would spare no effort under the burning scrutiny of the Caribbean's most powerful—and brutal, some say—tradesman. And just down the dock from the shipyard was the empty slip that the Lucia would return to any day now with new cargo. Maybe even this afternoon.

For a monied man like Big Tom it took a conscious effort to maintain the casual, bare-wood atmosphere in his office. He liked the dirt-kick quality. One of his wives would appear at the rear entrance with a northland wool rug, or a porcelain nude maybe—some campaign to bring civilization to the workplace. His hands would flutter like spooked herons—"Blast it! Take it to the mainhouse." And then her face would wilt into a scowl and he'd have to figure out how to make it up to her. Some nice smoke, or the powder, maybe.

He liked it here—the weathered-gray planking, the encircling veranda and the louvered doors pushed open on all sides. Here, he could think like a seaman, not some blubber-butt monk.

Out the east and west windows loomed the steep slopes of Crown Mountain, arcing around to form the bay, God's amphitheater. His office was a simple structure set into the base of the mountain, stilts out front, one story, a roof done in curved red tile salvaged from one of the ancient hotels gone to rot. From this spartan shelter he commanded Thomas Island and the largest known shipping line, Thomas Exports.

Big Tom lit a cigarette—fine mainland tobacco, machine rolled even, one of the silly luxuries he had come to allow himself. He exhaled, and the satisfying sting webbed onto the tip of his tongue. He was turning his jowly face back to the schematic of the Lucia when Bishop shuffled in on sandals, drawstring pants low on his gaunt hips.

"You look pounded," Big Tom said. "'Nother night sucking ale bottles at Sanders's, I'd say." His jaw muscles bulged rhythmically. He drew again on the cigarette. "Well, we can't have it both ways—can we?—your kinda social life, and on toppa that a job what's supposed to start at first light. You look pounded! Like New York City musta looked on Big Bang Day."

Bishop, five feet tall, rolled his eyes up at Big Tom painfully. "Sorry," he muttered. He was walking haltingly toward a round table in the corner, as if he had an equal limp in each leg. There a beaker of hot coffee perched on its rack over a candle stub. Big Tom watched the slow agony, the quivering hand taking the beaker and pouring sloppy spurts into a stained mug.

Bishop slurped, paused, felt no better, and slurped again. "I am sorry ta be late on ya," he said. His eyes stared dully into the room at nothing in particular. Bishop seemed to be searching in misery for each word, even the easy ones. "It was really work, ya know, ya could look at it like that—I was doin' a job what needed doing, that mess with the tug captain."

Big Tom's face relaxed, the folds of flesh easing down again. "You were working on our problematic Captain Bull? What, got 'im drunk—now he's hung over as you? Wouldn't be the first time he took to sea hung over, I'd say." He pointed a fat finger out the window. "The Lucia's still not in, ya see. If you bought us any time at all, well it ain't enough."

Bishop looked hurt. "I done better." He slurped. "I done better than that. I tole him we need a day was all, and he said no. He's got a Government schedule up and down the mainland coast what he can't break. He doesn't care that we got forty some red-leggers coming in any minute—that we'd have to feed 'em for a month 'fore he got back. Said he'd leave today with whatever we got already, he'd put off with an empty barge or two if he had to. These Government guys...."

Big Tom was nodding. He heaved into the walking stick, hobbling to a chair where he sat heavily and picked at the stuffing. "We hold red-leggers a month in the cells they'd rot away. Subtract the cost of feeding 'em well...." He stared at the ceiling, calculating. "They wouldn't be worth coconuts by time we sold 'em. Government wouldn't give us coconuts for 'em, nope. Timing, this business is timing. Some day, mayhap, the day will come that we can touch mainland with our own ships, our own cargoes, and pig-poke the Government. Ach."

"Ya, I tole him all that about the feed costs, and he didn't give a whit," Bishop said. "So I says to him that it's okay. We value his business—our official pipeline to the mainland—so much that we wanted him to have a send-off present, even if he couldn't wait."

Big Tom stopped picking at the stuffing. His eyebrows rose.

"Two fourteen-year-olds. Twins. I tole him I knew two teeners what would service him in any way was his pleasure."

"Girls or boys?"

"Girls. So I says let's have a few beers at Sanders's Shebeen, they gonna meet us there sometime, I dunno when...."

"You don't know any twins like that. Not on Thomas Island."

"But he don't know that." Bishop gulped now at the coffee. It was cooler. "So we get piss drunk at Sanders's waiting for the two kids—'Where are they?' I keep saying. 'They'll be here in a bit, I'll buy a couple more ales meantime.'"

Big Tom was starting to see it now. "I feel a fight coming on...."

Bishop grinned slightly through his stupor. "Right," he said. "Eventually, Captain Bullshit is coming back from the can, zipping up with one hand an' a bottle in the other. He's taking a swig an' he bumps into a table where Eric and Larry—the shrimpers?—they're playing chess and a coupla pieces get knocked over. And then Captain Bull gets knocked over and—well, when he wakes up today, he'll find himself in the brig owing Sanders 10,000 centimes for damages."

"There isn't 10,000 worth in the whole shebeen. If you broke every chair and every bottle, well, 5,000 centimes at most."

"Ya, but that's what Sanders is asking, 10,000. Hey, it could take days to negotiate him down. An' you gotta talk to the brigsman today—none of this bend-rules-for-the-captain, uh-uh."

"So Sanders and Eric and Larry are all in on this."

"Oh ya. It was quite a trick movin' that table in that captain's way, but we'd a gotten a fight going somehow."

4

Big Bang Day

TYM disliked this foolishness. She was not trained to be a teacher, had no inclination to be one. But every few months, her name came up in the rotation to fill in for Lupa and Manfred, the real teachers who seemed quite talented at escaping the classroom.

She would much rather be spearing boar, or plucking lobster off the sea floor. Anything but the classroom, those twenty sets of moist noses and wide eyes demanding wisdom. The little ruggers filled four collapsible benches under an open-air tent, which was dyed varied shades of green and brown to hide it amid the jungle vegetation. Collapsible was a dominant concept when you moved every few weeks, dodging enemies and following food.

"Todaaaay…." She let the word linger, as an announcement that the lessons were beginning. Finally even Pilsey, the jumpy six-year-old, had her grubby hands folded primly. "Today, we are going to talk about destructivism. Does anyone know what destructivism is?"

Silence.

Patiently, she began to pace in front of the class. She hooked her thumbs into her cut-off trousers and patted her long brown fingers against her thighs. She was bald, or nearly so—just a couple of days' growth. Being out of the sun, she wore no shirt.

"You talked about it before..."

"What, Jim-Jim?" She turned quickly. The older kid, maybe twelve, the one with no left hand, had said something.

"You talked about it before...."

"Yes, Jim-Jim, I discussed destructivism the last time that I was honored with teaching duty. But do you remember my rule? I want you to speak up when you have something to say—speak up loudly. But before you do, please raise your hand. I'll know to watch your lips. Remember, ah don' hear so good." She thrust her hip out and propped her right hand on it.

Giggles.

Tym pointed. "What, Luci?"

"Ummm...ah don' hear so WELL," squeaked Luci, the little one down front, naked except for sandals.

"Correct. Yes. I don't hear so well. Now, Jim-Jim, please define destructivism."

"It's..." His voice was croaking, sounding like it hurt. "It's, well, that things are getting worse."

"Well, not quite. There's more."

"Well, there was the Big Fire! Hundreds of years ago. The bombs that blew up most the mainland."

Tym was beckoning now, waving her hand in little strokes—come on, come on, come on—her eyes fixed on his rippling mouth. But Jim-Jim seemed to have run out of knowledge.

"Okay," Tym said, "that was very good, as far as you went. But you were lacking one idea: That sometimes things have to get bad, there must be destruction, before things can get any better. Out of destruction—historically, over long periods of time—comes progress. And this idea, this theeeeory, is called...what?"

Jim-Jim's hand shot up: "The Big Bang Theory!"

"Right." Maybe teaching wasn't so bad.

Tym adjusted the mirror again. She cursed the incorrigible

spin it seemed to have, dangling as it did from the overhead cross brace of her tent. When the mirror seemed nearly still, she dragged her stool a few inches to the left to follow the reflection. This repeated action had left several sets of zigzagging lines in the dirt.

She raised the straight razor again, head dipped, eyes on the glass, and proceeded to shave her head in short scrapes. She winced, slapped her hand into the pot of boar fat, smeared it onto her bristly dome, then started anew.

This could take half an hour, she knew, maybe more. Shave a little patch, stop the spin, drag the stool, shave. One of the extravagances of her youth—oh, ten years ago—had been braids down to her tailbone. But now practicality ruled. Just while swimming, the drag caused by hair merited the shaving. But add to that the danger of entangling it while sprinting through the island bramble—or of giving an enemy something to grab.

Every few days she dutifully chased her mirror around the tent. There was an answer to this foolishness of the spinning mirror, of course. Hanging the mirror from two strands of twine, not one. She would work on that—hoo, any day now—next time she found the spare minutes to hunt down the string.

Later, Tym would not think of the next sequence of events as continous time. She would remember it in a series of three vivid snapshots.

First, there was the numbing roar—an explosion of green tent canvas, singed rope, smoke and fire.

Second, unaccountably mobile, she was on her feet and bounding across the suddenly hellish tent yard toward the jungle.

Third, trapped. Flailing in a net like a frantic beast in the dark. Then a large mean weight fell upon her, another human, maybe two or three, and there was a flash of steel—in her own hand. Tym was going down in a hard way, but someone else was going to be sorry he had tackled a wild animal holding a shaving razor.

When she came to, Tym found herself shackled to a bench in the belly of a slave ship called the Lucia.

5

A Bloody Problem

QUINCE was wondering how to make himself bleed—preferably in the least painful, least obvious way. He sat naked on the mattress, really a large burlap sack filled with dried grass. He studied his dark skin, the veins in his arms, his legs, and his ankles, which were red rimmed from shackles. How would he draw blood?

He had told Dirk the plan, and now Dirk was squatting, looking exasperated in the far corner of the cell under the barred window. "Brains of a pig," he muttered, "you got the brains of a pig. Worse than that. You got pig shit for brains. Pig shit."

Quince studied the room again and found nothing of help: whitewashed cinder block walls, rebuilt from the ruin of some ancient hotel; two mattresses; a tiny window with Thomas Bay visible outside if you stand on tiptoe; the door, thick steel with a food tray slot; empty plates. The plates. Maybe he could bend one of the tin plates until it broke. He could slash himself with the jagged edge.

No. Ach. He hated this. He was a scribe, not a warrior or hunter. He hated blood, especially his own, and he hated pain. This made him think of doctors—their leeches and fever rooms and scalpels. He remembered himself as a little rugger in the waiting room of a doctor, a vile old bloodletter who seemed to thrive on fear and agony. When the doctor's assistant pushed through the door and motioned for him, little Quince had fallen forward in a dead faint onto the planking. His nose had broken, and ever since...ah, this was the answer, of course: Ever since, his nose had bled very easily!

He stood and snatched up an empty cup from the floor by the door. "Dirk, I have it. You will punch me in the nose. I will bleed, easily, I know it. Like Waterfall of the Wise—and it will only hurt a little."

Dirk still looked perturbed, but he pushed away from the back wall and stopped at an arm's length from Quince.

"I won't do it," Dirk said. He stared now at the floor, embarrassed to refuse his friend and cell mate, a fellow Rafer. "Your plan is dangerous—it will get you killed. They say we will be boated to the mainland any day now, so why not wait? On the mainland, there will be more places to run. On this island you will be found quickly."

Quince had been holding the cup under his face expectantly, but he frowned now and dropped his hand. "If we leave the islands, I'm afraid that we'll never see home again," he said grimly. "What is the word now—how many have died among us? Ten? More?"

And then Quince's vision was filled with a large brown fist, followed by a blinding light. He found himself on his back, staring at a cockroach on the ceiling. Tiny streams of moisture ran across his face and down his throat. There was a grumbly voice, Dirk's, and his head had not cleared enough to gully the meaning: "You bleed beautifully, my friend. Now go out and get yourself killed."

Jay-Jay was gnawing on his eighth pork rib when the screaming started. The portly young man slammed the bone to his plate, shoved his chair back and huffed himself to his feet.

He was locked into this corridor of malodorous green carpet, and it was his job—with no arms but a billy-banger—

to cruise up and down the row of steel doors delivering food, emptying slop buckets and handling the miscellany. Screaming red-leggers—that was miscellany.

The guard waddled down the hall, licking barbecue sauce from the stubble on his upper chin. A sweat mark crossed his broad shoulder blades in the shape of his chair back. He knew it was cell 243, those two red-leggers Dirk and Quince hollering their fool heads off. Hold a gang of pig-pokers for weeks like this, you get to know the voices. Even if they don't know any English, you know 'em by the sound.

He threw the crossbar back and opened the window. Dirk, the dumber one, was right there by the window practically spitting in Jay-Jay's face, for crissake. He was slapping his stomach frantically and pointing at Quince, who was rolling on the floor. On and on, Dirk was blathering in that Rafer tongue of theirs, sounding like, "Blad-de-la-de-la-de-la-de...."

"Back! Back ginst the wall!"

They don't know English much, but they know that anyway. Dirk edged back, still gibbering.

"What's a matter wichu, boy?" Jay-Jay shouted. That one on the floor, that one Quince, was always a pussy. "My Mama's slop gone to your tummy, Quincey-poo? Huh? Get up, jerkoff."

Quince lifted his head a little, all grimy from the floor, to look up at the window. He does look pretty pitiful, Jay-Jay thought, and what's that—stomach convulsions? Gawd, I don't want ta clean up more barf today. Pleeeease don't barf.

Just then Quince retched crimson down his chin and onto the concrete.

Jay-Jay's stomach tightened, and he worried about holding down his own dinner. He slammed the window shut, locked it, and ran down the corridor, making the floor quake. We'll be needing a stretcher for this one. And Big Tom's gonna be piss-angry if we lose another red-legger 'fore they ship off.

6

Taking Liberties

SANDERS Lafitte cracked the cap off a Liberty Ale and set the brown pint bottle in front of the mainlander named Farmington. Farm, as he was called by people who were not friends (the familiarity irritated him), scraped a fleck of cork from the lip of the bottle and tipped it back against his mouth. He sighed, and leaned onto his forearms against Sanders's oak bar.

"Someday," Farmington said, "I am going to ship you down a proper electric icebox—we've been manufacturing them for years. It would cost, of course, bringing it all this far. But I'd jump your mama for a cold, really cold ale right now...."

Down the bar, Eric opened his eyes. He pushed cigar smoke out his nostrils in contempt and lifted his chin off his shoulder. His beard came away looking matted and lopsided.

"Talkin' money, there, just you be careful with that bottle you're swinging about so la-de-da. You drop it, bust it—well whatcha think, Sanders? A thousand centimes?"

Sanders rolled his eyes toward the rafters.

"Things've changed, Farm, since you were here lass...uh, last. Um, since you last had a lass." As Eric straightened up, his drunkenness became fully apparent. "Juss one little ol' fight in here and alla sudden Sanders wants 10,000 centimes! Hah! Just fer breaking a few bottlès."

"Shut up." Sanders was wiping a glass.

Eric frowned and shakily checked his own ale bottle, finding it still empty. Sanders produced a full one for him, gratis, and changed the subject.

"These are cellar-cooled—just right, I say. Grew up on it. Any colder would kill the taste. Besides, there is an ice machine here on Thomas, remember. You brought it down, Dr. Scaramouch set it up for Big Tom in the mainhouse. And Big Tom, you know, he'd lend out ice if there was need for it."

Farmington wiped his mouth. He was a frail young man, black haired, pale skinned, strangely moist in the face, and there were many on Thomas Island who thought of him as more woman than man. His stay on Thomas Island was longer than usual this trip, as his transporter, Captain Bull, was having to settle some unexpected legal matters. Between his catalogue deliveries, there was little to do but sop up ale at Sanders's Shebeen.

"Dr. Scaramouch!" he said warmly. "I've brought the chemicals he ordered."

Eric hooted and wavered on his stool. Farmington's eyebrows rose in twin arcs, asking the broad question—what now?

"The chemicals!" Eric gulped, set the bottle down, and stared blankly ahead. "Here we got a blood business—blood, flesh, hair and bones. We sell 'em to the Government, them that we don't kill in the process. But fine! We gots the chemicals for the doctor—the chemicals not to heal, but to make pretty pictures. Dr. Scaramouch takes the clicker box you sold him and he takes the por-trait of one of the pretty Mrs. Big Toms, some harlot or other, and one of the wood whits will make a nice frame for it while he's not bleedin' fingers over a boat...."

The bar had fallen into that dead silence reserved for blasphemy.

"They're just red-leggers," muttered Farmington, the defensive mainlander.

"Ah, red-leggers, red-leggers, red-leggers." Eric drummed his forefingers against the bar. "Farm. Mr. Farmington, you ain't been at this long enough to even remember ten years ago in this business. But do ya hear talk of the red-leggers—way it used ta be? I hunted red-leggers back then—back when red-leggers was the runners from the Government. Had gen-u-wine rings 'round their legs from the shackles they broke on the mainland. You knew that? Now—hoo, now—Big Tom'll take anybody, native islanders. Hey, sell 'em to the Government. Work those farms southland 'til they dead. Work those farms, ey Farm? Hah."

Eric pulled on the soggy end of his cigar and pushed another cloud of smoke out his nose.

Moori lit Big Tom's cigarette, one of those machine-rolled numbers, and he eased back into the hammock where he could watch his feet swing up into the night and down again, back and forth.

"The boy will be home tomorrow," she said sweetly, reassuringly. "I can just feel it."

Ah, late evening on the mainhouse veranda. He rattled his glass—the wet clatter of rare ice cubes in whiskey—but he didn't want to sit up to drink. "God's honest truth, I don't think I miss Little Tom, the twit, af as much as I miss the Lucia."

"What a father you are...."

"Hey..." He grabbed at her standing there and playfully pulled at the bottom hem of her blouse so that he could see in. "We're talking about Little Tom, 'member."

"Okay, okay. But...oh yeah, Billister is at the grand door tonight. Sent me up to tell you the doctor is here." She pulled her blouse out of his fingers and spread it down even, patiently.

"Scaramouch?"

"You got the crabs again, or is he taking your picture these days?"

Big Tom was frowning. "Neither."

"Billister says he seems to have been printing pictures again—he has an envelope, a large one."

"Well, go get him for me, now would you?" he said, growing irritable. "We'll see what this one is all about, then tell Billister no more visitors, rest of the night." He watched her go, admiring her little ass and long legs, remembering what they looked like in bed. He liked his time alone with her.

Minutes later, Big Tom watched Dr. Scaramouch march importantly through the master bedroom onto the veranda, and there was that smell—something like cough syrup, a sickening odor he not only associated with the old doctor, but with needles, bleedings, polstices, and vomit. As important as it was to have a physician on the island, Big Tom was always queasy in close proximity to Dr. Scaramouch.

The doctor was as wide as Big Tom himself, but taller, and his salt-and-pepper beard gyrated now, a nervous habit. "Ah, Lashmaster! Good evening. Oh, a criminally good view of the bay from here."

Big Tom looked weary. "Lashmaster?"

The doctor cleared his throat. "Oh, harmless imaginin'. Think of bein' a lad on a longboat, or a scrootman on a skimmer. And always loomin' above is the strutting captain, Big Tom, the Lashmaster." He aspirated the words with as much genteel emotion as he could muster, but Big Tom still looked sour. "But nevermind. I'm bringing here a gift, just tonight mounted, and I'll drop it and run." The doctor waggled the large envelope under his right arm.

"It is a photo then?"

"Oh, well ya, a photo," the rotund physician said. "Of your beloved."

"Not Moori again."

"No. Hah! The Lucia. And you with her."

Dr. Scaramouch rattled the envelope open and drew out a gray matt board bearing a photograph of a dry-docked skimmer, nearly completed. It seemed to have been taken from above, meaning the doctor had stationed himself up

Crown Mountain somewhere with one of those telephotic lenses he'd ordered recently from the mainland.

Yes, it was the Lucia. Big Tom squinted in the poor light. "You say I'm in there somewhere?"

"Oh, ya. It was the Sunday before she launched. See, I had figured it was 'bout the last time to catch her out of the water for a year or two. Look there—the rigging's nearly all in place. And what surprise, but when I have the tripod set I see through the lens that it's you on that day you decided to work the skimmer yourself."

Big Tom's forehead rose appreciatively.

"That's you there." The doctor pointed a chubby finger, his beard bobbing excitedly. "Top deck, with a crate in your arms, loading down ta the holds, if I remember right. You and Bishop that day."

Big Tom sat up abruptly, spilling a splash of his drink. He grabbed one side of the photograph roughly and squinted. "Blime," the merchant said. Then he smiled. "You caught me at manual labor—can't have the crew 'er the wood whits see that, can we? Ha!"

Dr. Scaramouch laughed uneasily. "No, I guess you'll have to frame it yourself, huh? And keep her in the mainhouse, yer study maybe, then."

Big Tom looked at the wet splotch in his lap. "Moori! Hey, Moori!" Then he smirked, confiding to Dr. Scaramouch, "Perhaps she'll lick it up, no?"

Big Tom gulped from the glass and sucked in the night cool of his walled garden. All around him in a circle against the wall, mango and orange trees hunched against the starry sky. He stood in the precise center of the dark yard, at the intersection of two meandering paths. Forward, backward, left and right through the lush shrubbery, the tracks built of polished white stones faded into the night, looking like narrow beaches. Twenty-five years ago he had gazed down at his own blueprint for this garden and had imagined himself standing at the hub of a huge whirling pinwheel.

The thought returned to him nightly when he came down from the mainhouse for his meditative stroll.

Big Tom turned his head left, then right, and reviewed the collection of memories here, a gallery of ghosts assembled over the decades. Over there, for example: Bolted neckhigh to the orange tree at the center of the south wall was one of his favorite toys, a garrote. It was a fearsomely simple device—an iron collar that could be fastened to a prisoner's neck and tightened by a wing nut at the side. Slowly, if there were questions to be answered. Quickly, if he was feeling merciful.

Big Tom swallowed hard, twice, and felt the stubble of his throat. The garrote. That was how he had acquired Billister, the house boy. It was, oh, fifteen years ago (how old was Billister?). Billister's mother, Megan-Do, was a red-legger—had stolen a dory in desperation, but a skimmer found them after three days adrift. Nearly dead from exposure, she and her little boy. Even so weakened, the bitch Megan-Do left the world loudly, and Big Tom remembered turning the screw quickly to shut her up.

The boy grew up in the kitchen running errands, the only human Big Tom owned for any length of time, despite being in the business. All others he traded quickly. He made a mental note to find out when Billister's birthday was.

He dropped the daydream and walked southeast, crunching through the chill darkness over the white stones, breathing in the alternating odors of fruit trees, roses and rhododendron. Where the south and east walls met he came to a low hut built of long slabs of stone. He took the lamp hung by the door and lit it, turned the lock with his key and pushed.

The dank air was scented generously by the tall bins of topsoil and leaf mulch. Big Tom kicked back to close the door and stepped past the plywood bins to where the sacks of dung were stacked waist high. There sat the Cantilou, the oddest beast he had ever seen, enshrined on this little hill of burlap.

The Cantilou was feline, he supposed—part cat, anyway.

It sat proudly, paws forward, silky tan, tail thwacking in measured patience. But the face was the thing, and Big Tom felt a rush of surprise every time he spilled lamplight onto it. The face was nearly hairless, and except for the eyes it looked precisely like that of a human boy. The eyes. There were no irises as with normal eyes, and no whites, just deep black wells. Clearly they could see—they blinked under the flame—but how Big Tom could not guess.

It was Big Tom's private madness that he and the Cantilou talked to one another—not in spoken words, but in thought. The richest man in the Caribbean, barefoot at midnight, talking to a cat-boy in his garden shed. Mad.

You look happy tonight. Big Tom thought the words, tossed them to the Cantilou.

I am happy, yes, the animal replied in the same way. I sit on a mountain of dried turds, locked in a ramshack. And I am happy. You, however, have a brain pleasantly wet with whiskey, fine females, the richest house on the most desirable island in all the seas—and you are not happy. Hmmmn.

"It's just the Lucia, a temporary worry. I should captain her myself from now on...."

"Oh, it may be the Lucia just now. Hmmph. But then it'll be Moori next week. Or where to find more red-leggers. Or their going price. Or some new competitor putting up on Dead Island, maybe." The Cantilou blinked. "Forget the Lucia. She's quicksand to you—you put your all into her, or anything, and surely you will go under."

"Quicksand—pfffft."

The Cantilou thwacked his tail twice. "You know the best way out of quicksand? Relax. Do not struggle. Fall over and crawl away. Calmly."

The great door to the mainhouse was thick imported oak. The knocker in its center was a salvaged anchor, too small for a skimmer yet too intricate with swirls and emblems to have served a simple dory. Farmington guessed from its opulence that it had been designed for the lifeboat of a large ship and perhaps had never been immersed in salt water.

He pulled at the bottom arc of the anchor and let it drop—thonk, thonk.

Farmington realized that he was being watched—a feeling, really, but he was sure of it. He stepped back from the door and glanced down at his sandals and trousers to assure himself of his presentability. The cotton garments hung awkwardly about the slender mainlander, an unnaturalness that announced his origin immediately to any islander.

On the other side of the door a bolt slid aside and the mass of oak swung inward. In the polished foyer stood a sturdy young man, dark skinned, hair almost nonexistent, so short that his head might have been shaved just that morning. The youth did not speak, but his right eyebrow twitched, inviting an explanation.

"Uh, my name is Farmington, and I represent Cred Faiging, sales and delivery to coastal and island points." He held up a black-covered notebook as if it proved his credentials. The salesman wondered if the doorman could be Rafer, although that seemed unlikely. Most Rafers he had seen wore manacles, and those that lived in the wild, well, he had heard they wore nothing like the tailored tunic before him. There were other dark-skinned people, especially in the cities, but they acted and dressed like any other mainlander. "Uh, you know of Cred Faiging? The inventor, manufacturer? Um, you speak English?"

The doorman nodded politely. "Yes," he said. "I speak English. And Spanish, if you happen from Down Under, and Rafer, and a touch of Latin, too. What tongue would you prefer?"

"Hoo. English," said Farmington, forgetting his spiel. "Thank you. But I've come on a simple matter, if you would just call for your, uh, for Big Tom. Thank you." Farmington turned his pale head, gazing away into the blackness of the sprawling green lawn as if dismissing the doorman. But the dark man stood firm.

"Big Tom has left orders that he is not to be disturbed for the rest of the evening," said Billister.

Farmington felt tired suddenly, now secure with the

knowledge that he would not have to cajole Big Tom tonight—always a frightening duty. He swallowed hard, trying to rid himself of the souring taste of ale in his mouth. Perhaps another pint would help, he thought.

"May I just leave this, then?" Farmington tore a looseleaf page out of his notebook, a sheet bearing a drawing of a cylindrical contraption with piping and tubes leading out of it. "It's a flier on our latest catalogue entry, Mr. Faiging's newest invention created particularly with these parts in mind—the islands, all this water. A man can breathe underwater with that." Billister was holding the paper now, and Farmington tapped at the hand-drawn illustration, making the paper rattle.

Billister snorted.

"I've seen it work," Farmington said defensively, "and once he thinks about it, I'm positive that Big Tom would find such a device indispensible. Mr. Faiging calls it a Sustained Underwater Breather—SUB for short. Please do give Big Tom the flier." Farmington clapped his notebook shut and turned to descend the steps.

Billister studied the details of the drawing, the mouthpiece and gauges, the bulky tank. There was a word for the concept, and being something of a linguist he traced its origin back to the writings of Rutherford Cross: The ancients, before the Big War, had used such underwater tanks.

"Scuba," said Billister, and Farmington stopped in the yard and turned.

"What?"

"That's the Rafer word for it. Scuba."

"Rafers can't have...well, the SUBs have just been invented," Farmington said, doubt and recrimination in his voice. "So surely Rafers've never used a device like this."

"No. But that's what we call it. Those of us that can breathe underwater—twenty, thirty minutes anyway—those Rafers that can do that, it is said they have scuba."

7

When Bark Comes...

THE man looked near death.

The stranger sat, head lolling, oblivious. Three feet away, and Tym could barely touch him. They were both shackled at the ankles to a bench in the hold of a sea skimmer. The craft was at anchor now, but Tym guessed they would be underway again soon, judging from the dull thumps and muffled howls of the crew coming from somewhere above.

The light was not good—the slavers were not wasting much kerosene on prisoners—but Tym could see that her neighbor was a light-skinned man in his thirties. He had wavy blondish hair, matted with dried blood around a cruel gash above his right temple. She had seen this light skin many times—Fungus People, they were called by the Rafers—but this man clearly was paler than pale, quite sick. On the rare occasions that his eyes opened they were yellow and vacant.

What was most remarkable about him was the bit of skin-painting she could see curling up out of his shirt and over his shoulder. The Fungus People, as far as she knew, were not capable of much artistry, and certainly nothing like this. It was Rafer design. It was Rafer coloring. Skin paintings were for the telling of great deeds—but why would one be needled into the chest of a Fungus Person?

There was a divider panel between them, supporting their metal water cups in brackets on either side. The divider made it even more difficult to reach the sick one, although she could manage sometimes to put his cup to his lips. His tongue would respond instinctively, sweeping sluggishly from side to side, but most of the liquid would dribble down his chest.

His trousers were a mess, as he lacked the wherewithal to lift the bench seat and relieve himself in the trough running underneath. Four times a day, the trough ran awash with sea water, sloshing the human waste out the back of the skimmer. A cause for celebration. Up and down the hold in the dimness, those captives still feeling rambunctious would cheer the refreshing flood. Otherwise, there were long periods of painful silence, or moans, or a jabber of mixed languages—Rafer and unidentifiable tongues—as the perplexed and disoriented got the sad news from their more worldy fellow prisoners.

Far up at the aft hatch, the twin bolts clanked open and the door threw back, spilling a blinding glare onto the first dozen red-leggers. An unmistakable silhouette stomped through the oval of light: lean, bushy in the face, like the devil's scarecrow. Bark.

It was not feed time, which prompted a nervous murmur along the corridor. Unscheduled visits never ended well.

Bark marched at a determined pace, knowing his duty. When he stopped, Tym supposed that the first mate had come for the sick one. He hung his lantern on a hook screwed into the opposite wall, then placed his hand gently against the cheek of the dying man. But that was all. He turned quickly to Tym, and his eyes were sad.

He carried a set of leg irons in the same hand with a knobbed truncheon—obviously neither of them needed for an unconcious man. He mumbled something low, in that tongue of the Fungus People, and then he clapped a shackle around each of Tym's legs and let the chain between them clatter to the floor. Then he drew a key ring from his trousers and unlocked the fixed manacles that held her to the bench.

Tym uttered one of the few English phrases she knew, picked up from the Jesus People: "Oh, gawd...."

Bark responded in his gargly language. Seeing that she did not understand, he waved a large calloused hand back toward the open hatch. Tym obeyed, sensing death somehow. As if confirming her fear, the chain between her feet scraped morbidly up the floorboards.

Her fellow red-leggers tasted the fear. Moans fore and aft filled the hold. She passed down the row of shadowy faces, and some of them she knew—fellow island-hoppers taken in the same raid.

Ahead, someone was singing in Rafer—gawd, a dirge?—in a high crackly voice. Not all of the lyrics were intelligible, partly because of her damaged hearing, but as she neared she heard her own name in the piercing song:

"Tym, Tym, you must come to me,
I will slip you a weapon
To push into the belly of your murderer."

Well, Tym thought to herself, that makes a lousy verse. But Bark won't know that, will he? As she passed another divider panel, she found the crevassed face of old Crin-Claw, the huntress. So—they have taken even the best of our fighters, Tym thought, and she felt sadder still. There seemed to be little left of civilization, less and less reason not to die.

Tym let herself stumble over the leg iron chain and fell into the lap of the aging woman. Crin-Claw's hands were quick. She pressed into Tym's right palm a metal object, which wedged between the heel of her thumb and the base of her middle finger.

Bark was on her immediately, yanking her up by the armpit and shoving her ahead. Tym glanced down at the object the huntress had passed to her: half of a broken tosser disk. Ach. Useless as a throwing weapon. It did have four of its tines intact, however, one of them digging into her finger and drawing a droplet of blood. Fine, at least she would be less likely to drop it—but let's hope there's none of the Gila poison left on it. Maybe she should just bury the disk into Bark's chest now and let the bangerbrook begin.

Tym stole a look over her shoulder and decided against it—Bark's truncheon was aloft now, perhaps his suspicion aroused by that fake trip. Behind the first mate, Tym saw Crin-Claw's face—the quivering lips, the sunken mouth, fade into the blackness.

Bark shouted, impatient, and Tym stepped through the hatch into the eye-searing white.

The young captain, the one they call Little Tom, had left her alone in the master's cabin. He had waved his hands about, saying something about Bark, and then disappeared out the door.

The cabin was a stunning example of the functionless preoccupations of the Fungus People—gleaming brass, polished wood and porcelain everywhere. A fitting abode for a young skimmer rat like Little Tom, a vain pig-poker who apparently razored his beard away daily as he must have seen mainlanders do. Clearly it could not be because he was a swimmer—such a pathetic physique.

The portholes were open, allowing a brisk breeze into the room—it was rough weather out—but there remained the unmistakable scent of burned ganja. The red-eyed young captain must be half gullybonkers, she thought. I wonder if they've raided our ganja fields as well as our people.

Tym glanced again at the piece of tosser disk in her right hand and decided to leave it there. She would make quick work of Little Tom, run above and hit the water before any of the skimmer rats could react. The drop of blood at the base of her finger had grown to a tiny trickle now. The pain meant nothing, but the blood might give her away prematurely.

She stepped toward the basin, and the leg iron chain rattled across the new floor. Ach. How would that affect her swimming? She could swim with many times the weight, that would not be a problem, but she could part her ankles no more than two feet—not enough for a proper frog kick.

The water jug was a perfect white sphere with a bottle stem on top, affixed to the wall by a teeter hinge. When she reached for it, the floorboards at the door squeaked. She dropped her right hand to her side, crying "Oh, gawd," and hoped that he hadn't seen the tosser disk cupped there.

Little Tom laughed and swaggered in, eyes painful-looking, shirtless, drawstring trousers. He yanked the jug off its hinge and stared at her up and down—cutoff pants, T-shirt, the swimmer's chop-cut hair. It was the way a man looked at a woman when his thinking was sexual.

Tym felt a sickness growing in her chest. She stumbled backward until she fell into the captain's bunk, and she started again, afraid she might have dotted the sheets with blood. Tym had to cup her hand now, trying to keep the disk out of his sight, as a tiny pool of warm liquid gathered there.

Little Tom was speaking again, in gentle tones, if the Fungus People's tongue can be thought of as gentle. He held the jug out to her, and Tym took it cautiously in her left hand. She splashed water onto the puddle of blood building around the tosser disk, and she threw the mixture at her mouth and swallowed. She splashed again and again, hoping any blood dribbling down was diluted sufficiently not to alarm him, hoping he would step closer—perhaps just two paces.

Tym pictured herself thrusting the metal shard into his throat before he had a chance to cry out. Between splashes of water, she sucked in deep breaths, feeding her body extra oxygen for a long underwater swim. Any moment now....

But Little Tom backed away, and Tym sighed—her first chance gone. The entire ship was groaning now with the stress of filling sails. Now would be the best time for the kill and escape, she told herself, with the crew above at its most distracted. Ach.

Little Tom pulled the cabin doors closed, then produced a key from his trousers and threw the bolt to lock them. The captain hop-skipped boyishly by her—too quickly for the slash—and fell back onto his bunk, legs dangling over the side.

Then came an abrupt movement that shocked Tym, even though she was nauseatingly aware of his intentions: Little Tom rolled his knees up to his chest and whisked off his pants in one fluttering motion. The stoned young shipmaster laid back lazily, staring into space, confidently waving her to him—he seemed to have done this before. His pale legs were parted, swinging easily along the side of the bunk. His penis was rising like a new mushroom.

Tym wondered if these people were always so artless with their sex. She breathed deeply three times and went to him.

8

A Runner, A Writer

QUINCE scrabbled through a jungle of bougainvillea, not daring to take the dirt-and-shell road that wound down the hillside from the medical buildings. He paused, kneeling in the blackness, listening for any human noises through the riot of creeking tree frogs. There were no signs of humanity, save for his own heavy breathing, sounding like rhythmic sobs.

He peeled off his hospital gown, a smock so tattered that it really covered little of the body. He mopped his brow with it, then rolled it and tucked it under his arm. Dark skin made a better night cover. Scratches be damned—it was better to have a few thorns in the fanny than to risk recapture. Red-leggers fared badly enough as it was; red-leggers who dared to break out before sale to the mainland, it was said, would suffer a cruel torture at the hands of the pig-poker-in-chief, Big Tom. His walled garden at the mainhouse was renowned for that.

When Quince hit the beach he rested again. The sand was still warm from the day's sun-scorching, but the night sea breeze here in the open was a relief. His stomach was twisting—a wretched mixture of anxiety and the sourness of the blood he had swallowed to simulate sickness. He crouched in the shadows of the jungly shrubs at the beach's edge and tried to decide his next move.

I am just a scribe, Quince thought to himself resolutely. I make stories, I write history, I teach. This is work for a warrior, a hunter. Perhaps Dirk was right. I will die on this island. He pictured his friend in that cell over the ridge of Crown Mountain—dull-minded Dirk, the steady laborer, determined to ship quietly to a farm worker's life on the mainland. Who was right?

Just east up the beach, barely 300 yards away, were the shipyards and main docks. Tied up there, among Big Tom's little skimmers, were the three barges and their tug lashed together, black against the glistening waves. Capture by Big Tom's marauding beasts was a miserable enough experience. But it was said to be a pleasure cruise compared to the barge ride to the mainland. Those few red-leggers who escaped the mainland and returned to the Out Islands carried back nightmarish tales of this Captain Bull and his pig-poking enforcers with their billybangers and snub shotguns.

To the west the beach buildings were more sparse, decrepit little ramshacks dotting the west side of the harbor for miles. The choice of directions came easily, if for no other reason than Quince's instinctive repulsion for the slave barges. West. He would find supplies in one of the shanties, then steal a boat and skim away.

Jersey Saple knew that someone was approaching his house from the beach path. It was as if an extra sense had awakened in him over his ten years of blindness. Especially in territory familiar to him—his house, the garden and outhouse area in back, or the boardwalk and twenty yards of scrubland out front running down to the beach—Saple could even identify the intruder before he had a chance to rap on the splintery door sometimes, if he knew him well.

This extra sense could be explained scientifically, he supposed, as the old blubberburst Dr. Scaramouch huffily insisted. Perhaps in his perpetual visual haze—dim light during the day and blackness at night—Saple had become attuned to infinitesimally small sounds, or vibrations, or odors, that never registered with sighted people.

Perhaps so. But Saple liked the charm of something more mystical—the idea that he had acquired a gift of vision somehow. The Jesus People, or even the Rafers, would say that it was God given in compensation for his unjust blinding. Ah, that was a much better story, Dr. Scaramouch, a much better story.

So it was that in the perfect stillness of his threadbare study, Saple "watched" the approach of this stranger from the beach. He was not only unable to identify this person—mmm, it is a man, he was sure now—but he quickly became convinced that they had never met. The man's bearing, his way of carrying himself, his attitude, were absolutely foreign.

Oddly, the stranger seemed to be avoiding the boardwalk, risking the wrath of caugi cactus, hooker weed and shell fragments against his bare feet. Bare feet. Hmm, not only bare feet, but Saple was not sure that the intruder was wearing any clothing at all.

The stranger was lingering now at the front door, a simple ill fitting frame of silvery wood that served little purpose but to hold a swath of rusted metal screening over the entry—which kept out those bugs that weren't particularly intent on getting inside anyway. The visitor's hesitation did not last long. He simply pulled at the door handle and let himself in.

Saple's curiosity advanced into a state of alarm. On Thomas Island, courtesy and legality were strictly observed, as the penalties for infractions (usually, as interpreted by Big Tom) were severe. A gouged tongue, perhaps, or a severed hand. Or, as Saple found out not long after arriving, blindness. For the first time since detecting the intruder, Saple moved—he pushed back against the rollers of his desk chair and came to an accurate stop at the floor cabinet behind him. He opened it.

The intruder was still in the tiny front room, where Saple had a hammock strung for sleeping and the walls were banked with disheveled shelves of books, folders of loose papers and odd bits of wood and twisted metal scavenged from the shore.

Now he is a burglar, Saple mused, and I can blow his belly out with nay a warning shot. The blind man's hands were shaking under the weight of his snub shotgun, so he propped the short, ghastly barrel on his desk, nudged among his latest writings on alternative forms of government.

The weapon had washed up two days after a minor capsize in the harbor. Saple had broken a toe on it during an evening jaunt and spent the next day brushing and oiling the rust away. Now it would have its first firing, and Saple found himself hoping the charge would not blast out each end with equal force. A banger of such minimal craftsmanship could really be trusted only by a person standing far to the side of its barrel. It was a cool night out, but Saple could feel the sweat trickling into his beard.

He waited until the invader was well into the study, too far to escape back into the front room and out the door. There. Saple lit one of the striker matches that he kept around for the convenience of guests and held its tiny roar aloft in the blackness.

"Ho, there," he said to the frozen figure before him, "sit down aback a you in the chair, and move slow or I'll be painting that wall red at your expense."

Quince's nerves were screaming from the shock of surprise, but his tongue was wooden, mute. Behind a marred and littered desk he saw a middle-aged man, wild haired and scrawny, with one of those tiny torches in one hand and an ugly banger in the other. He was grumbling something, like the sound of barking dogs, in that tongue of the Fungus People.

Saple could taste the tension, but his order was not being obeyed. He ran his forefinger across the two triggers, one for each barrel. The problem could be resolved so quickly, safely: Blam. But a few more problems would be created. The mess. And an inquiry about the banger, a slaver's weapon found but not returned. Could he prove it was not stolen?

Saple tried again. "Mayhap you know that I'm blind—these eyes are whiter than stones, I'm told. But you'll be asking yerself why it is that I'm able to point this blaster right at your coconuts, huh?" He waved the gun toward the chair. "Sit there, or soon you'll have to squat to pee."

Quince understood the motion, at least, and sat, his nerves still howling. "There...there was no light on in the house," the Rafer said in his own language. "I meant no harm. I needed...food, maybe clothes—yes, I had a mind to steal—but I would be gone then, quickly."

The bushy face of the Fungus Person showed astonishment, then thought. And Quince got another surprise. This time, when the blind man spoke his words sounded smooth and warm, not like the barking dogs at all. The sense of them was halting, but understandable. It seemed so odd to see a Fungus Person speaking Rafer. Unnatural. Like watching a poorly operated marionette.

"You are Rafer," the Fungus Person was saying, "and now I think I understand. There is only one Rafer on Thomas Island who is even close to a free man, and you are not him. That would mean you are a runner. You have broken out of the cells?"

"Yes...well, not quite," Quince replied, deciding that the man with the gun was not going to be deceived. "From the infirmary. They had thought that I was vomiting blood—which I was, but not from hemorrhage. I had swallowed blood to feign such an illness."

"And once in the hospital, they ignored you—thinking that you had the belly rot?" Saple held firm to the snub gun propped on the desk, trying to assess the danger. He touched the dwindling striker match to the wick of the desk candle.

"Oh, more than that," Quince said, enjoying a chance to tell of his cleverness, even under the circumstances. "When I stopped breathing, I was taken for dead and wheeled to a cooler-room."

Saple snorted. "You fooled the doctor—the big one, Scaramouch—with that? He knows of Rafer breathing, this scuba that some of you have. He has vowed to make a medical study of it."

Quince looked puzzled. "It was just another of the jailers watching me in the hospital. He said that the doctor could not be found. He was distraught, actually—saying that this Big Tom of yours would be violently angry that another of us was dying. But there was no big doctor."

"Then you are lucky to have gotten this far—to the sea, the boats. But now, as you must know, you will die if you are caught, even though Big Tom will not be able to profit from selling you to the mainland. An example to the others—that's the thinking."

"You are releasing me?"

Saple sighed and raised the snub gun, pointing its jagged maw at the ceiling. "Yes. I think so."

"Why? This could bring you trouble, no?"

"It would bring me trouble only if I were found out," Saple said, struggling to find the correct Rafer words. "But no matter. I am not faithful to Big Tom. He put my eyes out for articles that I wrote when I first arrived on the island, articles about his selling of red-leggers—Rafers, other runners from the mainland."

"You, too, are a scribe? But who would read such articles if they are not allowed? Certainly not mainlanders, where the Government is buying humans for farm work."

Saple sighed. How could he possibly explain it all?

"Well, yes, I have been many kinds of scribe in my life. Both for the Government and for—well, those who call themselves the Ungovernment. I came to Thomas Island as an itinerant Government bureaucrat, writing inspection reports mostly, for the Department of Transport out of New Chicago. It was quite dry material, really. I would much prefer writing poetry when—"

"A poet! I should have guessed!"

Saple grunted. "Well, during my travels I had developed a rather bifurcated career, you see. The Transport reports went to New Chicago, and the poetry circulated among less reputable audiences. I found that using a pseudonym, I could express frustration in my poetry that was never vented in my Government assignments. Then I began writing articles, too, about the conditions I had found during my travels. Not all mainlanders believe in the slaving, you know—or the Government at all. There are Revolutionaries—no one with much power, mind you—but it was them that I was writing the articles for. To be circulated among the Revolutionaries, to inspire them."

"But one of these Revolutionaries betrayed you?"

Saple shrugged. "I think the Department of Inspection simply put two and two together, finally. I was assigned to Thomas Island when they did, and the inspectors sent notice to Big Tom—asked him to settle the matter. So Big Tom searched my possessions and found notes I had been gathering about his slaving company."

"And still he did not kill you?"

"No, he just ever-so-mercifully burned my eyes out. Now, he allows me to dwell in this abandoned ramshack, and even looks the other way when his house boy smuggles provisions to me. Big Tom is an odd poker, a curious mixture sometimes of violence and beneficence. A mind doctor could spend his career on Big Tom."

"How is it that you speak Rafer? Do all of these Revolutionaries speak our tongue somehow? We had thought it impossible for...excuse me, but your race is known as the Fungus People."

The blind man laughed. "No. I learned it from Big Tom's house boy. He taught me his language and I taught him mine, even how to write—which is something I can not manage in Rafer."

Quince squirmed in his chair. "I should find a boat quickly," he said. "Can you afford to give me food?"

"Not necessary. A mile west, near the point, you will find the skimmer of a fisherman named Murdoch. He keeps it well stocked for long hauls. But...oh, gawd...." Saple's lids closed over his milky eyes. He sensed movement again down the yard, near the beach, and his heart shrank as he recognized the figures striding toward the house. He rolled back on the chair to the floor cabinet, shoved the banger inside and slid the door closed. “Go! Now!”

The last two words were shouted in the Fungus People’s tongue, but Quince read the panic quite accurately and sprinted out of the ramshack. Down the hill, silhouetted against the glowing beach, were three tall men with snub shotguns glinting in the moonlight. There was nowhere to run.

9

A Dousing

JAY-JAY pointed a fat, quivering finger toward the corroded building at the bottom of the clinic lawn. He shouted at his sister, "Git down ta red-legger cells and watch 'em. An' I don't care of they's sick ta dying, nobody else's making it ta hospital tonight. No one else's out less Dr. Scaramouch himself says so, and he'll be plenty piss-angry about the escape."

Lily, a female rendition of her rotund brother, sagged her pudgy face into scowl, letting him know he didn't need to use that tone of voice with her. She marched off to the holding cells, each side of her buttocks pumping up and down testily. "Ah didn't let no red-legger out, nah," she said into the night, as if to no one in particular.

Jay-Jay pushed angrily through the beaten-aluminum swing doors of the clinic. His breath was rapid and anxious now, growing into an audible whine. What a mess! A red-legger he had brought to the clinic had busted out. An orderly had run to Big Tom's compound to get the search started, and Jay-Jay couldn't find Dr. Scaramouch anywhere—not in his office at the other end of the hall, not in his private quarters adjacent to the office, not down drinking at Sanders's Shebeen, as one would expect this late.

Jay-Jay jiggled down the chipped linoleum hallway straight under its three bare lightbulbs. He glanced into each green-painted patient room, most of them empty, thinking the doctor might have decided to make a rare midnight round. Wheezing louder, the jailer stopped at the end of the hall next to the office and leaned against the wall, his sweaty back cool against the cinder block. He pulled a hand down his hammy face and wiped the perspiration on his shirt sleeve.

The cellar door, just there to his right, jogged his memory. It was so rarely entered, by orderlies or jailers anyway, that it had grown almost invisible in its disuse. But he remembered the doctor's odd hobby—the clicker box that makes pictures of things just as they are, better than the most meticulous brush painter. He recalled the doctor hunching behind his tripod up on the hillside of Crown Mountain, sour-smelling, wide-brimmed straw hat pulled low over his eyes, explaining in long-winded scientific terms how the photo box worked—the numerous lenses and celluloids and papers and chemicals imported, of course, from the inventor and manufacturer Cred Faiging.

Jay-Jay had shaken his head at the irony: Only during light of day is there proper sun to expose the photo film to take a picture; and only in the dark of night, in a sealed room, can the chemicals be employed to do their magic. And Dr. Scaramouch explained that he had set up such a dark room—a darkroom, he called it, running the words together and pronouncing it as if Jay-Jay should be familiar with such a thing—in the dirt-floor cellar of the hospital. He had boarded over the windows and caulked around them with shipyard resin just to ward off the moon and starlight. He even ran a water line down, for crissake.

Jay-Jay heaved himself off of the wall and tapped tentatively against the metal door. He called out, "Dr. Scaramouch!" and sensed immediately somehow that his voice had met no human ears.

He pushed, and the door fell open easily. The scant light

fell down the wooden steps, illuminating another door at the bottom.

"Dr. Scaramouch!"

Again no answer.

Jay-Jay, extremely conscious of his weight now, put one foot onto the first step of the dubious stairway. It held rather steady, only a slight shiver. He grasped the handrail and paced delicately to the bottom, where he turned the doorknob and entered the black room. There was absolutely no light, save from the doorway, and of course that was the point of a darkroom, he told himself. Instinctively he felt for a light switch on the wall to his right but found only bare studs and cobwebs. He heard dripping water, and there was an acrid chemical scent to the air.

"Dr. Scaramouch?"

He stepped farther out onto the dirt floor—he could see nothing in front of him now—and paper crackled under his feet. A whispy something stroked at his face, and Jay-Jay squealed and wiped at his jaw, thinking of spiders, bats, who knows what. But when his nerves subsided and reason returned, he reached out for the string hanging from the ceiling and gave it a pull.

An amber-colored light blinked on amid the low rafters just above his head. And there at his feet lay the hulking Dr. Scaramouch twisted in the dirt, a stretch of electrical wire tight around his neck. His face was a dull blue, his eyes popped open, surprised. Paper and tipped chemical trays and four-inch-square celluloids were littered all about, the sign of a wild struggle. A twine strung with damp photographs had been yanked to the ground. Water dripped into a metal sink.

Jay-Jay fled up the trembling stairs to tell Big Tom's men how the escaped red-legger had buggered Dr. Scaramouch.

They were a fresh set of cuffs, sturdy quarter-inch steel darkly burnished. Hefty. For the arms and legs, both. The newly uncrated cuffs were the sort that only a high-volume trader of red-leggers would have in stock.

The shackles were bolted to the dock piling with the three-quarter-inch shafts that the ship-making wood whits called "deathdicks." Each bolt was topped with an octagonal nut, screwed into the wood with a whale wrench.

Quince was already sobbing the morning they clapped him in. Half a dozen of Captain Bull's naked musclers pressed his legs and arms into the metal cradles, slid the cuff covers into place and drove another set of bolts through the lock holes. The low tide was swirling at Quince's feet, and when he looked straight up, there was Big Tom leaning into his cane and staring down his beard at him from the dock. Quince shackled down in the rising water; Big Tom peering over his belly at the rebellious red-legger.

Big Tom coughed softly and spat, and the silvery bullet smacked into Quince's chest and sped down through the curly hair. The slaver was well versed in the mechanisms of hope, and it was he who had demanded that the monster bolts be used to secure the cuffs to the piling. Shackles that had been merely locked by key gave the captive a glint of hope, albeit unwarranted. This would not do—the terror must be total and unabated, and only the thick bolts driven home permanantly by a muscley bargeman would produce the proper level of shrieking despair.

Big Tom wanted Quince to see death now, to see it cruelly and inevitably, hours before it actually would come.

He stepped back from the edge of the dock, and his three guards, snub blasters at their sides, moved in unison in the same direction. They were the ones who had found Quince in front of Jersey Saple's ramshack. They were Big Tom's men, islanders, as attested by their leather boots to guard against shell fragments, the dungarees, and the high-collared blouses that kept the mosquitoes at bay. They were easily distinguishable from the slave bargemen who populated the docks while they were waiting to ship off for the mainland. Such bargemen had an aversion for garments, and wore them only against the most extreme sun or cold. This day the bargemen found perfect for swaggering about the docks and beach with their own snub shotguns—naked save for the occasional belt or calf strap bearing a hand shooter or knife. There was a grand amusement to be had today, the dousing of a Rafer.

His back and legs were bruised now, battered against the piling by the wave action, and his eyes stung from the salt and sand. Quince had begun to regard the wave action as an insidious evil, smooth and unrelenting, a bully smacking him into the wooden pillar, whop...whop...whop.

Quince had provided quite an entertainment for the bargemen and guards throughout the day. But now, with the sun dying, Big Tom had ordered them all away. Quince understood the extent of that cruelty—he was to die without hope or human contact, helpless, alone, strangled by the inevitability of surging nature. The only perceptible trace of mankind was the occasional burst of guffaws from the island's pub, upland a ways. The laughter provided no solace—he already was dead and forgotten, even in the minds of his tormentors.

The waves this evening were not breaking in the protected harbor. But they rose inexorably up the scribe's face now, shushing through his hair. Quince had hoped, at the very least, that the deadly tide would wash the sting of spit and urine from his hair. But it did not. The indignity still burned, and he would die now in the red-shimmering waves at sunset.

Quince sucked in long breaths between the waves, packing oxygen into his blood as he had been taught since childhood. He had the rhythm against that evil flow—immersion, breath, immersion, breath. The panic set in when he began to miss between waves—occasionally, even at its nadir, the lolling sea buried him. Quince strained his lips toward the red, blackening sky, pulling fiercely at the bolted cuffs, wrists bleeding down there.

And finally there was no more air. His Rafer lungs would last him half an hour at most, and already his heart was thrashing a grim tattoo up his spine and into his head—a-wump, a-wump, a-wump.

Quince knew his religion—better than most. Had taught it to the hundreds of youngsters for whom faith comes easily; was fluent in the scriptures of the god Rutherford Cross and well versed in the deeds of Cross's son Pec-Pec. He had always considered himself a religious man, with all of that knowledge framed out to perfection. But now, with the sea water gnawing at his bulging eyes, taunting his lips to open, Quince was surprised by a rush of calmness, a warmth and ease he could only attribute to his faith welling up in proportions he had never known.

Out in the darkening murk of shifting green water, Quince saw a large white body glide by. The scribe thought briefly, without fear, of the vile feeder beasts who owned the night waters, but as it passed again he saw it was not one of them. On the third pass he could see clearly the monster dragon fish, thick as five dock pilings, red, green and gold fins trailing yards behind. And mounted atop the glorious fish, precisely as described in the scriptures, was the dark-bearded Pec-Pec, the god-man son of Rutherford Cross. He wore a bemused expression as he wafted past on his sea-steed, unable to speak but clearly intending, My, how fortunate that I wandered by just in time.

Pec-Pec pulled the streaming dragon fish into a sharp turn and slowed to a hover by the manacled scribe. He thrupped his fingers across each of the bolts gripping Quince's limbs to the dock, and the black little shafts spun and backed out of the piling wood obediently. The manacle covers fell away. Quince mounted the grand dragon fish behind Pec-Pec, and together they swept into the black ocean.

In the morning, Big Tom ordered that Quince's body not be unshackled. Leave it there in the low tide muck. Let the fiddler crabs do their work.

10

A Shift of Ballast

For Sailors, oh the murder wind!
For Healers, the Trygulkul flu,
for Sounders, it's a shattered skin,
the bones not tossed, the bones gone rot.
But what's the fearsome, gnawing beast
that feeds upon the men who press
the borders of reality?
It inhales fear and suckles gloom—
the madmen speak to Cantilou.
—Rafer nursery rhyme, translated by Jersey Saple

LITTLE Tom, naked and brain-numb, was staring at the ceiling of his cabin, entranced by whispy little ganja ghosts dancing across the woodwork. His nose was twitching, as if from some imagined rotten smell. He beckoned to Tym with a lazy roll of the wrist, legs open.

Tym obeyed. She stroked the back of her hand down his inner thigh to signal that she was there, and his penis grew even more upright. In the same motion she worked the broken tosser disk out of her palm, then sucked away the smear of blood, drawn by one of its tines, from the base of her forefinger.

She had meant this to be simple—pound the shard into Little Tom's throat, then escape topside. The younger deserved the death. For the rape he intended. For the slaving. For the communities demolished.

She envisioned the moist plunge into his neck. Hitting bone halfway through. The gurgle. It would be over quickly, and she would be alone then in a slaver's cabin with a warm rack of flesh. Was that enough?

Well, perhaps not. And without further thought she gently took his erect member into her hands, waited for the blissful smile to spill across his vacant face, and pressed the tosser disk's deadly tines into it until they popped out the topside in four little geysers of blood.

Little Tom bolted up to a sitting position, paralyzed by a scream too big for his throat. And that was when the entire ship seemed to explode. The floor fell away from Tym's feet and was suddenly behind her. Mirrors, maps, chart instruments, and drawing leads showered the cabin. Then came the real buster—like an earthquake—when the deep wooden gut of the Lucia burst under the shifting weight of her ballast bars.

Tym was airborne, then pounded against the cabin wall, then sliding down into the splintery rubble. An avalanche of black metal bars poured through the upturned flooring as if it were paper, and Tym watched as the stunned shipmaster was buried up to his chest in ballast.

Just as suddenly as the disaster had struck, the Lucia was silent again, shifting unsteadily now in her irrevocable capsize. The portholes, submerged, burst from the water pressure and twisting of side beams. It was that spray that awakened Tym to action, and she began pulling the heavy bars off of the semiconscious Little Tom. The slaver was bleeding slightly from the nose—probably some internal damage, Tym told herself. She squinted in the stinging sea spray and pulled frantically at the leaden bars, tossing them one at a time over her shoulder.

Little Tom smiled weakly, appreciative of the effort. He lifted a limp left arm in a pathetic attempt to help free himself. His smile faded when he saw what Tym had really been after: the trousers he had flung onto the bunk. When the wirey Rafer unearthed them she tore away the pocket containing his key ring and left the slaver to his fate. The sea was rising within the cabin in angry swirls, a veritable sewer of objects coveted by these Fungus People.

Tym's shoulder began to beat a painful throb from the bashing she had taken, and she stopped knee-deep in the maelstrom to concentrate on shoving that agony aside—cope with it later.

She blinked and cleared her head, then scanned the vertical decking for the rents and gouges that would allow footholds as she clawed her way up to the shattered cabin door. Mmmm. It was possible.

Little Tom moaned and splashed his hand sadly in the rising water. "Waaaait. Unnh. Hey. Wait." And the little Rafer he had tried to rape was gone.

In the blackness of the corridor, Tym did not have the patience to allow her eyes to adjust. She scrambled by memory—at the expense of numerous toe stubs and shin raps—down the long row of slave holds.

The wall of shackled humanity was now the floor, turned under her, and she decided the most expedient way to move down the line was to step from the edge of one slot divider to the next. As she passed over each frantic red-legger, Tym attempted encouraging words, but most often they were lost in the collective howl of doomed people. Under their seats, the water duct was shooshing with seawater, probably backing up from the aft drain hole. The slave hold would soon be submerged.

Tym counted her way over fifteen slots until she estimated that she was in the right place. Then she squinted into the blackness below her to see each occupant, sometimes offering a reassuring pat on the shoulder, sometimes having to struggle out of a panicky red-legger's grasp. When she came to an empty hold, she knew it must be her own and, yes, the unconscious Fungus Man, the one with the remarkable skin-painting, was in the next one.

The air seemed flavored with fear now, made worse by the odor of the human waste being backed up the wash gully by the rush of seawater. Tym straddled the slot, and below her the young man lolled, oblivious. She pulled the pocket cloth away from Little Tom's key ring and ran her forefinger across each key until she found one that seemed the right size for the ankle shackles. She thrust it into the slot and turned. No good. The next key was the same size, she tried again and was rewarded with a satisfying steel snap. The ankle cover slid away and she released his other leg with the same key.

The chorus of shouts and whimpers was becoming overwhelming even to Tym's deafened ears. She hopped to the next hold, where she found a middle-aged red-legger, an overweight Rafer whom she did not recognize—a cook, or some other campman, certainly not a swimmer or hunter. She pressed the key into his eager hand.

She cupped her hands over his ear. "Unlock them all," she shouted in the Rafer tongue. "The land people first, then the swimmers, then the scuba breathers." She watched his rolling eyes and wondered if he could act responsibly on the distinction. When he sat forward and unlocked his own cuffs, Tym decided she would have to surrender the matter to him. One person could only do so much.

The unconscious Fungus Person, unaccountably honored with a Rafer skin painting, would be her responsibility. She placed a foot in the rising water on either side of his chest, positioned the base of each of her palms into his armpits and pushed until his back rose against the rough wood that had been the ceiling before the capsize. Tym was breathing heavily now, the air growing thin of oxygen.

She kneeled, placed her shoulder against the stranger's abdomen, and heaved him up. When she was upright, she curled an arm around his right leg, letting the other dangle down her back, and began the awkward stagger, slot divider by slot divider, back toward the dim light of freedom.

The Lucia's upturned bow point dipped beneath the choppy sea. It went much quicker than Tym had imagined it would. Suddenly, from her standpoint on the wide beach of Dunkin Island, there was nothing but the broad expanse of furiously shifting water under a depressing gray sky.

Tym was immobile as she watched from the beach, every arm and leg joint screaming with the pain of overexertion. Alternately, she tried to envision the scramble of slaves in the Lucia's hold and she tried to forget. She could do no more. Her head lay on the rising and falling belly of the rescued Fungus Person, her legs lapped by the surge and ebb of the sea. Pictures of the horror flashed into her mind, and she drove them away again.

Surge and ebb. She smiled with satisfaction at her cruel use of the tosser disk; she sobered again at the realization of the tormented deaths happening just now, beyond the reach of her depleted body.

She stared up at the swirl of gray clouds. Again and again she replayed in her mind the scene with Little Tom. The violent capsize, bashing into the wall, the floor exploding and the avalanche of metal ballast bars. Tym pictured herself clawing the bars away, looking for the shackle key. The bars of battered metal she threw aside. And then she remembered the odd detail she had mentally filed away for calmer times: those bars.

She had supposed the ship's ballast would be lead, an extremely heavy and common metal. Naturally. But these tons of metal bars had been tossed about, bashed through decking, in a way that no shipbuilder would imagine in the worst of nightmares. The bars were scarred and twisted and beaten, and underneath their dull black surface paint was the unmistakable glint of gold.

11

The Dream Vessel

BIG Tom pressed the tip of his drawing lead into the U-shaped sharpener on the edge of his drafting table. He whittled it to a sharp point. The shavings dittered into a cup screwed just under the sharpener, where they would be collected eventually for remelting.

With a wad of rubber he erased the line he had just drawn, repositioned his flexible snake rule on the paper, and rechecked the curvature. Ah. Then he drew that segment of the hull line again, satisfactorily thin and precise this time.

The merchant-shipbuilder faced the open veranda windows of his stilted office building, a perch from which he could watch for ships coming in—the Lucia, ah, that would be a blessing. But the Windon Wait or the Darwip, out to scout for her two days now—word from either of them would do.

So it was that from this lookout he was likely the first person on the island to see the Darwip heading into harbor from out east—even at such a distance identifiable by its single yellow streamer flying from masttop. Big Tom dropped his drafting lead and hobbled to the telescope pointing seaward from a tripod. He swung the telescope to the left and tightened the brass wing nut on the joint to stabilize it once he had found his mark.

The Darwip was full sail, yet there were four or five idle men on her foredeck—which would not be, unless she had picked up passengers. Extra crew meant wasted wages. Especially while full sail, all of Big Tom's sailors had duties.

As the skimmer drew nearer, he thought he could make out the tall frame of Bark among the laggards, and that would mean that the Lucia was disabled at least—and possibly down. Big Tom could feel his heart beating, and he argued with himself over whether to grab his cane and hurry down to the dock.

It would not do to appear unduly concerned about one skimmer—his son aboard notwithstanding. He heaved himself up onto the stool at his drawing board and took up the lead again.

Taking shape on the paper before him was a seagoing fantasy, a ship scaled to roughly twice the size of any vessel ever seen in the Caribbean. Why, if ever the timbers could be had to build her, she might even hazard a crossing of the Great Ocean itself. The timbers. Yas, that was the problem. All that the Government would ship to him came from the closest sources—yellow pine from the Southland forests, which was too small and weak to make a reliable craft over 200 feet or so. And even with the better timbers, what design could keep such a monstrosity from falling apart under its own weight? He dropped the lead and sighed.

This was more thinking of a madman, he knew. Wouldn't it be better to start a draft of the Lucia II?

The door at Big Tom's back threw open and he heard a single person step in tentatively. He did not look up from his drawing.

"Come in and sack ya in a chair, Bark," Big Tom said, scouring the rubber wad over a smudge on the paper—making work for himself. "Glad ta see you're near 'bouts in one piece." He heard an irregular shuffle heading for his frayed easy chair, and then the long form of Bark, bent over some, entered his line of vision. His black beard was wilder than ever and fanned out over a once-white blouse, now gray from a sea-drenching and terribly ragged. He eased himself into the chair carefully.

Big Tom looked directly into the first mate's pain-squinting eyes. "You've not been 'ome."

"Ma kin wait. In this shape, I'll not do much for her anyway."

Big Tom chuckled uncomfortably. A mild breeze wafted through the room, seeming unreal, impossible to enjoy.

"The Lucia—she's down, isn't she?"

"Ya," Bark replied, his voice sounding high and anxious, "with a lot of crew an' cargo. Six men of our own, an' I'd guess ever last one a the red-leggers."

Big Tom emptied his lungs out his nose in a whoosh. Couldn't have been much worse. But the knowing of it was not unlike relief. From his pocket he drew a slender folding knife and clicked it open. He glanced at Bark and noted the sweat droplets collecting in his eyebrows.

"And my boy?"

Bark tried to sit up straighter. "Dead—down with her. He done it to himself, Big Tom, a fool's suicide—forgive me speaking of kin, but it's so. Smoke-headed, an' ordering us full sail inta storm. Bumping a Rafer girl below decks...."

"Ho up!" the trader grunted, and Bark wondered if he was going to pay now, for telling too much of the truth too quickly.

Big Tom pulled open the pencil drawer at the base of the drafting table, drew out a silver cylinder and screwed its cap off. His knife blade fit into it neatly, and when he eased it out it was covered with a ridge of fine white powder. He placed the dull side of the blade against his upper lip, under his nose, and when he inhaled violently, the powder disappeared. He thought to offer a snort to Bark, his friend and fellow conniver for decades. Hmm. Not yet.

"Now," said the big-bellied man, working his rubbery lips side to side and brushing the last of the white dust from his face, "start again, at the start."

Bishop had heard most of the story down on the docks, where he had elbowed his way to the center circle. There the telling would be the best, with the least exaggeration. Scrawny though he was, no one denied Big Tom's assistant the right to hear it straight from the survivors of the Lucia.

And now the sun was down, and Bishop was pacing the veranda outside Big Tom's office. The boss had dragged his drafting stool out and was sitting there, belly pressed against the rail. He had everything he needed laid out—knife, cylinder, and a bottle of mainland whiskey—and had said nothing for thirty minutes while he sopped his brain like Bishop had never seen.

A few minutes back Linsey, Big Tom's third or fourth wife—Bishop could never keep them straight—rapped at the entrance. He sent her away, telling her not to count on Big Tom to come home till sunrise. Which was true. That much powder was likely to keep his mind running all night, even if it did go rudderless from the alcohol.

Bishop stepped up and down the planking, his mouth open in an O, his jaw locked into a concerned scowl.

How does Big Tom do it? When he finally spoke, he addressed the worry that had been tying Bishop's mind in knots.

"I dint tell Bark about the gold," Big Tom said, tilting back the whiskey bottle. "Everyone knows the Lucia's ballast shifted, but not a word 'bout anything else unusual on that score. She went down too fast for anyone to see."

"Half-a-billion centimes!"

Big Tom was just about to inhale another knife-load, but he stopped. "Look at it this way: You and I put the gold onta the Lucia in the first place, cause everyone 'spects we store it under the mainhouse, the prize for the first pig-fuck to knock off Thomas Island. But if the Government ever collapses, like some of those barge boys gossip? We'd already have it all in the bottom of the fastest little skimmer in the Caribbean."

"But she's down in fifty, mayhap seventy feet of water...."

"Where no one can get at her—that's the saving part of it. Our gold is safer at the bottom of the sea than even in the mainhouse." He inhaled the little foothill of powder. "Ah. Jeeze."

"Oh, gawd, Big Tom! If the sands shift, or she breaks up, or if a current spreads it all up and down..."

"Ya, ya, the gold's safe for now, but we got to bring it up soon. So here's—mmm—so here's my idea. Let Captain Bull out of the brig and tell 'im the damage at Sanders's is forgiven. Goodness of Sanders's heart—he'll go along, no?"

Bishop nodded. "I 'spect he hopes ta keep his lease with ya, Big Tom. So I'd say he'll go along."

"So before any more red-leggers drop dead, or escape and then drop dead, we'll get 'em all shipped off to the mainland. We're not waiting on the Lucia no more, so let's get the others out of here before we lose the whole lot of 'em. Tell Captain Bull he's to alert the Government that we have need of a new doctor. And have that little lad—Farmington is his name?—run a rush order to his boss Cred Faiging. We're to have some equipment down from his compound on Captain Bull's next barge run south."

Bishop was silent, his face fixed into that same gape, trying to figure it. "Winches, right? Faiging 'bout made his name manufacturing winches. But there can't be a portable what's big enough to draw up the Lucia."

"Na." Big Tom pulled a leaflet from his pocket, unfolded it and handed it to his assistant. The slaver tipped the whiskey bottle against his flabby face.

Bishop's eyes widened at the diagram of a Sustained Underwater Breather. "Oh, gawd."

12

The Linguists

THE blind journalist and poet Jersey Saple had thrust himself into his sun reader outside his rotting ramshack near the beach. The sun reader was shaped like a storm-blown tent, a box made of thick scrap, sail canvas and wood framing. To follow the path of the sun it pivoted atop a length of piling left over from dock construction. The sandy yard was dotted with caugi cactus, but Saple's feet never encountered their unforgiving needles, either from a gift of "vision" or a gift of memory.

He withdrew his head of tangle-hair from the dark frame, letting the cover shroud, which was tacked to the top of the box, flop over the hole he had occupied. In an exacting motion, he turned his head twenty degrees to the left and shouted, "Ho! It's Billister, at seventy-five feet!"

The throaty reply that came indeed was young Billister: "Oh, clearly I made it to fifty feet. You should have your eyes checked."

Saple harumphed, mushed through the sand to the opposite side of the sun reader, and there he released the latches that held a square frame to the back side of the box. He slid a pinpricked sheet of parchment out of the frame and returned it to the portfolio lying at his feet. He selected another page, clipped it into the frame and latched it back onto the box.

"I can never keep these writings separate," he grumbled. "Specially those what come before the coder system I started punching into the bottom corners—mmm—back eighteen months or so."

The wirey man reentered the box up to the waist, with the shroud down his shoulders. As his sweat-dripping nose brushed along the sheet of paper stretched across the back of the box, his damaged eyes could just make out the patterns of searing sun dots poked through it. He heard just outside the sun reader the rustle of a tote bag laden with canned goods and fruit being eased into the sand. He swallowed, thankful.

Billister was at his side now, and the young Rafer heard the muffled voice inside the box declare, "This is the one! Hoo, I'll mark it now. The theories we discussed—what, two years ago?—I was telling ya the principles of voting what the ancients used."

Billister watched as the blind man felt about for the oil cloth sack he had laid next to the post of the sun reader. It was a ritual they never spoke of anymore—a few tins and pieces of fruit pilfered from the larder of the mainhouse. Saple tried his hand at surf fishing and container gardening, but it was not enough to keep even a slender old hermit alive.

Assured of dinner, Saple returned to his reading. Fidgeting, Billister drew a sheet out of the portfolio that had been flopped in the sand. He held it up against the midday sun, admiring the precise rows of clustered dots. "One day you should teach to me your prick writing," he said, louder than usual to penetrate the canvas.

Saple grunted and tore the shroud off his back. "We will call it dot writing, please. It is a visual form of Braille, the tactile writing used by blind people way back when. By night I can write—all I need is stylus and paper. But daytime is the only time that I can read. For these sorry eyes, it takes the pure strength of the sun to penetrate the punctures I have put into the paper—the dot writing. Please, not 'prick writing.' More proper it would be to call what you do 'prick thinking.' Hah. I like it! I will write it up tonight: 'Billister, prick thinker of Thomas Island....'"

"But I'm serious," Billister said, rattling the parchment—Saple tolerated his habit of making unnecessary noises to announce where he was standing. "What is the point in having a library of writings that no one else in the world can translate?"

"It is a good question that, ahhh—" here Saple switched to the softer sounds of the Rafer tongue "—that there is no safe answer for. I lost my eyes for scripting much less than is recorded on these pages. There will be a use for them someday, ya, but for now they will just be my recollection, my second brain. Okay? Besides, knowing the dot writing would be even less use to you than that Latin what you've been studying."

"You wish you could read at night—why not just feel the holes with your fingers," Billister asked, "the way blind people among the ancients did?"

Saple held a withered hand aloft. "With these old bones? Hmph. Blood circulation bad as it is, I'm lucky I can feel well enough to find my pud. Besides, the Braille the ancients had was raised bumps. Much easier to feel than tiny holes in paper."

Billister picked a sand burr from between two toes. He decided to drop the subject, although he continued to speak Rafer. "I heard that there was an escape the other night," he said slowly.

"Quince—that was his name."

"Then it is true, that the bulliards found him here. That you had spoken to him?"

"There's not a thing ullegal, ya know, about having your home broken into by an escaped red-legger." In a shadowy kind of way, perhaps borne of imagination, Jersey Saple could see the young Rafer before him, shaved head nodding now sullenly.

"They doused him, ya know. He is dead."

"I know," Saple interrupted.

"...for killing the doctor, Scaramouch..."

"He'd a died the same just for the escape." There was a palpable death of enthusiasm between the two friends. Saple pulled the hair away from his face distractedly, trying to make the salty scraggles stay matted to the sides. It was a habit left over from sighted days, pulling hair out of his face. When Billister turned to leave, the writer reached out and clapped him accurately on the left shoulder, stopping him.

"You must know," Saple said, "that there was nothing I could do to save the man. I was sending him up to take Murdoch's boat when they surrounded the house. My only regret is that we dallied briefly in discussion. A few extra minutes, and..." The journalist's voice was low, almost a whisper, even though they were the only free men on the island to know the language.

Billister sniffed and walked toward the beach.

Saple stood helpless, knobby knees poking into the sunlight from ragged holes in his drawstring trousers. "Not a thing I could do, Billister, but I give ya this—he didn't kill Dr. Scaramouch. I'd mentioned the doctor to him in passing that night—and Quince had never heard of the blubber-butt bastard!"

The blind man heard the footsteps pause in the sand, and then he tracked their silent progress southeast—fifty feet, seventy-five, ninety....

13

The Photograph

BIG Tom stepped into the dank, natural perfume of the garden shed—rotting leaves and fertilizer—and steadied himself against the seed bins. The aisle seemed to be swaying under his feet, something like walking the bottom hold of a storm-thrown skimmer.

When he had stumbled his way to the cat-boy Cantilou, he felt that recurring, uneasy surprise—a wash of cold saltwater prickling his scalp and rushing down his spine. The feline sat paws forward, motionless except for its eyelids lapping down over those wide ebony pupils-gone-wild. Big Tom bent at his thick waist and marveled again at the total wet blackness of those eyes.

The little-boy lips on the animal's near-hairless face did not move, but there came the voice: "So, you think I am your madness, Big Tom?"

"Unh?" The merchant scratched at the front of his sweat-moist blouse.

"The skimmer is down and the crabs are feasting on what the feeder beasts did not bother with. The Lucia is well on its way to driftwood. But the dying won't stop—will it?—until you let her go. That's your madness." The Cantilou whacked its tail on the manure-filled burlap.

Big Tom wiped his nostrils between thumb and forefinger. "A fool 'ud let the gold go. It's mine, an' my secret."

"Ah," replied the Cantilou, closing its eyes, "too many died, and not enough died."

"Wha?" Big Tom squinted at the beast. "You mean me? Or who? Wha riddle is this?"

The Cantilou's eyes remained closed, and it appeared then nearly lifeless.

Billister had a theory that there were two sides to the mainhouse. Not like front door, back door. But two ways of viewing the mainhouse, two aspects, depending upon who you were.

There was the illusory version that Big Tom and his wives and visitors saw—a breezy, open-air mansion, three tiers of polished wood, rattan and verandas. The servants saw the other side, of course—the whiskey bottles and vomit; the grain and fish and salted beef to haul up from dockside storehouses; the putrid garbage mound out back, fenced in and populated by a family of vulture macaws.

It was a notion that Billister entertained as he made his rounds of the building, pushing his two-wheeled maintenance cart before him—trash bin in the center, wipe rags and spray bottles of wood oil and glass cleaner hanging off either side. Working the mainhouse, Billister imagined, was not unlike it would be working backstage in one of the New Chicago theaters that Jersey Saple spoke of. Clean this, fix that—create the illusion of luxury inside a pile of boards and stones and mortar.

Billister had oiled the left wheel of his cart, for this was not a day to be making unnecessary noises around the mainhouse. Big Tom had finally slouched in from his office down the hill after a whiskey bender and, probably, a nasty measure of the powder. He had entered with his arms slung over the shoulders of two of his musclers, his feet dragging, nearly useless. He had been sweating like a docksman at noon, and his skin was fish belly white.

Poor Big Tom, mourning his son so. And the loss of his

newest skimmer. The man never showed any emotion but rage. Sorrow was vented with a good mind sopping.

So Billister tip-toed in and out of the bedrooms emptying trash baskets, whisking at the floor with broom and dust pan, and wiping ashtrays. He could track an evening's amusements throughout the house just by reading the cigarette butts—who was where for how long.

In the pale half-light of the anteroom to Big Tom's bedroom, Billister righted a mahogany end table. Probably it had been upended by the careening master himself. Cautiously he paced into the bedroom. The windows had been thrust aside to allow in the curing fresh air, and someone had graciously hoisted the mosquito netting over the four-poster. Big Tom lay there on his back, wheezing and oblivious to the midday light streaming in.

Billister mashed his lips together and scanned the expanse of gleaming oak, trying to recall what areas of flooring would not creak as he went about his duties. He decided to empty the near trash basket, the one beside the headboard, and not risk venturing along the window side of the room. When Big Tom awoke, he would be in no condition to quibble about the housekeeping anyway.

In the basket there was nothing but a half-dozen torn and crumpled pieces of a photograph. It would have to be one of the late Dr. Scaramouch's works, of course—how odd to destroy one—and Billister felt a mournful unease settle into his chest as he knelt to remove the pieces. Sad, the murdered doctor. The houseboy sighed and the depression deepened in the tomb-quiet room when he realized what had been the subject of the doctor's photograph. Each shard of gray mounting showed a different section of a sleek new yacht in dry dock—undoubtedly the Lucia, for no other skimmer was so experimentally broad. This would have to be that photograph the doctor delivered the very night he was killed in the chemical room below the infirmary, the darkroom he called it.

What the trade master had obviously destroyed in a raging

despair, Billister decided to make whole again and return to him at a happier hour.

Tacked to the rough paneling at Big Tom's left was the original blueprint of the Lucia. Pinned to the wall below that was a photograph of the same skimmer, once ripped into six pieces and now remounted, the pieces glued flat and meticulously realigned. The white tear-gaps that remained had been inexpertly touched up with drawing lead. From fifteen feet away, one might think the photo had never been mangled.

Tacked to his drawing board before him was a sheet of drafting paper, wide and blank.

It was Sunday morning, and Big Tom gazed lazily in a hangover fog from the board to the motionless shipyard below. Most workers had the day off, as had been the custom since Jesus People worked the island generations ago. Only those in essential positions were on duty—Sanders Lafitte, for instance, down at the pub. And Big Tom considered that he could use an ale or maybe even two.

No. He returned to his ruminations over the Lucia II. From the scant witnessing that Bark had given him, he had to decide where he had gone wrong—if it was a bad design at all. Had he really been the victim of monstrous chance, as the excitable Bark had suggested? If he had not exiled the Jesus People from the island, he knew, they would be saying that the sinking had come by God's will, some sort of cosmic comeuppance. Ach.

Big Tom heard the shouts of Captain Bull's bargemen on the hillside. He hissed a long sigh, pushed himself back from the drawing board, and treated himself to a machine-rolled cigarette. This is what he had really come to the office for, and he could set aside his dalliance with the Lucia II.

Outside, leaning into the veranda rail, he sucked on the cigarette, thought how good it would go with an ale, and watched the procession winding down the shell-and-gravel main road. In front marched a haughty little toad-like man, huffing out an unintelligible count that seemed to make sense to the red-leggers shuffling behind. They were march-manacled, wrists to waistband and then to each other as well, front to back. For this no leg irons were needed—it moved things along, and an en masse escape was impossible. It was better that this be done on a Sunday, as some workers were still unaccountably haunted by the sight of the very commerce that fed them and their babies.

Big Tom listened to the count from the little, fat man. It sounded something like "Oad, umpa, thail, tu…, oad, umpa…." Around Rafers long enough, he supposed, and you pick up a few words.

From that, his thoughts drifted to the young Rafer, Billister, just the night before. Big Tom was barely aroused from a day's bedridden stupor when the shave-head kid proudly presented him with the Scaramouch photograph, pasted together and retouched. The house boy's eyes had glinted and begged for approval. Big Tom had twisted strands of his beard irritably, thanked him gruffly, and dismissed him.

But Billister had insisted on presenting the commander of the Caribbean with one more gift—a titillating shred of gossip to consider, that Quince the red-legger might not have buggered Dr. Scaramouch as everyone had suspected, that the escapee had not known of any such doctor. Not that Quince would have died any differently, Billister noted in his diplomatic smoothness, but it did raise the issue of whether there was some other murderer on the island.

And now Big Tom sucked in cigarette smoke, enjoying the satisfactory sting webbing across the tip of his tongue. His red eyes followed the procession, scores of ragged men and women, most of them gray-black of skin and all looking sickly and sad. A half-dozen of Captain Bull's men kept pace alongside, jabbing at the laggards with the tips of their chopped shotguns, jovial at the prospect of getting off to sea toward the carnal lures of mainland.

Big Tom spat at the thought of having to keep the redleggers in the holds so long, and he wondered what discount he would have to surrender when they were sold finally to the Southland farming concerns. Money would be pig-ass tight until the gold was recovered. He wondered often about those farms, how they managed to keep a man secure yet working the land at the same time. And he thanked chance, or God, or whatever there might be to thank, that the red-leggers kept escaping and returning to their island homelands to be harvested again and sold again…

The first of the red-leggers reached the barges dockside, and Captain Bull's men were detaching each of them and shackling them to stubby little posts spaced three feet apart on the barges. The barges themselves were not much more than rusty clusters of metal drums lashed to beams and boarded over. They looked dangerous to the ship-making mind of Big Tom, although he had heard of nay but a few sinking or even flipping over.

Captain Bull would be in the pilot house of the tug now, where he had retreated huffily when he was released from the hoosegow. He seemed to know he had been held on spurious charges and was grousing loudly when he was set free from the little ramshack jail. His bargemen were irritable themselves, but they calmed him down with a good ribbing. Better to get out and forget.

The last of the procession of red-leggers was snaking down the road now, and manacled at the very end was the one that Big Tom had come to see. That last manacled man—out of place, like a flower in the trash heap. Dazed, beaten about the face but healthy and muscular, a clean white tunic. Billister.

In the thought muddle of a mind bruised by whiskey and powder, Big Tom had argued with himself over whether to kill the house boy. From some painful corner of his brain came a stark admonishment—no. He had spared him as a baby some fifteen years ago and he would do it again now.

He did wonder, though, which was actually worse—a quick death, or the slow death that was the lot of a redlegger? He sucked on the cigarette butt, burning it down to his pinching fingers, and flipped it over the rail.

Yes, Billister, he thought, the doctor's murderer is still among us on the island. And the murderer is me.

Inside, he ripped the photo angrily—into four-dozen pieces this time, a shower of little shards falling into the trash basket. His hand shaking, Big Tom flicked open his pocket knife and steadied it against his large belly. From the drawing table drawer he snapped up the metal cylinder, screwed off its top, and wondered where he was going to find a new house boy.

14

A New Mission

ROSENTHAL Webb's lungs were gurgling with each breath and he felt feverish, but this was not a meeting to miss. There were only five other faces around the Revolutionary Council table, the others no doubt busy with mounting administrative chores.

We're all getting stretched rather thin, Webb thought to himself.

Winston Weet was getting flushed in the face as he ranted to the council, and Webb instinctively knew to begin paying attention to the speech again. The round-faced orator was finally getting to the point. It was as if Weet's guts constricted whenever he measured his words carefully, and this tightening forced blood up into his face.

"...and if the very existence of the Revolutionary movement owes itself to the theory that Government must serve its people, as opposed to the people serving the Government, I propose that our priorities should lie with the dismantling of the work camps."

"He's getting philosophical again," Eliot Kohrn grumbled to himself.

Weet slapped the edge of the conference table. "I'm beginning to believe that we're wasting too much time here tying ribbons and bows. The camps should have turned open and voluntary the day we nipped the Monitor's head off."

Virginia Quale broke in, "And the schools broadened, and scientific inquiries begun...."

"No," Weet replied, whapping the table again, "none of those before freedom of the individual."

"But as yet, we have so few of our own people in place in New Chicago," Quale objected.

Weet frowned. "Sometimes I think we're being more careful—ya, more paranoid—that the Monitor ever was. Who's ta say that the populace will want us for leaders once we announce ourselves anyway? Why must we be in total control of New Chicago? Or is it that we're afraid of what the populace will want—just like the Monitor?"

Webb tried in vain to clear his lungs with a cough, but spoke anyway with a slightly strangled sound: "Ya, the theory of it all is amusing ta bat about, but I say this—" he coughed again "—I say we're down to no man power to even start such a mission. Ho, we can send a few freelance musclers to Chautown, have our people in New Chicago wire 'em authorization for this and that. But it will take a lot more than cable messages to prevent a massacre. Remember, there's still a tangle of bastards in Merqua what would want the Monitor's systems intact, even if he ain't."

"You go, Rosenthal," said Kohrn. "You who's so quick to jump into a mission, farther the better, when it's the homeland what needs fixing. So quick to send Gregory off an' then complain of man power."

"My health like this, with this mud in my lungs, I couldn't possibly start out," Webb answered. "As fer Gregory, he'd be right for the job, the right temperament. But I can't apologize for just asking him to contact a shipbuilder. He shoulda reported back by now. I say let's hold up on this 'til we hear from him."

Quale looked undecided, and her eyes darted from person to person around the table.

"I say we go on it now," Weet huffed. "You have an able

muscler down on Level Five right now—doin' nothing but petting his willie. The big booger, guy with a scar on his nose—what's his name?"

Webb's face drained. "Fel Guinness? You've never been in the field with 'im. Disaster. A savage with a banger or knife when that's needed. Fine. But trust him to a diplomatic matter? Disaster."

"Perhaps you should have sent Guinness to strong-arm the shipbuilder, that Big Tom," Kohrn put in. "Then Gregory would be here to recruit a team outta Chautown."

"Disaster. Guinness on his own? Disaster."

When the debate fell cold, Quale said, "So. I propose a vote: If Gregory is not back within a week, Fel Guinness leaves for Chautown."

Not necessary, Webb said to himself. He could read the five other faces, and he had lost.

Webb rapped on a narrow plank door on Level Five and heard a muffled "Unh" respond within, which Webb took for permission to enter. When he stepped in, an object whirred past his ear and whacked into the door. A Rafer tosser disk bit into the pine, forming a perfect line with three other disks down the center brace.

"Thass pig-pokin' dangerous," Webb said, keeping his voice steady.

Fel Guinness slouched in his cot, leaning against the far wall. Unlike many denizens of the Revolutionary hideout, he had the tanned, weather-beaten look of a man who had spent much of his life out of doors. He had a strangely small head and large lips. He was frowning now, his right index finger still poised in the air from making the toss.

"Ah dint use the poison, Mr. Webb. That would be dangerous."

Webb studied the inscriptions on the disks. He suspected that eventually someone would copy the nasty little weapons, but these were authentic Rafer.

"Where did ya get 'em?" Webb asked.

"Traded an old banger for 'em a while ago."

"Hmph, doubt that," Webb replied. "A proper Rafer wouldn't have a use for a banger, wouldn't go near one."

"Oh ya. Guy I got these from weren't a Rafer. He'd killed a few, though."

Webb sighed. He was tempted to give Guinness a lecture on Revolutionary policies, but he thought better of it. Guinness already knew them well.

"Likely we'll have a mission for you to run in a week or so," Webb said. "So next time ya go prowling, don't go too far."

Guinness pushed his hands into the mattress and sat forward. "This got something to do with that big ship you keep talking about? That ship what's gonna sail some of us over for a taste of European radiation, count of ours ain't good enough?"

Webb leaned against the dresser, feigning patience. The room had a close, rotty smell, and he wondered if this room alone could be fouling the air of the entire complex. There was little decoration, save for the weaponry belts and bangers hung from nails around the wall. A small photo of a large-breasted woman, the blurry sort of porno snapshot sold by the street corner ruggers in New Chicago, was tacked to the wall beside Guinness's cot.

Webb coughed. "Nah," he said. "This is a run down ta Chautown. Need a team put together—I'll give you some names of reliable men down there, time comes. The team will do the enforcing once we announce the dismantling of the forced labor on the Southland farms. Any trouble, make it work."

Guinness scratched at his crotch. "That I can do," he said.

"But I tell ya," Webb said, pointing a nubbed finger into the air, "this ain't a license to whack an' chop anyone what don't kiss your toes."

"Me?"

"You been warned," Webb said, turning to go.

"Hey wait, Mr. Webb!"

"Ya?"

"Show me that new tattoo?"

15

Filling an Order

MORNING in the mainland mountains, even on an early summer day, was much too cold for a skinny, young man to be standing outside in his underwear. This thought was on Farmington's mind as he shivered on the rim of a small swimming pool at the downhill end of Cred Faiging's compound.

The hillside had been cleared of trees and surrounded with high electrified fence against all outsiders—scavengers, Revolutionaries and Government people alike. (Faiging, the renowned inventor and manufacturer, treasured his privacy and independence.) The grounds were dotted with long and low manufacturing huts, the main laboratory-residence, and the garages beyond. The scrubby grass was criss-crossed with muddy vehicle tracks running between the structures.

The sun was bright but warmed little, and Farmington, in drenched undershorts, was enjoying very little privacy. The aging, yellow-and-white-haired inventor was strapping a tank-and-hose contraption onto the younger man's back. Faiging's assistant, a drawling stick figure named Kim, was dragging up a duffel bag of other gear.

"The trouble with showin' those brochures around," Faiging was saying, "is that once in a witch's moon you'll make an immediate sale. Big Tom don't know that the only

SUB we have is the prototype. But we can't be disappointing an eager customer, can we?"

Farmington's entire pale body was shaking. "He wasn't... eager enough to pay...cash this time," he stuttered. "Seemed odd to me. Always...he always paid cash before."

Faiging sucked in his pocked cheeks as he considered the point and released them again with a comical pop. Like Farmington and many other southlanders, he razored off his facial hair every few days. "Ya said they was a load of red-leggers what Captain Bull brought up. See there? Big Tom's got plenty of money—we can wait for the delivery. Just you get expert at using the SUB, while I see can we throw together a couple more. By time I'm done, you'll be able to demonstrate your merchandise like a proper salesman."

Kim was pretending not to notice the cold little bulge in Farmington's pants. She lifted each of Farmington's feet to strap them into a pair of downward-curving paddles fashioned from old tire rubber. Next, the mask, a thick piece of window glass surrounded by more rubber and sealed to the face with a coating of gum to keep the water out. She secured it by tightening a strap across the back of his head.

"Captain Bull's due back in Edenton in juss three weeks," the younger man said, his nose stopped up by the mask. "Reckon you'll be done then?"

Air whoosed out of the hose as the inventor pressed the mouth piece for a final test. "This I call the air-stager," Faiging said, fitting it into the salesman's mouth. "Think of it as a mouth switch—you suck in, it'll feed you air till you stop. And yeah, I can make a couple more—if the inspectors leave me alone meantime." Faiging and Kim exchanged sober glances. Farmington noticed and wondered what kind of heat the old man was drawing this time.

He breathed in on the mouthpiece and filled his lungs with stale-tasting air, then heaved it out again. Seemed to work. Mouth only—don't breathe with the nose—that would be one of the hard parts.

"How'd you think up a machine like this?" Farmington asked.

"Like a lot of my inventions," Faiging said, rapping the tank, "I just plain didn't. A scavenger, a scummy old bugwart name of Alistar found it nearbout the coast. Didn't know what it was, but knew I'd have a use for it. This tank's an original, ancient stuff. The hose was rotted, just enough there to copy the design."

Not at all reassured, Farmington jumped into the pool feet first. The water was just thirty feet across, muddy looking. It was formed by sloping concrete walls that were hard to see and easy, he had found out during his earlier swim, to scrape knees on. Before, when he had just dipped into the pool, the visibility underwater was virtually nonexistent. Now, he could see at least a few feet away. He stood up, thrust his head out of the water, and nodded his tentative satisfaction to Faiging.

"Good," the inventor called out. "Now go to the deep part—try out those foot paddles."

Farmington obeyed, swimming down, hands out front in case he encountered another wall. The paddles supplied remarkable propulsion, but at a depth of twelve feet or so he could barely see his hands in front of his face. The water was seriously numbing his body, too, and Farmington hoped that vision and temperature were not going to be such a problem in Caribbean waters. The breathing was not too bad, though—an easy hissing intake; a flatulent-sounding rush of bubbles on the exhale.

His right leg brushed against seaweed, and Farmington thought that odd in a concrete pool. He swam upward for better light and turned himself upright in the water to look: A long black band with white speckles was wrapping itself around his ankle. He screamed a torrent of bubbles, losing the mouthpiece, and scraped the creature away frantically with his left foot paddle.

Arms and legs flailing, he scrabbled up the hard bank into the grass at Cred Faiging's feet. He rolled onto his back, the tank propping him up, and examined his numb legs for fang marks. "Snake," he stammered. "Pig-poking speckled...big ol' snake."

"Dammit," Kim said, hooking a thumb into her dingy denims, "I thought water moccasins might a got in there! You rest up, and I'll try to rake 'em out."

"Thanks," the salesman said, watching her boney little rear end wobble away.

Faiging knelt and swept aside the blood on Farmington's knees. The scrapes didn't look too bad.

"You did that just right," the older man said, "letting the air out like that."

"Huh?"

"In deep water—you rising fast like that—I figure if you didn't exhale, your lungs 'ud burst."

"Mr. Faiging...uh, gawd. Never mind."

16

On the Bottom

THREE streamers flew from the mainmast of Tooth of Horan, one blue and two orange. The skimmer pointed out at just 125 feet, but with three small cannons starboard and three backboard, she was the most heavily armed—and the most sluggish—of Big Tom's fleet.

Bishop sipped coffee from a metal cup and chewed lazily on a sausage biscuit brought up from the crew slots. At such a peaceful summer daybreak, Bishop thought to himself, hard to believe there was tragedy here just two months back. The Tooth of Horan was anchored fore and aft, just a mile south of that low lump of sand, rock, and jungle called Dunkin Island.

They had spent yesterday locating the wreck of the Lucia. Bark had sight-reckoned the area to be searched, and swimmers scanned it in a criss-cross grid with the new Cred Faiging diving masks or the old-style glass viewing bowls. And now a yellow net bob marked her 140-foot hulk, seventy feet below. She had appeared intact, but with light falling the actual search of the downed skimmer was put off until today.

Bishop's morning peace did not last long. Big Tom's growl rumbled from below—"On deck, lagbellies! On deck!"—as he pounded the walls of the crew's quarters with his fists. And then the bearded trade master burst up out of the hatch, fresh and clear-eyed like Bishop had not seen him in months, an eager black bear done with hibernation.

As the crew grumbled into a loose assembly near the starboard rail, Bishop considered that it was nothing like the military-style assembly he imagined the Government would require. If it had a navy. They were a sag-eyed lot, and these clothes they had slept in quite needed an airing. But they fell respectfully quiet when Big Tom waved his meaty arms over his head. They numbered nine, total: Big Tom captaining for this expedition only; Bark as first mate; Bishop; the Tooth of Horan's usual captain, a round young woman named Altia, demoted temporarily and fairly silent about her indignation; her usual first mate, Mark Ontario; the Tooth of Horan's usual three crewmen; and Farmington, looking as if he'd prefer to be on land.

That one Farmington, Bishop thought, he looks awfully out of ease—something about these new breather tanks.

Big Tom cleared his throat with a loud harf, and shouted his speech into the steady sailor's wind: "We will be starting a search today of the Lucia, which holds the leavin's of my only son. But it's a search about which I have not been full in the telling, for reasons you'll gully right rapid. Some among you, I'd wager, are those talking that it'd be more right-minded to let the bones lie with the Lucia, a captain an' her ship forever. But her ballast…hmph…well, she went down with a bellyful of gold, and we're here to bring it up a hoist-load at a time."

There was a gale of spontaneous conversation. Altia mumbled, "I knew it." A dubious claim.

Altia lowered the dory over the side, and tied it off at the aft anchor rope. That would serve as a station for the divers.

Farmington shuffled, sickly looking, to the gasoline-powered air compressor center deck and yanked at the starter rope. It sputtered to life, then leveled out into a gargly hum.

He clapped its feeder hose over the valve of the first tank and tightened the screw ring.

Bishop watched Farmington with a suspicious eye, as the two of them had argued the day before about this process.

"How come is it," Bishop had asked the young salesman, "that you expects a man can breathe out of such a little bottle of air for half an hour?"

"Because the air is compressed—uh, mashed together—into the tank by this machine until it actually holds as much air as the entire ship does below decks. Think of that!"

"But below decks a this skimmer," Bishop had replied, "how come is it that I could breathe for a week withou' coming up, huh? An' you says your bottle of air won't last a whit of that?" Farmington had not completely thought out his response before Bishop spat and lurched away.

Now, Bishop shoved himself off the backboard rail and decided to busy himself with assembling the spare winch into a side hoist. The tripod-boom-and-pulley rig would bring the gold up ten bars at a time.

Bark clapped Bishop on the shoulder and whispered, "If I'd a been Big Tom, most of my fortune in the Lucia, don't know as I'd have let her outta the harbor. And let Little Tom captain her? Never."

Bishop crossed the deck, dragging the pulley gear in a sack behind him. He exaggerated the hunch in his shoulder on purpose—the one arm hanging lower than the other. Some of the Cell Island trugs said it made him look animalistic—cunning and powerful. Yes, the ladies were paid for favors both physical and mental, but this particular point he chose to believe.

There were only three air tanks for Farmington to fuss over. Cred Faiging had sent an apologetic letter with Farmington explaining that the unexpected order had temporarily depleted his stock.

Farmington had delivered the letter and kept to himself his reservations about life-critical equipment that had been manufactured in such a hurry. He recalled with trepidation the procession of factory workers entering the low huts at

Faiging's compound. They were grime-faced mountain folk with bad teeth and split fingernails. Geniuses at assembly, Faiging claimed. And so far the tanks and air stagers and gauges (originally boiler parts) functioned flawlessly. So far.

Farmington had taken each of the SUBs to the bottom of Faiging's muddy test pool—once it had been freed of moccasins—so mayhap there was nothing to worry about. He had given them another trial run while teaching Bark and Big Tom how to use the tanks in the shallows of Thomas Harbor.

The three of them would make the first dive to scope out the skimmer, cut some exploratory holes, and set up the hoist line: Farmington would make the dive because of his expertise with the breathing equipment, Big Tom because of his builder's knowlege of the Lucia, and Bark out of the unspoken notion that a first mate should take part in setting aright a mess he helped create.

Big Tom shouldered one of the three harnesses, but Farmington said no, and pointed to the rig with six lead weights lashed to the front belt. The other harnesses only had two.

Farmington looked embarrassed. "Um, bigger men, they float more easily—the extra weights compensate."

As they strapped on their harnesses and belted the tanks into them—Bark towering over the two of them, looking puzzled, Big Tom looking impatient—Farmington reviewed aloud his teachings on use of the gear. Admonitions against panic. Stay together, to watch for emergencies. Breathe slowly, evenly.

He tried to sound authoritative, but his stomach knotted with the uncertainty of what would happen with the breather tanks at a depth of seventy feet. That was a lot of water to have on top of ya, a lot of pressure, far from a man's natural grab of air.

They splashed into the Caribbean blue cold, and Altia threw their tire-rubber foot paddles after them. They were too awkward for a man to stand in on deck.

Big Tom coughed, shouted an anguished "Hooo-ahhh" at the frigid sting, then silenced himself by biting into his breather. On a hemp line, Altia carefully lowered to him a heavy cloth satchel of saws, drills, and ropes. Bark splashed around folding the sling that was tethered to the winch line, which he would take to the bottom. Farmington led the way over to the dory, then down the aft anchor line into the blue bubbly quiet.

Now Big Tom understood the point about the weights. Even with the six slung under his large belly, and the extra weight of the tools, he had to work to push himself deeper as he followed Farmington, one hand pulling along the anchor line. The foot paddles provided astounding propulsion, but when he paused he would slowly begin to rise again. His thoughts flickered to Moori, her ranting about all the ale he consumed, and then the sea floor and the Lucia came into focus.

Big Tom's renewed vigor seemed to fade as he descended into the gloom where his finest skimmer lay. The horror of her sinking was not real until this moment. She lay on the bleak sandy landscape exactly as she had last been seen—fatally weighted onto her backboard side by her precious shifted ballast. A word came to Big Tom's mind, dark-sounding and foreign: Port. That was it. A Rafer word. Rafers, he remembered now for some reason, called the backboard side of a skimmer port.

The Lucia's top deck faced away from them. With Farmington still in the lead, they left the anchor rope. Big Tom dropped lower than the rest, compelled to do just this one thing—touch her keel. And he did that, ran his hand along the wide beam sadly, the way he would stroke the spine of a lover.

Then, like a mountain climber freed from gravity, he glided up her hull to join the others where the starboard rail arced up like the rim of a canyon. Big Tom was taking a breath every two or three seconds—too much, he knew. He wouldn't last the thirty minutes. The cold did it. And the distress.

Farmington was looking excited, his head twisting back and forth from the Lucia's deck below him to Big Tom approaching. The young man's black hair rose into a dancing mop that jerked with each turn. Bark rose over the rail, too, and waved Big Tom on.

When he topped the rail, the trade master saw. The skimmer's nonbouyant debris was already fanned out across the rippled sand. A narrow slice of the backboard decking was missing. Not fractured by impact. Not eaten away arbitrarily by the Caribbean's fabled sea worms, the giant gluttons that would just as soon make a meal of a mast as they would a man.

No. The decking had been pried away precisely as he, Farmington and Bark had planned to do—by intelligent hands. The reason was obvious, and Big Tom knew immediately that the gold would be gone.

As he stared in shock, Big Tom drew the air-stager out of his mouth as if discarding a cigar he had lost the taste for. He scanned the looted yacht defiantly, a minuscule stream of bubbles trippling out of his lips, as if he dared the sea to take his life as well as his wealth. Farmington issued an audible squeak through his mask and jammed the mouth piece back between the fat man's teeth.

A tiny dragon fish trailed colorful fins across Big Tom's mask, and he swatted the little beast away irritably.

17

A Reflection on Tongues

Sun reader dotscript
Portfolio 14
Page 27
Jersey Saple

FURTHER historical notes, linguistic in particular, for possible inclusion in history of the Rafer race. Fact, theory and lore collected by self and Billister from interviews with incarcerated red-leggers.

The Rafer language, formally known to its users as Guller, appears to be an amalgam of ancient tongues, including American Indian dialects, Spanish, a whit of English, and a large measure from a pre-war European country called Africa, more specifically its sector called Sierra Leone. They are a darker-skinned people than the predominant mainland race, which itself is undoubtedly a mixture of ancient bloodlines. The Rafers owe their isolation and proliferation, in part, to homelands remote from the ravages of Big Bang Day (islands south and east of mainland Merqua, as well as swamplands rimming the Gulf of Texaco).

The Rafer gene pool has remained to a large part distinct. This is due in part to their religious devotion to the writings of an ancient named Rutherford Cross and to his "son" Pec-Pec, as well as an aversion to systems and regulation inherent in the current mainland government.

Guller would seem to have had some effect on mainland English. Witness the ancient word Guller itself, which aside from naming the language, also is a Rafer word meaning wisdom, understanding or fluency. To be fluent in Guller would have meant, to Rafers of long past, to have education, to have wisdom. It would seem to be the derivation of the mainland word gully, which of course carries precisely the same definitions. The word gully, by the way, is not to be found in any of the prewar English writings impounded in New Chicago, or in Revolutionary archives.

Government linguists, prone to disparagement and degrandizement of the Rafers, have argued that the word derives somehow from gullible, which would require that in the course of doing so it took on a nearly opposite definition. That would make it a rare case, indeed.

18

The Disc Spin

"WATCH again. Watch me—closely." Tym tapped her chest, indicating herself, not at all sure that the blond young man with the vacant stare knew a whit of the Rafer tongue, even before his injuries. She was glad now for the patience she had learned during her occasional classroom duties, the methodical persistence required to teach a child-like mind.

For the first time in her life she wished she knew enough of the Fungus People's language, that sound like barking dogs.

"This is called the disc roll. It will make you strong—here. Strong." She slapped her slender forearm. She paused, and then slapped her thigh. "And here. And it is a good defensive stance, impossible to attack."

The man squatted naked outside of Tym's bunker, obediently making an effort to concentrate. His wounds had healed into flat, silvery patches of hairless flesh, a round one on his forehead and a long salamander-shaped swath running up the back of his head, neck to crown. His left eye and the left side of his mouth sagged slightly with reduced muscle control. His head cocked to the side, like a spaniel begging for comprehension. A brilliant chest tattoo spiraled off to entangle his neck, arms, and crotch.

Tym sighed and began the maneuver. She stretched out over the soft earth, a black mixture of rotted jungle vegetation that would prevent the bruising of an inexpert student. She propped herself up on all five points—two feet, two hands, and her chin extended as far out as possible. Then slowly she lifted her chin and right hand, waiting for the blond man to observe. As she touched her chin to the ground, her right foot rose. As her right hand touched the ground, she lifted her left foot. So went the pattern. She repeated the motion, first slowly, then more and more rapidly—always two adjacent appendages in the air—until she resembled a spinning coin waddling against the ground.

When old Sey-Waage approached, Tym broke out of her spin and into a cartwheel. She rolled up his chest, flattening him to the dirt. She came to a standing stop on his sternum, one foot poised daintily above the gray thatch of hairs sprouting from his Adam's apple. Sey-Waage sputtered with mild surprise, although it was not the first time he had been used as a fighting prop.

"Gragi, this you can do, and you must try—to keep your body fit," Tym said to her student.

Sey-Waage hacked and rumbled his lungs under Tym's spindly yet deadly heel. "May I rise, please," the elder asked, "before you flatten my swallowpipe?" It was a high-pitched voice, but smooth and girllike.

"Ya," Tym replied. She stepped back and brushed the flecks of dirt out of the patch of Spanish moss that grew from his chest, then helped the elder up. Three tiny calliamaw feathers dangled from his leather necklace, and one of their shafts was now bent. With a deft flick of two fingers, Tym straightened it as she brushed at his chest. She hoped he wouldn't notice right away. He would find out eventually, of course—the next time Sey-Waage stitched and cleaned a wound with the feather—but perhaps by then he would not recall how the quill might have snapped.

To distract him, Tym returned to her demonstration. She

had never known the old man to resist watching a lithe female body in motion. With the two men watching her now, young and old, she resumed the disc spin, kicking up a circle of peat as she whirled, rapidly this time, into a blur.

Sey-Waage stole a glance at this young one that Tym had taken to calling Gragi. The elder had been able to heal this Fungus Person's mean head cuts, but obviously there was a rotting fever under the surface that did not allow his mind to reach full awareness. For an injured Rafer, the cure for such damage would be tedious but obvious, and none could do a better job of it than this old Healer.

But the mind of a Fungus Person was altogether different, an unfathomable maze that he would more quickly wreck through his blundering than repair. Tym had to be persuaded that her Fungus Person friend needed to return to his own people, his own Healers.

When Sey-Waage returned his gaze to the romp dirt, Tym had disappeared. His lips twisted in mock disgust at such a school child trick. The revered Pec-Pec, it was said, was able to literally disappear at will—one instant there and the next gone. But young Tym, a mere younger, just a Gatherer, a provider of fish and rock crawlers, was not so capable. She had spun off somewhere the second he had glanced at Gragi, and now she was hiding. Timing—almost as good as actually disappearing, if you catch your observer off guard.

Let's see. Sey-Waage squinted and detected a minuscule rain of dirt particles settling to the ground. His eyes followed their line and came to a many-trunked banyan tree hunched at the edge of the clearing like a twelve-legged cat. Ah, that would make an amusing spin-climb for an immature young woman. The elder pointed into the leafy upper branches, even though he could not see Tym, and cried, "Hak, must be a jellyfish in the sky." His visual hunt for her had taken less time than a heartbeat.

There was a disappointed rustle of branches, foul cursing, and Tym dropped out of the tree.

As Tym marched back, Sey-Waage turned his back to her and stepped away from Gragi and toward the village.

Showing his back like that was a message to Tym that something vaguely troubling was in the air. As he moved his knee joints burned, and he told himself that at age 128 he should not be feeling old—mature, but not old. Perhaps it was the fatiguing sadness. The physical ache one feels for the decline of civilized people.

From this vantage point, looking up this hillside of Jonni Island toward the south end of the village, the elder could see nearly all of the huts and tents. He was awed by the varied designs, demonstrating influence from all corners of the Caribbean and beyond. All of the inhabitants were Rafers, all of them island-hopping nomads—but even then, what a hodgepodge of humanity!

The low tents with the hooping supports under a primitive stretch of animal skin—those would be from the remote Litus Archipelago, south and west of here, one of the few island regions said to be damaged irrevocably by the firebombs of the ancient war. The sturdier structures of tile and thatch would belong to more well-to-do traders, indigenous probably, who had never had the misfortune of being sold to the mainland to work the farms—had never lost their spouses to despairing remarriage, or their trading brass to envious neighbors, or their tongues to the slavers.

But most peculiar of all of the island's structures was the new bunker Tym had just built for herself and the blond one. Its sloping walls were made of bricks of metal the color of the sun.

Tym was at his side now, a slender shadow above him against the electric blue sky, breathing hard, a defensive tone in her voice: "It will revive his coordination. It will give him a talent to survive by."

Sey-Waage cleared his throat, a harumph meant to express disapproval. "Any child can learn the disc spin. Any child can learn to wheel away into the treetops." He paused to let the barb sink in. "But your Gragi has an adult body, an untrained one, an incapable one, with a damaged mind. It is not the same as teaching the disc spin to a child. He will not learn."

"Gragi improves every day," Tym told the Healer. She was pleading, wringing her hands in the lap of her soiled trousers. "He makes sounds sometimes—I think they might be words in his own tongue."

"Babble. Blither."

"But it sounds the way that the Fungus People speak, like a kennel of animals."

Sey-Waage snorted, signaling his final pronouncement on the subject: "The blond one needs the medicine of his own people, the Fungus People."

"But he was aboard the slave ship! That is how they care for their own. They will sell him to the mainland, like any other red-legger. Perhaps it has to do with the tattoo—the death sun. Perhaps they think of him as part Rafer."

Sey-Waage held his temper. He resisted the temptation to ask her if she pitied the blond one more than her fellow Rafers, whose population was being decimated by the slaving. Five Rafers, he wanted to remind her, were not able to scrabble their way out of the holds of the Lucia alive. But such a comment would start an argument, one that Tym was not capable of winning, and the elder decided to spare her that embarrassment.

"To never get well," he said, "to never regain a full mind—that to me is a worse kind of slavery. It is a risk, one that must be taken. We do not know his past, save for the odd story written by the plains Rafers in Gragi's tattoo. And we do not know his future."

Sey-Waage could tell by the rise in her voice that the young woman was finding the impertinence to press the point. So he changed the subject, the privilege of an elder. He pointed by clapping his index finger and middle finger together in the direction of Tym's bunker.

"You tell me that this is gold," he said, "the measure by which Fungus People value themselves. If it is their power, then it is a power that can be used against them. Have you thought of that?"

Tym frowned, puzzled, and Sey-Waage wondered if she

was frivolous enough to worry about losing her sparkling new bunker.

"But I have used it against them," Tym responded. "It could be the gold of no one but the chief of slavers, Big Tom. It was I who showed our swimmers, our raftsmen, how to take this power from him. Now, among people of his kind, lack of power will be his undoing."

The elder was nodding his head, agreeing politely. "But now Big Tom's power is standing idle," he said, pointing again with the clapping fingers. "It makes a sturdy home for you and your handsome pupil but no more. It is not even a practical home, for it lacks ready mobility. There are people among these islands, though—Fungus People, even—who would be willing to help us in exchange for some of this gold."

"But..." Tym paused to consider the grotesque proposition. "That would be using it just as the Fungus People do."

"Ah," the elder responded, smiling. "Hmmm."

Behind them, Gragi was down sweating in the dirt, practicing the disc spin. Arms, legs, and chin slapped into the dirt awkwardly, disastrously. He looked like a child smashing ants. A goat walked by him on its way to munch on the underbrush. It gave Gragi a quick glare.

Sey-Waage wondered whether he should mention to Tym the chest feather she had broken.

That night, Tym had almost lapsed into sleep when she awoke with a start in her hammock. Gragi was standing at her side and had cautiously caressed her right breast. Then quickly he climbed in with her, setting the hammock swinging dangerously in the dark.

He was against her, naked as well, breathing hotly, a flush Tym could feel all the way to her toes. He stroked at her hip gently. His intentions, and arousal, were apparent.

Gragi's tattoo rippled with the excited breathing, and Tym remembered the peculiar story that Sey-Waage had translated from the art script contained within the swirl. It began, "The bearer of this death sun is a valorous man among the Fungus People whose continued life I hearby grant…." It was signed by Tha 'Enton, identified as a Rafer warrior and musician from the western plains of the mainland.

Tym hesitated. Oddly, she considered accepting Gragi—the tongues among the villagers could not wag any more disapprovingly than they already did. She studied his pale eyes for the understanding of what he was doing—that would help her decide. And when the answer came to her, Tym realized that old Sey-Waage had been right. About Gragi. About the gold. Everything.

19

Parting

AS they neared the coast, Tym lowered the hinged mast on her catamaran—let the breakers, suddenly roaring just under them, carry their craft to the beach. Even under a new moon, an erect white sail could catch the eye of a beach wanderer, and that would not do. As she and Gragi lay clinging to the elastic beetle vines webbed between the two pontoons, Tym wondered why she had not thought to bring a dark sail for the night work. Her mind was in pain with this business about Gragi and—ach—too many lapses could be fatal.

Tym watched Gragi bowing headlong into the billows of sea foam, innocent eyes pressed shut, mouth open in a silent scream and filling with white water, draining, and filling again. During the hard sail over the last two days he had been so cooperative, eager, even, to meet a fate which he had no mind to comprehend. Now he leaned emphatically into the surf, vest and leg skins sopping in the wind, a lamb being born into a cruel and foreign terrain.

The pontoons skid-scratched into the sand. Tym pointed past Gragi's nose to the docks east up the beach, and the lights of the pub house. She shoved him out of the cradle and he staggered into the cooling sand. He stood there dumbly, hair glistening even in the moonless dark—looking back at her, expecting her to lead him into this new life. He let out one sharp, barking whine—a sea lion croak.

Tym vaulted into the sand, too, her hands planted on the edge of the webbing, and proceeded to push her catamaran back into the surging sea. Quickly, she told herself. This must be done quickly.

But before she was even hip deep Gragi had splashed his way back to the boat's webbing, his safe nest. Tym cursed and pulled the catamaran once again toward the beach. She wanted Gragi safe in the hands of his fellow Fungus People, but not at the expense of her own life—or her enslavement. This foul island....

On the sand again, Tym dragged the catamaran toward the camouflage of the rolling dunes several yards upland. Gragi caught on and helped, then delighted in the game of kicking at the sand to erase the furrows left by the pontoons.

Tym shed her skins and left them in the boat's webbing. But Gragi, she decided, was too light skinned to be running around bare in the dark. Gragi's eyes lingered on her, and she knew he would follow unquestioningly. Her throat tightened.

A quick survey of the upsloping terrain gave her an obvious destination—the tiered wooden structure halfway up Crown Mountain. It threw light from its many tall windows like a Ligkh High Priest's lantern at a pyre ceremony. She would take Gragi up there and abandon him, where he could never thrash his way back to the waterfront. Given a chance, Tym was sure, Gragi would swim after her to his death. He must be lost away from the sea.

She took his hand and pulled him farther up into the shadowy dunes. Gragi followed with an overjoyed, twitching grin. His grip wrapped her hand powerfully.

The scream came just as Big Tom's eyes rested on the clepsydra, the water clock. Its copper filigree pointer had edged its way to 10 P.M., but Big Tom had no confidence in its accuracy these days. Sometimes Moori filled the clepsydra's drip bowl precisely by the sundial in the garden; when it slipped her mind until too late, she would fill it only part way with a cavalier shrug.

The house boy Billister had gotten it right every evening, Big Tom was thinking. And then the scream.

A desperate, tearful howl shattered the night's serenity. Doubtlessly, there was no one in the house that did not think of Big Tom's torture trees in the garden below.

The merchant moved quickly on his stubby legs, his crimson robe flying open behind him. Down the polished staircase past the row of decaying oil portraits; past the pillowed pleasure room with its pull curtains; down another staircase, the showy one that fanned into the foyer. He yanked open the heavy double doors.

On the porch stood a blond young man facing into the night, sobbing, his shoulders quaking like a cantering horseman's.

20

The Interview

BIG Tom could not stand the pudgy jailer's whine, nor his urinelike odor, so he hoped this could be dispensed with quickly. His nose still twitched with his first-thing-in-the-morning knife-load of powder. While the tradesman doubted that there was any better standpoint from which to greet a new day, the drawback was that the powder seemed to heighten each unpleasant sensory experience. Wind chimes became annoying gongs in his ears; Bishop's ratty visage became a painful, surrealistic painting to his eyes; a sour-smelling body became rancid mountains of meat under his nose.

In this nerve-jangled mood, he followed the bouncing mass of flesh named Jay-Jay down the lockup hall, with Bishop and Moori trailing behind. As if a merchant's everyday life did not present enough problems, a madman showed up on his porch last night howling to the stars, and it took four musclers to cuff him and drag him into the red-legger holds.

"Right 'ere in number three," the fat jailer shrilled as he clanked open the window to check the whereabouts of his prisoner—procedure before opening the cell door. "Lucky this was to happen soon after the lass ship-off, else I don' know where we'd a had room for him." He fit a key into the lock, and heaved the slab of metal back.

Big Tom hesitated at the door and turned to Moori. She was still squinting with sleep, whisking along barefooted in one of the long cotton dresses she wore about the mainhouse most mornings. "Why don't you stay here, 'til we see what he's about?" Big Tom said.

"Oh gawd." It was Moori's plaintive tone, the one that usually persuaded her husband to do her bidding. She stabbed a finger toward the cell. "Lookit. He's just sitting, head down, probably just brain-burned from too much powder last night—something like that. Made him gullybonkers. What'll I tell the others? That a blond banshee rattled my house like the island's never seen—but Big Tom chopped his throat afore I ever got ta see him? Haw! I'll tell ya, I can not go back without a full look at this tattoo they're talkin' about."

Big Tom scowled, glanced at the silent prisoner, then back at his number one wife, this frowning red-haired lady with the freckled face. He shrugged and motioned for her and Bishop to follow him into the cell.

Bishop was swinging a truncheon, almost scraping the tile with it, he was so short. He put a boot against the prisoner's shoulder and pressed the guy's back to the wall. The young man was awake, his eyes so bloodshot that it reminded Big Tom of a long bout with the ale bottles. The stranger had been so maniacal the night before that they left him cuffed, ankles and wrists. During the night he had shed a set of skin wraps. The matted fur skirt lay to his side, and the vest dangled by its armholes from his wrist chains. A wild picture whirled across his chest.

"What's your name? Where'er you from?" Big Tom was using his interrogation voice. Authoritative, with underlying menace.

The prisoner's dry lips parted, quivering. "Greggie," he said.

"Greggie?" The merchant's tone was mocking.

"The long way," the prisoner stammered, "you...ah, you

say it 'Gregory.'" He showed a faint smile. "You...do you all here speak English?"

The three islanders glanced to each other wide-eyed, and broke into laughter. Gregory looked bewildered, but then ventured a small laugh himself.

Bishop let his foot fall away from the prisoner's shoulder, leaving a smudge on his skin. "Boss, he's a retard, all right," Bishop said. "Like Jay-Jay said, he's a retard—look." Big Tom's assistant pointed with his truncheon to the round scar on Gregory's forehead. "An' it looks to be, from that skin picture, that the Rafers had hold of him. Gawd knows what they did to 'im."

Big Tom grunted and wiped at his nose. "Stand up, lad."

Gregory pushed himself up weakly, his back scraping up the rock wall. "Where...where is Tym?" he asked. "The water woman, the dark lady?"

Moori answered quickly, "Greggie, you're on Thomas Island now, and we don't know where you came from." As she spoke his name, the prisoner's face fell into a gawk of complete trust. Their eyes met, and Moori knew that she would not allow the man to be killed. She leaned her face forward to inspect the detailing of his tattoo, and the prisoner took that to be some gesture of kindness.

"From?" Gregory's face brightened even more, happily oblivious to his iron-laden wrists. "I am from Blue Ridge, on the mainland of Merqua. I come from under a mountain."

Bishop haw-hawed, and Gregory looked hurt.

"True," the prisoner said. "True, true, ya, true. Grew up there."

Moori was starting to say, "We could let him..." when Big Tom broke in: "Thass a long way, son. The Blue Ridge, thass up north even of Chautown and inland. A long wander, I'd say, to end up on my porch."

"It was the Government sent me," Gregory replied. He stared at the ceiling, hoping the fog would clear from his mind. "Government, Mr. Webb, said to come."

Bishop was sitting on the floor mattress, chuckling, assured that there was no physical threat. He tapped his club onto the dingy tile. "You wouldn't be the Monitor, would ya—run the Government yerself?" he asked, toying with Gregory. "Monitor, I thought he was 'sposed to have three heads or something."

The sarcasm did not escape Gregory. He arched his shoulders defiantly and replied, "The Monitor—he's a dead pig poker. Dead. An' I'm sent by the new Government, ta find a builder what can make a ship ta cross the Big Ocean."

Bishop and Moori giggled, but Big Tom's brow furrowed into four erratic, worried rows.

21

A Raid

OPERATING the forty-foot skimmer Kapinta was a family affair. Lyle and Nob, fraternal twins, were arguing on the bow as she plowed along on three sails—Lyle formally the captain (more conservative, wiser) but only nominally in charge, and Nob the grunt (flashier, but an ale hound). Younger sister Belinda, the first mate, had a hand on the helm.

Lyle was kneeling, fiddling with the right eyepiece of his binoculars. He was not sure if the problem was focus or sea spray, but he glanced from his brother's blouse to his own and found nothing clean enough to wipe the lenses with.

"Dunkin Island's been more picked over than a corn cob," Nob complained.

Lyle scanned the island's tree line again, pressing his nubby cheeks back in a smile, happy that the focus had improved. "Big Tom said to gather up the red-leggers double-time this swing out an' he'd pay a bonus on top of the bounty, ya? Well, if my theory proves right, we'll find more 'n we can hold right hereabouts, not two days out of Thomas Island. The boss'd be pig-grin pleased at that."

"How ya figure it, though?" Nob asked. "The entire fleet came out after the sinking! And then Big Tom came out hisself on that six-shooter The Tooth of Horan to look at the wreck. If there's even a mosquito left on Dunkin Island that ain't been buggered, we'd never find it."

Lyle stayed focused on the hump of land growing bigger in the spyglass. "Brother, if you got even a pea for a brain..." he paused for effect "...make some soup, honey, 'cause it's gone to mush. You heard the rumors about the Lucia. Somewhere there is a booger of truth—about most of the red-leggers escaping instead of drowning like they shoulda; about some missing gold. Now, think: Why is Big Tom in a hurry to sell more red-leggers—because he's got to build another skimmer? He's got dozens of skimmers!" Lyle slapped at the deck under him and continued. "No. But could it be that he's short of cash? Ah, mayhap."

"An' you think maybe some of those red-leggers are still hid out on Dunkin?"

"Or the nearabout islands. Or maybe they was gone and come back—like for the gold, if they seen something during the wreck. Maybe there's even dozens of 'em around, got they little peenie boats all put together already and go zip back and forth like they lived here a hunnerd years."

"Oh, if they had boats already, they'd a lit off by now," Nob said, scratching in his beard doubtfully. Unlike his brother the captain, he rarely shaved.

Lyle handed Nob the binoculars. "What ya make of this? The birds—halfway down the eastern slope?"

Nob squinted through the glasses and followed the crown of Dunkin Island down to his right. Four large birds soared in slow circles just above the tree line. As each in succession banked and caught the sunlight, they flashed brilliant plumage—blue, green and red. Their heads silhouetted against the pale sky were shaped like large spring hooks.

"Well, damn," Nob said, "vulture macaws."

Lyle shrugged his shoulders in mock modesty, as if it were possible his deductions were wrong. "Ho, well, it's just that I've never known 'em to flock very far from humans," he said. "Seems to me they take a liking to a fresh garbage pile, often as not."

Nob snorted and wiped his nose on a sleeve. "Hmmn. Often as not, ya."

Lyle pointed grandly toward the birds over the backboard side and Belinda dutifully corrected her course.

Just short of the beach they anchored, loaded their gear into a small inflatable raft, and the three swam ashore with the raft in tow. Lyle handed out the equipment in bored, routine motions: two of the hoop-shaped whip traps per person, four handbombs, and a snub gun apiece. They already had knives strapped to each calf—standard wear. Each piece of equipment bore the oval Cred Faiging stamp—would have seemed inadequate without it.

Being lighter on her feet, Belinda was assigned to sprint up the beach and climb the opposite side of the ridge. Nob followed Lyle straight up into the troublesome mangrove and pigtail vines. Knives out, they quietly snicked their way through the tendrils, knowing that a machetelike slashing would raise an alarm.

Once inland, the sea breeze was lost, and the jungle pressed close with its envelope of steam. Their noses dripped sweat. No words were spoken. The captain signaled orders to his brother with minute flickers of the hand.

When Lyle judged they were high enough, they cut to the right, scabbing the hillside until they came to the trail they knew they would find. In some ways, Lyle often said over an evening ale, humans are the simplest beasts to hunt.

The slavers followed the trail up again until they came to the right spot—a clearing where a patch of sunlight glared onto the path, followed by a section of deep shadow as it plunged into low underbrush. In the shadow, Lyle lay the hoop of his first whip trap, nestling the rim under the leaves, then reeling out the trip wire, and hooking it to the charge pin on the opposite side.

Farther up the hill they found the ratty camp. It was empty, but told the silent hunters something about their prey. A dubious lean-to had been built by vine-lashing three cross supports to the arcing roots of a banyan tree and then thatching them over. Crude wooden roasting tools lay about the rock-rimmed campfire coals. The vulture macaws clawed at small skeletons with their vicious talons: primarily small fish, perhaps a couple of tiny wild pigs.

Seasoned outdoorsmen did not live here.

Nob was startled to suddenly find Belinda grinning among them. She had appeared silently, like a khaki ghost, breathing normally despite her jog up the ridge. Lyle pointed the two of them in opposite directions and drew circles in the air—the signal for them to plant their remaining whip traps at the periphery of the campsite. That done, they toured the border together to review where the traps lay. If a melee broke out among red-leggers and slavers, it was strategic to know the location of the crippling devices. To stumble into one during battle could prove disastrous.

Then came the most mind-numbing part of the hunt. The wait. Lyle crouched at the trail head, Nob squatted near the small trash pile to keep watch on the east approach to the camp, and Belinda searched once more—fruitlessly—for hidden weapons, and then planted herself on a stone near the dead fire.

The sun rose, the flies hummed, the vulture macaws had for lunch the same thing they had had for breakfast.

And finally Lyle's whip trap blew—like a distant shotgun blast—down the hillside, the first one he had hidden. The vulture macaws took to the sky in a blue-green clatter of wings. The slavers broke into a quiet hunter's trot single file down the trail, handbombs bouncing on their belts, until they reached a black circle, still smoking on the path. Ten feet to the side of the trail, hurled into the underbrush, lay a grizzled man in shock, thoroughly cocooned by a webbing of minuscule barbed wire threads.

To step into a whip trap is rarely fatal, for to set a killer snare would defeat the purpose of slaving. The charge detonated by the trip wire actually is directed away from the victim, in the shape of a circle. The blast throws out an intricate, spring-loaded netting of barbed wire thread which instantly compacts again around the hapless person or animal that set off the charge.

It is a painful and stunning entrapment, but to struggle against the restraint is even worse—the effect of dragging hundreds of miniature knives across the skin simultaneously. Instinct will not allow that more than once.

The three slavers approached their wire-bound quarry cautiously nevertheless, scanning the jungle for more fortunate companions. There seemed to be none.

Belinda began clipping the wires away, cooing softly in a universal language designed to calm a new prisoner. Her hands darted about his body, methodically snipping the metal threads and peeling them off like bloodied briars. As each hand or leg came free, Nob set a cuff in place.

As the prisoner's shock subsided his breathing grew shallow and rapid. His maniacal eyes followed Belinda's hands and an occasional whine gurgled deep in his lungs when she tore away the barbed strands. He wore filthy drawstring trousers, and his bare feet were in sorry shape—where they weren't bruised there were red-cracked calluses.

Lyle kicked around in the surrounding pigtail vine looking for hand weapons. Instead, he found a length of cloth wrapped around three small sea bass.

"The pig-poker netted hisself a right sorry dinner," Lyle called to his brother and sister, holding the fish up by their tails. He tossed them farther into the vines and tramped back.

Belinda had cut the prisoner's head free, and Lyle worked his fingers into the matted, sun-scorched hair and pulled his face out of the dirt. The captain winced at the open sores under the blond gnarls of beard, the cracked and peeling skin.

Nob grunted. "Ya think he could be off the Lucia's crew? Bark said there weren't but a few red-leggers in the holds that weren't Rafers."

"Pig-brain," his sister responded as she finished up the wire-clipping. "He was crew, he'd a had a dozen chances to get hisself rescued. They's had more skimmer traffic here lately than Thomas Harbor. This's one we can sell, I'd say."

"Ya, but juss one," Nob said, slapping at Lyle's thigh, "not the great harvest some of us was expecting."

Lyle was soberly studying the stranger's face, and Nob slapped him again, encouraging him to join the banter. The skimmer captain declined with a silent shake of his head, and he carefully eased the wild-eyed man's head onto the blast-torn jungle floor.

"You can pig-poke what you was expecting," Lyle murmured. "This one was on the Lucia, all right—but mayhap a swagger that was not eager to be found, if the rumors are true. The one we've whip-trapped here is Little Tom."

22

A Reward

WHEN Dr. Scaramouch died and the jailer's pudgy sister Lily was assigned to tend the clinic, Thomas Island and the surrounding atolls cooperatively fell free of serious disease and injury.

It was as if the islanders knew better than to grow ill without a proper physician in the vicinity. Or perhaps it was that they were developing no fewer maladies than before, but they dreaded surrendering themselves to the ministrations of a woman whose surgical qualifications amounted to hacking chickens in the kitchen and feeding unidentifiable slop to the red-leggers in their cells.

It also was likely that the islanders began turning to the healers who had been operating discretely for centuries on the Out Islands—Rafers, some of them, Jesus People and the like. Such physicians had been pushed into semi-exile by the disbelieving mainland-style "civilization." And now, surely, some under-the-weather islanders were finding superstition-laced treatment preferable to guaranteed modern-day incompetence.

So it was that Lily's only patient that night was delirious and in no position to argue or plead for a change of venue. Leather thongs bound his hands and feet to the four corners of the clinic bed to keep him from scratching at his wounds and breaking open the stitches.

Big Tom, standing bedside, brushed the flecks of white powder out of his moustache, snorted back hard one more time, and pressed his bearded chin to his chest in an expression of horror and disgust. His son splayed out before him had more wounds than a Nganga man's mastabah doll in the dancing-knives ceremony. The tiny rends in the flesh had been stitched closed with fat black thread in wild, random-looking patterns that soured Big Tom's stomach.

"Gonna scar beautifully," Big Tom mumbled, hunching down to stare wide-eyed at the chaos of needlework around his son's left nipple.

Lily was nervous in the presence of the trade master, but she managed to roll her eyes upward in mock annoyance, hoping such familiarity would alleviate the tension. She lifted a corner of the white towel covering Little Tom's crotch and paused for a warning: "Big Tom, now, none of this here's my doing. And I 'spect the infection's dying back some."

Big Tom's eyebrows rose and bounced in a civil manner, inviting her to proceed. Lily lifted back the towel, and suddenly Big Tom felt detached, as if he were viewing the scene from the ceiling of the hospital room. Tracer lights criss-crossed his vision. For scarcely ten seconds he watched as Lily gingerly cleaned the row of black puncture wounds festering on his son's penis.

Big Tom staggered for the door and pushed it open. Lyle and Nob were arguing in the hallway, and the conversation stopped, each of them mid-sentence. Both of them toyed with smouldering stubs of the machine-rolled cigarettes Big Tom had given them minutes before.

The merchant unzipped his fly, reached in, and withdrew a leather wallet. He whisked out a wad of centime notes without counting them, stuffed the wallet away and zipped up again.

"Here," Big Tom said, only glancing at the faces of the two slave-boaters. Big Tom pulled the wad of bills into two, as if tearing apart a lettuce head. "Here," he said again, handing each of them an undetermined reward, "an' thanks for my son. Hmmph."

Big Tom lingered to gaze out the windows onto the black lawn outside, an unknowable powder-inspired meditation, and then he shuffled toward the exit.

"Thought you said he woont have no cash, huh?" Nob prodded his brother.

Lyle was not remorseful. "You work on Big Tom's level," he whispered, lest the merchant was still in earshot, "a few thousand centimes don't matter a whit. But think of it—this here's the same we'd make for bringing in fifteen or more red-leggers. Just for trapping one body." Lyle eyed his brother's fistful of centimes and finished shuffling through his own share of bills. He stuffed his take into his front pocket.

"Hey!" Nob shouted.

"Shhhh."

"Hey!" Nob slapped Lyle on the shoulder. "How much was that? We splittin' this, right? Even?"

"Shhhh."

23

House Boy

SLOWLY, Gregory learned how to be house boy for the mainhouse. He stood patiently over the garden sundial until it marked 5 P.M., and then he clamored up the stairways with his gurgling watering can in tow. He filled the balance basin of the clepsydra carefully until its intricately sculpted pointer indicated the correct time, and immediately the same water began its steady ploit, ploit, ploit into the catch bowl. The water clock then began its twelve-hour sweep across the hour board, charting the passage of time for all evening observers.

He learned from Big Tom's musclers how to unload the deliveries from the mule wagon, where to stash the potatoes, the salted beef, the cases of ale and whiskey. He learned how—and how often—to refuel the generators that kept the mainhouse aglow at night.

He learned that Big Tom was insanely protective of his walled garden, seemed to save even the manure-spreading for himself. It was the merchant's private botanical kingdom. Above all, Gregory was to stay away from the little shed built of flat stones in the corner.

Mintie, one of Big Tom's plumper wives, taught Gregory how to butcher chickens. With great pride he plucked them and whacked them apart, then rubbed into their meat a paste of garlic, black pepper, lemon juice and cilantro. Some evenings Gregory would sizzle the chicken on the wide brick grill built into the back patio. He would feed the entire household—Big Tom, wives, musclers, sometimes a guest. For the rest of the night, Gregory would wear the scent of garlic and smoke like a badge of honor.

He found Big Tom a frightful man, wide and gruff, pressing him for stories of Merqua's mainland. Gregory would not talk to him any more than necessary, and he found it convenient to pretend to be more dim-witted than he was.

Moori was .different, scented and elegant. She would stroke his hair and ask about the mountain he used to live under. The more Gregory tried to tell her, the more confusing the story seemed to get: that he grew up under a mountain with windmills on top of it; that his people were the "Ungovernment," but he had come to the island representing the Government; that the Monitor was dead, his head bitten off by a large fish in the canyon where the despot had been hiding.

Moori would shake her beautiful head and walk away. Eventually, Gregory learned not to tell her the truth either. He felt a warm welling in his chest when she showed an interest in him, and he grew distressed when she threw up her hands in disgust and stopped asking questions.

It was an involving life for Gregory, if not a challenging one. He lived on Thomas Island with an ever-present sense of loss, however, an anxiety that pressed close to this throat in the darkness of his room when he tried to sleep, making his breathing come hard. He had lost Tym, the dark woman who had dragged him out of the water. And before that, he had lost his home, the Blue Ridge. He wondered if he could have them both sometime—Tym and the Blue Ridge together—but that seemed impossible and made him fret even more.

Gregory turned the pieces of marinated chicken carefully

with long wooden tongs, inviting an angry crackle in the coals as the fat ran off. He knew that next morning it would be time to force back the bin cover on the side of the brick barbecue and sweep out the ashes. They were building up too much.

Big Tom and a guest arrived on the patio chattering and rattling bourbon glasses. The tall one with the beard, the visitor, gave Gregory a chill. The recognition was mutual. The man was motioning toward Gregory with the whiskey glass, mumbling something to Big Tom. Big Tom squinted and laughed, and the pair walked jovially in Gregory's direction.

"Gregory," Big Tom began, "this is Bark, one of my top skimmermen. He thinks you've met before."

"Hi, Bark," Gregory said, not looking up. He proceeded to turn all of the grilling chicken that he had just turned.

The tall man with the silver-speckled black beard closed one eye as he studied the new house boy. He pulled at his drink. "Ya, I'm sure now. Gregory, you were aboard the Lucia when she went down. You shoulda drownt, so how is it that you washed up on Big Tom's porch some weeks back?"

Gregory shrugged and kept himself busy with the grill.

"You say he was leg-ironed in the hold when the Lucia went down?" Big Tom asked.

Bark snorted. "And barely conscious." He pointed to the scar on Gregory's forehead. "From that, when it were a fresh wound from 'is capture."

Big Tom took Bark by the arm and steered him out of Gregory's listening. "On the Lucia, you originally picked this one up off an island—he was running with other red-leggers?"

"Ahh, no. Seems to me not. He had to be the one we blew out of the water just before the Lucia went down. We had sighted a skimmer 'round the southwest Out Islands, thought 'er a pirate or a powder runner, one without yer banners. So when she tried to make away, we turned the cannons to her.

"Second shot—can ya believe it?—must have hit a fuel tank. She blew her hull and dropped right quick. This house boy of yours bobbed up in a float vest, his head knocked open."

They were inside now, and Big Tom rounded the bar and sloshed more bourbon into each glass. He slid back the top of a cabinet against the floor, extracted two handfuls of ice cubes, and dropped them into the glasses, too. He bounced his eyebrows at Bark to point up the extravagance.

"You said fuel tank," Big Tom stated. "Fuel, you mean, as if she carried an engine?"

"Oh, ya, the blast was that big. Warn't no kerosene tin for the lanterns, I'd tell. Spread decking for a quarter mile."

Big Tom pressed at his nostrils between thumb and forefinger. "If his skimmer was powered, then either it was licensed by the Government—or was Government—or...."

"Or was an Out Island pirate," Bark finished. "Or was a powder runner."

Big Tom smiled and stroked his nose again. "Wasn't a powder runner I know. A couple have lit in and out since you sank that one."

Bark's voice was starting to rise, sounding defensive. "Well, if she was Government, I had no way to know—don't go reporting that to Captain Bull to pass along, now. An' I soon had sorrier things to worry about, anyhap."

Big Tom returned to the French doors to watch Gregory poking at the grill.

"He's scared of me," Big Tom said, taking a sip. "But he tells Moori tales about the Government—about fighting against the Government, about working for the Government. Doesn't always make sense. Said once he'd come looking for a ship builder. Also said once the Monitor was dead."

Bark was growing easy again and the alcohol was beginning to warm his limbs. "Sounds like a case for the new doctor when he gets here."

"Ya. Any day now. After he puts the lift back into Little Tom's willie, he can look at Gregory."

Big Tom glanced down at his drink and up again to stare at the dim-witted man turning chicken pieces. In that fraction of a second, impossibly, Gregory had disappeared.

24

Arrival

THE bargemen, those swaggering apes with the snub guns, all remarked upon what a bad time of year it was to be transporting red-leggers. Their conversations were the sort that farmers have as they worry over their crops.

"They never seem to draw in the centimes like an autumn run will," huffed Buehl, the senior of the three men stationed to work Billister's barge.

Billister remained shackled to a stubby post for the entire four-day sail to the mainland. Quickly he was reminded of the origin of the term red-legger: the skin under his irons was becoming inflamed, itching.

The only slave among them to be freed of the manacles was a woman about fifty years old. She had passed out on the second day of baking exposure. Buehl produced a key from his trousers, snapped the unconcious woman's cuffs open, and rolled her off the edge of the barge.

On the third day, amid much grumbling, the three bargemen erected a makeshift shelter over most of their captives, a few tarpaulins lashed together and hoisted atop teetering poles. Then Captain Bull, hollering from the lead tug, ordered the other two barges to erect coverings as well, to protect the cargo. This prompted even more resentful bickering.

They puttered into Chautown resembling a chain of seaborne circus tents.

Billister had expected the mainland to seem more...main. There was a harbor not remarkably larger than Thomas Island's. The meandering coast misted out of sight north and south and easily could have belonged to an island instead of a continent. Somehow, Billister wanted to see towering cliffs, mountains looming beyond—a cumbersome chunk of land.

In the last hour of the trip the wind picked up, as if tranquility were verboten here even for the weather. The stubby tugboat out front sliced into the low swells, and the three barges bobbed after it obediently like quarter-acre ducks following Mama. The sky had turned gray, a shade lighter than the sea. The tarpaulins snapped and sputtered in the wind. Billister nodded sadly, pegged to this large raft, and watched the sea spray spatter his leg irons to a grimy black.

Near port, the tug's engines died to a low cough. Captain Bull marched in and out of the pilot house shouting commands inaudible over the wind and splash. They gurgled past a battery of rust-eaten cannons, impotent reminders of ancient times, then eased up to a crumbling concrete dock rimmed by fairly recent creosote pilings.

Billister briefly forgot his circumstances in his awe of Chautown. At dockside he could see avenues of elegant residences, pre-war matrons crouched behind their iron grill-work fences. Intermingled were the utilitarian touches of the modern age: artless stonework, corrugated steel roofs rusting under the salt breath of the ocean.

Even more astounding to Billister were the motor vehicles murmuring over the pavement. He had heard of them, of course, but only a handful of the two-wheeled varieties had made their way to the islands. Here they lumbered irritably, all of them the same beaten four-wheeled, Government-issue gray. Open-topped personnel carriers, produce wagons, one-

or two-passenger cars for Government officers or honored citizens.

Billister found himself again chained with the others single file, front to back, walking awkwardly on numb legs that moved like ghostly crutches up the roped gangplank. The younger in front of him twisted around and opened his lips furtively to say something, but Buehl was there instantly punching him in the kidney. It was a wound that would not show—important on sale day.

At the top of a concrete ramp, dozens of the open-air trucks waited. The red-leggers were loaded in, freed of all restraints but the wrist cuffs, the leg irons laid carefully in growing piles by the tailgates. A guard with a heavy pistol hopped onto the tailgate when the truck's engine started. His clothes were almost a uniform—light gray cotton, pressed, the trousers belted with polished black leather and a matching holster. The guard seemed easygoing, even a bit of humor in his eyes. This was a mainlander, a bona fide Government man.

They were saying goodbye to the barges.

25

Negotiations

THE catamaran's twin pontoons were running low in the water, and Tym cursed at the craft's sluggish response as she tacked toward the inlet.

She had thought old Sey-Waage was napping there in the webbing, his eyes closed, his graying beard poking skyward like the tuft of some drab jungle bird. But the old Healer was chuckling now, a sound something like creaking deck wood—only the catamaran had no deck.

"If all goes well," Sey-Waage said, "we will be lighter than a water spider on our way out. If this Fungus Person shares our wisdom."

"And if he does not?"

Again the creaking laugh. "Then perhaps you and I will share him for dinner."

Tym smiled. Cannibalism was somewhat rare these days among the islanders, but the practice always showed a resurgence during desperate times. It was amusing to contemplate—the insult of consuming one's enemy. In a way, that was easier to accept than what they were actually about to do: Ask an enemy for assistance.

Tym checked that her knives were still snug in her thigh straps and the tosser disks were sheathed in the leather pocket stitched to her G-string. She let out the rope tethered to the corner of the blue-gray expanse of sail, colored to blend with the morning's first light. She corrected the rudder and grimaced at the clumsy rush of water twelve inches below her bent knees.

This little sea fly should barely touch water, she told herself. But look at it drag.

To enter the cove, the catamaran had to round a spear-point of beach, and as they did so Sey-Waage flicked his right hand and clapped his pointing fingers together. "Ah, there," he said.

Tym looked at the elder, puzzled that his eyes still seemed to be closed, and followed the line of his bony fingers into the underbrush. A Fungus Person stood in the shadows with a rifle, his face smudged dark green in a pathetic attempt at camouflage. She drew a disk from the sheath and cupped it in her right hand as a precaution. She judged the throw to be seventy-five feet—even moving, she probably could thok his throat out; undoubtedly strike his chest. Unless he sights with the rifle, she decided, she would do nothing.

The catamaran rounded the point without a shot fired or a disk flung. Beyond, in the center of the south-facing beach, another Fungus Person stood at the end of a low dock, its wood weathered to gray. An old dory was lashed to the dock, apparently belonging to the thirty-foot skimmer anchored a dozen yards out, a bulky, unremarkable craft. Perfect, in its unassuming appearance, for a black marketeer.

The man wore high black boots, faded denim trousers and a billowy white blouse. His face was sun-reddened, the eyes surrounded by a permanent web of wrinkles.

The man propped a rifle against one knee, an automatic, Tym guessed—the kind fed by a rounded clip. The sight of its vile steel made Tym sick. She had seen many, always in the hands of Fungus People who did not mean well. Her tosser disk was still very much ready.

Tym threw him a dock line, and although it had a satisfactory loop on the end, the stranger tied it in a square knot around a piling. This made Tym even more uneasy, but if a quick escape were necessary, she would just whack the rope.

The Fungus Person motioned them up onto the dock and said something in the tongue that sounds like barking dogs. When they returned blank stares, the stranger fumbled with the Rafer language: "The man who sells your people's, uh, ganja to me said that you would come." It seemed to hurt his lips to make understandable sounds.

Up beyond the trees, Tym could see a wooden shelter on stilts. Fungus People seemed to abhor even harmless forest animals as much as Rafers detested the banger weapons.

The man flashed a quick, ceremonial smile and pulled the clip out of his rifle. "I know that your people do not like guns," he said, "that having one here might be an insult. But I must take, uh, precautions."

Sey-Waage was still scanning the woods. "We also know that this is not the only banger among us," the old man replied.

The Fungus Man shrugged. "My name is Franklin Delano Roosevelt Jones," he said politely. "Your people prefer to call me Delano, as it is a sound most at home with your way of speaking. It is an honor to be visited by a Rafer elder, and I hope that the guns do not offend too much. So. Why have you come?"

"We want a ship," Tym blurted, and Sey-Waage winced that she would be so undiplomatic as to get to the point right away. "We want a skimmer faster than any in these waters," she added.

Delano pointed with his chin. "That little two-stick you're sailing—they've done Rafers nicely for centuries."

"And there are many among us," Sey-Waage said, "that would say we should not attempt anything more—that to build larger, to embrace the complexity, the technology, would be sacrilegious." The elder grinned and scratched absently at his bare chest. "I am not among them, of course. I am of the opinion that if our people are to survive among the islands, we must have skimmers that will outrun and outmaneuver Big Tom."

Delano hoisted his right leg and planted his foot atop the piling where he had tied the catamaran. Tym backed away casually, wanting to put distance between herself and Sey-Waage in case a fight started. The Fungus Person was starting to sound surprisingly fluent in the civilized tongue, and she could not shake the feeling that something was wrong.

"Hoo. To hammer up a proper skimmer—hunnerd, two hunnerd feet?—well, timbers like that just aren't grown on these islands," Delano said. He was directing his comments at Sey-Waage, which further irritated Tym. "And the wood whits for it...."

"If we must build the skimmer we want, the Rafers will learn to do the work," the elder said. "We have specific capabilities and design requirements with which you may not be familiar. But to obtain the knowledge for the building of these larger vessels, to obtain the timbers and hardware that we would need from the mainland—that would take a Fungus Person, one who knows trading, one who is not particularly allegiant to the wishes of the mainland Government. That, Delano, would be a person such as you."

Delano laughed and tossed his ammo clip up in the air and caught it again. "I appreciate your directness," he said. "You don't skin a pig with a penknife, do you?"

Sey-Waage nodded.

"But it wouldn't be news to you," Delano said, "that I do frequent business with Big Tom, a powerful man who would not be amused to have such a skimmer whisking around the islands if he didn't own it. What makes you think I wouldn't tell him that the red-leggers were building a ship like that?"

Tym's eyes had squinted almost closed and her words quivered with mounting fury. "Red-leggers, Delano, are runners from the mainland. Or they used to be, until Big Tom decided his flesh harvest wasn't big enough and started to take islanders, too. Red-leggers...."

"Tym. Tym." Sey-Waage was wagging his pointing fingers at the catamaran, uneasy with this angry talk. "Just show him."

Tym sighed and leapt onto their skimmer's near pontoon. She slid back the cover to the storage hold and removed a gold brick, which she thumped onto the dock. "This is how we will pay," she said. She unloaded the gold bars from alternating sides of the boat, maintaining balance to keep it from flipping. When she was done there were ten bars in a neat row at Delano's feet.

The Fungus Person's eyes were wide. "I…heard…a rumor that…."

"Yes," Sey-Waage broke in. "The gold was Big Tom's. The reason that you will not tell Big Tom about our desire for a skimmer faster than his fleet is simple. You will take a share of gold in return for helping us build the kind of skimmer that we desire, and for training our people. And Big Tom is the last person you would tell about it. I suspect he still considers the gold to be his, no?"

Delano was nodding rapidly. "He'd rip my gizzard out with his teeth to get it back. Wouldn't matter how I came by it."

26

Changing of the Guard

BILLISTER carried with him guilt, many forms of it.

As he worked the tobacco field, he tried to think back to his youth. Even just to two months before, for that matter. Hadn't he known? Hadn't the solemn parade of red-leggers, tens of thousands of them, marched directly under his upturned nose? He had been aware of something, that something was out of kilter in his pampered upbringing on Thomas Island.

He hunched in the steamy field with the other red-leggers, a chain rattling between his ankles each time he stepped to a new tobacco plant. The farm supervisors, "Ag Agency superintendents," had taught him how to sweep his hand around the stalk and tear a cluster of leaves away without damaging the entire plant. They had not taught him how to do this without damaging his back muscles.

The arrangement was that if he worked Ag duty for five years without incident, he might become eligible for a better assignment. They spoke dreamily of the indoor jobs available in Supply and Transport. They pointed to themselves, former field workers, they claimed.

But even aside from the work, it was a ghastly, regimented life. Meals of overstewed vegetables, with the rare shred of pork. No news sheets, books, or anything written—much better to pretend to be illiterate. Into bed, and up again, as the wailing sirens dictated.

Billister was not sure any human would last five years.

Priming tobacco, this was called. He and many people of his own race were primers, up to their elbows in gluelike tobacco juice. In the heat-warped distance the barbed wire fences stood sentry.

Billister was regarded with suspicion even by fellow Rafers. Occasionally he pronounced words oddly, words in his own native language. He had that manner about him—too gentlemanly, almost effeminate. His skin was soft from a protected life, and on the first day anyone had seen him—on the day of loading on Thomas Island—his fellow red-leggers had actually detected perfume, one of the incomprehensible products of the Fungus People. And he had appeared clean shaven, head and chin!

Those field workers who knew a touch of English made a play on his name—Blister, they called him, after his first day of picking. Who was this soft stranger?

If they only knew, Billister thought—thwack, he tore away a handful of tobacco leaves—they would remove my limbs just like that. He handed his shoulder bag of leaves to a field runner, who laid them on the portable conveyor belt that followed the primers up and down the rows. There the stems of the leaves were bunched around a stick and then run through a gasoline-powered stitching machine. Later, the racks of leaves were piled onto a cart and wheeled over to the curing barns to be hung.

An Ag Agency pickup truck rumbled down the dirt road between the pines and the field. It skidded to a stop at the point nearest to the primers. The red dust cloud, momentum-borne, drifted over and past the truck like a tidal wave. Odd.

Billister turned to look, wiping his face on his shoulder (he had quickly learned not to use his gooey forearms). A supervisor jabbed him in the side with the butt of his snub gun, and Billister doubled over, near vomiting, remembering the day he arrived on the mainland—the man chained in front of him trying to speak, punched in the kidney. The crisp pain produced a hallucination: the red earth between the tobacco stalks superimposed over lips of the young man who had tried to speak to him. Moving lips, trying to say what?

Weakly, Billister grabbed a few leaves, a poor effort. But the supervisor, wearing the gray cotton uniform and a straw hat, seemed satisfied.

Three men hopped out of the truck. They were not Ag Agency. They wore loose jump suits, swung rifles at their sides irreverently, and had wide utility belts slung around their hips, hung with hardware like Billister had never seen.

Billister decided he would keep his head down, stealing a glance only when his bag was full again and he had to stand erect to deliver his pickings to the field runner. There were two supervisors in this field and fifteen red-leggers—ten primers, three runners, and two operating the stitching machinery. The supervisors were talking with the new arrivals in low tones. A cigarette pack came out and they all lit up.

Eventually, the supervisors were led back to the pickup truck, looking bewildered. The oldest of the jump-suited men walked authoritatively to the stitching machine, studied its controls, and shut it off. Suddenly the field was ringing with silence. For the first time, the primers' feet could be heard whispering across the earth.

"English!" the jump-suited man shouted. "Do any of you speak English?"

The workers stared, motionless. Billister hesitated, but decided the other red-leggers already had a low opinion of him—he might as well cooperate with the Fungus Person. "Here." He raised a gum-covered arm.

The man trotted over. His shaven face was tanned, sweating, and there was a scar on the tip of his nose. His head seemed small for his body size, and a cigarette dangled from his lips, dead center. Crescent moons of moisture had formed under his arms.

"Hallo, the name's Fel Guinness," the stranger said. "Those two men, are they workers?" It was an odd accent. The man's breath smelled of ale.

"Workers?" Billister found the question peculiar. Obviously they were workers. One man had been shoving the bulky machinery down the rows on its rubber wheels while the second man aligned the leaves properly on their hanging sticks.

"What I mean is, are they supervisors like those two"—he jabbed a thumb over his shoulder—"or are they workers? Red-leggers. Laborers not here by choice."

"Ah," said Billister, feeling faint from the pounding he had taken a few minutes before. "The rest of us are, uh, workers. Yes. All of us."

The man raised his voice to a shout: "Then you will all please proceed to the barn." He pointed to the wood-frame structure a half mile away, down the dirt road at the edge of the field. Then the man about-faced and trotted back to his truck.

None of the red-leggers moved. Then Billister remembered, and shouted the instructions in Rafer.

The business at the curing barn went quickly. When Billister and his fellow field workers filed into the dim enclosure, the two supervisors stood in the center of the room. Their mouths were gagged, their hands bound behind them. Two ropes were looped on the end, fitted around their necks, and the other ends tossed over a high rafter, up where the racks of tobacco were, dripping moisture onto the crowd of curious observers.

Then Fel Guinness's younger assistants hoisted the supervisors three feet off the ground. Billister watched them kicking, pumping silently save for the dry rustle of gray cotton, the scuffing of leather, and the creak of rope.

The field workers were speechless. Guinness was smiling, sucking his cigarette down to a butt. He laid an arm around Billister's shoulder, saying, "Tell them we are from the new Government. Tell them that they are free. That we will take them into town now where we will feed them properly, until they decide how they will spend the rest of their lives."

Billister turned to the gaunt, distrusting faces in the low light and wondered how to explain the ways of the Fungus People.

27

Education

GRANDFATHER had been the one who claimed to fly. He had put the youngster Tommie on his lap (the nickname Big Tom came later, with his ample belly) and angled his open hand into a beach wind flecked with spray and sand. He explained there on the wind-creaking deck how a ton of steel could rise off the ground under its own power.

But Grandfather also told him the story about Jagger and the Beanstalk. And that men had walked on the moon. Hoo.

So Grandfather, the daft, old man with legs bowed and vibrating, told the youngster how he had climbed into a canvas and bamboo carriage with a twirling shaft on its nose, and had crashed the contraption into the welcoming swells of the Big Ocean.

Grandfather let on, the breeze tugging at his scrappy tufts of hair, that his very experiments had brought the Monitor to decree that flight by humans was impossible. And, furthermore, illegal. Humankind could not benefit by flight out over the unknown waters.

Big Tom spent his childhood ship-baiting on these narrow islands running parallel to the mainland coast. The Outre

Banks. As the youngest male of the family it became his ten o'clock chore, just before bedtime, to hang a lantern from a mule's neck, and lead the beast up and down the beachside dunes.

In the dark chill of early next morning, he would find a baffled and bedraggled wet captain in the kitchen regaling the adults of the family with the story of a ghostly, bobbing buoy that had signaled safe harbor to his ship when there was none. Of course, come daylight the unfortunate captain's beached skimmer would be found—picked clean even of its brass fittings.

Father and Grandfather would be quite demonstrative in their outrage at the seaman's misfortune, tossing fistfuls of sand and cursing to the rising sun. Then they would sell the soggy captain some rotting sculler, and he would make his way homeward with tales of the killer ghosts of the sand dunes on the appropriately named Outre Banks. Once, they even sold a captain his own lifeboat, freshly repainted.

Big Tom had worked the mule trick for his family two years before he realized he should demand a share of the booty. He immediately began to collect a small percentage of the spoils—sure, why hadn't he asked before, Grandfather wanted to know. And with that, Big Tom took his first step into adulthood. The misty fantasy of childhood began to fade, and it was perhaps coincidental that at about that time he saw his first Government man.

Grandfather had been hearing tall tales about the Monitor since his own childhood, so the bull-faced, three-headed ruler already would have been impossibly old by the time Big Tom was a professional boat-baiter. This age business led Big Tom, in his maturing wisdom, to conclude that the famously secretive and paranoid Monitor was actually a succession of furtive rulers, perhaps a family dynasty not unlike his band of Outre Banks scalawags.

The Government man arrived in a little borrowed sailboat he had awkwardly tacked across the inner sound from the mainland. McTaggart was his name. He was a smooth talker, pasty-faced, thirty-five or so. His eyes glowed with the fire of a true believer as he preached of the imminent arrival of order in the outlands, as he called them. The frontier. There was a bustling new capital in the middle lands, New Chicago. There was commerce. Defense and security. Work assignments for all.

(This was old news to Grandfather, who grumbled that New Chicago was supposed to be a pitiful crosshatch of mud ruts. But nothing about the Government had pleased Grandfather since it declared that flight was impossible a couple of decades before.)

The Government man made vague references to the pirates who would no longer terrorize such innocents as the inhabitants of this little coastal fishing community—that was how they subsisted, wasn't it—fishing? Grandfather nodded yes, uneasy as the Government man scratched notes into a little book.

And then the emissary McTaggart wobbled back into his sailboat and floated away. No other Government men were seen for three or four years.

They did see, however, an increasing traffic of drifters—the first of them mere malcontents uncomfortable with the growing influence of Government where once there was a robust survival-by-wit. Many of them bought boats, any old dory that would carry their bobbing souls a few miles down the coast. As the fleeing men and women grew more desperate over the years, heartier craft were in demand. As a young adult, Big Tom took to designing and building twenty- and thirty-foot skimmers—quickly and roughly pounded together—and selling them at outrageously inflated prices.

In the year that Grandfather died McTaggart returned, and Big Tom was glad that the old man was not around to see this. A large chunk of coastland, including the Outre Banks, were now part of Government District Eight; with McTaggart its governor—actually, the only lawman at all.

McTaggart was going gray now, earlier than most, his face eaten by the sun and an inch-long scar curving up the right side of his lip, bitten there by a panicking runner. He arrived in an odd contraption, a boat twenty feet long but without mast or sail. At the stern there chugged an engine, mechanically related to those in the land-autos that were now grinding up the trails of the mainland, it was said.

The Government man lifted the lid of the engine for Big Tom to see the inner workings of "the little whore-banger," as he called it. Big Tom grunted admiration. McTaggart said that there would be no engines licensed for civilian boats. And Big Tom agreed that that would be a good thing. Privately, he envied the potential of the throbbing machine, but he began to see rather clearly how Big Bang Day had come about.

Big Tom had begun to carry a hip flask, a flat silverplated number bartered away by a well-heeled desperado. He and McTaggart traded nips there on the sound-side dock and the Government man used his loosened jaw, eventually, to complain about the frustrations of overseeing an outland territory, one more populated by people fleeing the Government than loyal to it.

Big Tom harumphed a few sympathetic sounds, passed the bourbon a few more times, and almost mortally gagged when McTaggart told him: "I know this, that ya sells sea craft to the disloyals."

"Ho, now...."

"Awww, hold on. You're a solid, longtime local. An' by the way, sorry to hear of the old man."

"He didn't care much fer the Gumment, ta be honest."

"Like I say," McTaggart continued, "I'm not in a choicey situation, our sector being in its infant stages. But the Monitor says that part of the mandate of the outland governors is to stop the runners. Grab 'em, ship 'em back for labor assignments."

"Hmmph."

"And I have no security force as yet, but a budget for bounties."

"Ah," the young Big Tom said, imagining the body of Grandfather just now being sheet-wrapped to a slab of slate that would carry him to the ocean floor. "And just how much would that bounty be?"

28

The Timbers

CAPTAIN Alfred Jerome-Paul sucked at his coffee, brain-numb, hoping that Churchill the cook was keeping a proper check of the supplies being loaded on. Those three rousers he had met last night were now edging up the gangplank, nudging their way past the docksmen who shouldered sacks of flour and potatoes. The three of them looked as ragged and blood-eyed as the captain felt.

The captain blew his nose on a blue bandanna and tucked it into the back of his trousers, letting it trail out over his belt. Cold coming on, mayhap.

Last night. Captain Jerome-Paul had fully intended to make an early night of it, just one dip of the wick at Madame Augusta's Trug House, Portland's safest and most genteel establishment on the Blain Street red-light row. Just one poke. Maybe a pop of rye. And he would dog back to his tidy aft cabin for a nightcap and then plenty of bunk time.

That had been the plan. And as often happened when Captain Jerome-Paul hit the streets for a pop and a poke, it turned into many pops and many pokes, all up and down Blain Street until well past three A.M. It amazed him that he awoke this morning in his own bunk. His head throbbed, his wallet was thin, and his pecker burned like a fireplace poker. How he managed to get back to the ship he would never know—unless these three youngers slogging up the gangplank had the story.

He slurped at the coffee again, forcing it down too hot and scorching his esophagus. Too old for this, he thought. Time to give it up to the likes of these boys. The three youngers boarded, each of them swinging a duffel, and the captain resurrected a dim memory that they had talked him into an illicit lift down the coast—for a sizeable fee.

Captain Jerome-Paul had observed that these three were rather free with the centimes from the moment they had met at Madame Augusta's. The talky one, who seemed to be the group leader, had been buying a stream of those weak house cocktails for the ebony-haired trug Bestilla (the captain's favorite—and there was a minor sting of jealousy here). The other two were singers, in a loose sense, a bastard's howling opera. They took their trugs two at a time, returned to the center lounge to tell all about it, then took two more back for another roll.

If it was possible to bust manners at Madame Augusta's, these three had done it.

And now, this morning, the captain had rolled out of his bunk, squinting painfully even in first light, and ordered the dockside craneman to load the last of his cargo—the shipbuilding timbers he would off-load at first port, Norfolk.

The talky stranger—the captain remembered his name to be something like Dolan…no, Delano—dropped his duffel to the boards. He approached the captain in sure and careful steps, a thumb hitched in his drawstring as if he had a tired putter down there that needed fresh air.

"Morn," Delano said.

"Ya," Captain Jerome-Paul replied. "The same morning when I last saw you, no?"

Delano coughed a laugh. "My buds and I have to count the days by sunrises, elst we'd neer keep 'em all straight."

"Then you nay be sailors."

Delano ran the tip of his tongue along his lower lip and looked back at his two companions: Jackie, admiring the parade of supplies being shouldered up the gangplank; Will, in the process of pacing off the massive deck, stern to bow.

"No," Delano said. "As I said last night...."

The older man shrugged, lips twisted, his pickled memory useless.

"...we're landers, got to make Chautown before our travel papers expire."

Captain Jerome-Paul snorted. "Ya. Let's pretend I believe that. For a fee...."

"Ten thousand centimes, we said."

"...For a fee, I can believe you're Madame Augusta's left knocker."

"Mmmm," said Delano with a knowing smile. "Or Bestilla's?"

The captain's lined face sagged grimly. He pointed a finger toward Delano's nostrils, saying, "I'll have to put you off at Norfolk, after we makes the wide swing around New York."

"What? No radiation suits? Ha."

"And you'll sleep with the crew in the forecastle. Ya?"

Delano saw that the captain did not want to be humored. "Ya. In the forecastle. Hmph. From the fuckusall to the forecastle."

Delano leaned onto the doorjamb of the forecastle, the bunks inside all empty except for Jack in his top slot, backboard side. Maybe he wouldn't mind Jackie's persistent complaining, he thought to himself, if the little red-haired pig-poker didn't whine like that, in that squeaky voice—about everything.

"They gots five crew," Jackie was saying. "Five swagasses, an' we gotta make do with us three? Hoy, I tole ya I could handle any ship, but this's one like a fairy tale. Two hunnerd feet and more! Jesus potatoes."

Delano stared grimly into the darkness of the cramped, sour-smelling room. Jackie was oiling the last of the three snub guns, his knobby fingers gliding a cloth back and forth. He poked a shell into each barrel and clapped the banger shut.

"You look in the captain's quarters yet?" Delano asked. "It's licensed by the Monitor like any other ship—framed there on his wall over the tilter jug. She's got anchor winches fore and aft like any other—so what if they's 200 feet apart? And sails and sheets and masts—so what if it's three masts, 'stead of one or two? Think of it like this: The three of us will make three real crewmen. Out of their five, they've got captain and cook—which we don' need for a little skim down ta the Blue Islands. We'll make do on Will's slop for a few days, done it afore."

Jackie was arranging his duffel bag to neatly cover the snub guns on his bunk. "I saw the timbers down inta hold," he said, looking worried. "With those little deck hatches, I can't figure for Jesus potatoes how they got such long timbers down there."

Delano laughed, flecking his thumb at the white paint peeling up from the jamb. "There's an aft hatch, Jackie, half below the water line. Dockside, they loaded the timbers by crane, then caulked the hatch shut."

Jackie slid to the floor frowning, contemplating the ingenuity. "A hatch flat against the stern, caulked? Hoo. These timbers, they big enough for what you was thinking to build?"

"Ya, but thass my business," Delano said. He was looking grim again. "And Jackie, long as I'm paying the freight, don't talk Jesus—that sort of thing upset my mama."

"But ho, Jesus potatoes—they's fine. With whole peppercorns…?"

"Ya, I know. But don' talk Jesus, okay?"

29

The New Doctor

IN the deadly heat of late August, mainland visitors were rare. It was the slow season for commerce, especially trade involving perishable goods, human or otherwise. But an elaborate spectacle such as this could not have originated in any place other than the mainland.

From his strategic office perch, hunched over a drawing board, Big Tom probably was first to see the strange skimmer angling for Thomas Harbor. He had just honked down two knife-loads of the powder, and the delicious numbness webbing through his throat made him doubt his perceptions a little.

Hoo. The ship was some kind of harlequin nightmare. It was a two-master, normal enough, but there were no sails to the wind, not so much as a handkerchief. Top mast, there was no flag, but a couple dozen posts around her rails waved bright and flapping streamers in blue, red, and yellow. They seemed to be a taunting send-up of Big Tom's own banners, the system by which he identified his skimmers from afar.

The merchant grunted, pushed back from his drafting table, and tilted his telescope toward the odd craft. On 150 feet of deck there was not a crewman to be seen, yet the gaudy skimmer was angling accurately for the mouth of the harbor. Big Tom considered that perhaps it was under engine power—some special leniency decreed by the Monitor—but that would not explain the absence of crew. There was something strange, too, about the skimmer's deck: the shape, perhaps, or the arrangement of its boards. Even in the telescope, he could not make it out.

Down in the shipyard, the faint skeleton of the Lucia II was taking shape. But Big Tom watched the thundering building process falter, and then clatter to a halt, as the ant farm of wood whits turned their attention to the sea spectre slicing through the harbor. Already eager for the start of noon break, fifteen minutes away, the workers were surrendering to the temptation to drop their tools and gather, gawking, on the wharf. Big Tom made a mental note to rail at today's crew chief—and perhaps he would dock the payroll for the quarter hour.

Big Tom sharpened the focus of his telescope. The pilotless skimmer had now berthed itself comfortably and accurately. Anchor chains fore and aft released themselves on cue, then winched back a bit to steady the yacht. Anchoring at dock, that was odd. But piling ties were now unnecessary, which was fortunate, because there was no crew to throw them.

Big Tom felt a flicker of fear in his chest. He cursed his luck that this otherworldly intrusion would come just as he had slipped comfortably into a powder-induced euphoria. It was a fragile state at best, and there was nothing worse than being high and aggravated at the same time.

Then he snorted a self-deprecating laugh. Hoo. By that standard, he admitted to himself, there was no good time lately for a set-to. He wiped at his nostrils, sighed, and turned for the door.

At the docks, Big Tom could not see over the dozens of heads. Like a common dockside muscler, he elbowed through to the front where a railed gangplank bridged the way from the dock to the foreign skimmer. No one had dared mount it.

The crew chief was there, somewhat embarrassed to find his boss at his side when the work shift was still on clock.

"Who set the gangplank?" Big Tom asked him, deciding to save the other matter for later.

The crew chief shrugged, and flecks of sawdust dropped from his shoulders. "It juss fell," he said, perplexed, "like it was on balance or something and teetered over." He held his browned forearm up in the air to demonstrate, and let it waver, then fall.

The day suddenly seemed impossibly bright to Big Tom, the steamy air motionless. His vision shimmered with glints of pure white light. Even a skimmer set to full sail would have a hard time of it in today's dead air, he thought.

He stared at the gangplank—not your average throw-boards. The rails were intricately carved mahogany, a pattern that reminded him of the back of an ancient rocking chair he had bought for Moori on the mainland. The tread of the walkway seemed to be fresh, black rubber—excellent as a foot grip, but another exhorbitant detail fashioned from rare material. This was not a mere workaday vessel.

He placed a cautious foot onto the rubber matting, and it felt firm and oddly welcoming. He had experienced many emotions about sea skimmers, but never such an overt friendliness. It was a feeling he instinctively wanted to resist, for his intellect—some haggard corner of his mind—was still squirming in fear.

As he topped the gangplank, the murmur of docksmen and wood whits died to a whisper. Big Tom held up the palms of his hands, motioning for the others to stay on the dock.

The skimmer's deck was polished mahagony as well, and at the sight of it his mouth fell open. In many ways it resembled any other finely kept skimmer top: precise coils of hemp, handsome masts, and thick piles of neatly folded canvas tied in place. But the striking feature was the shape of the deck itself. It was not flat. The gleaming boards swept upward from the center, dovetailing into the rails on each side. It was as if the deck had been crafted from half of a monstrous barrel.

Big Tom stepped onto the deck, expecting to slide on the slick embankment. To his surprise, he found himself standing at an angle, perpendicular to the deck as if the skimmer had its own demented law of gravity. His large stomach soured and his breathing began to come hard, as if all the weight of his belly were drawing against his lungs. He scratched under his beard.

The merchant tried a test. He tip-toed down to the center of the empty deck and found himself upright like the masts. Then he paced slowly up the far curve of the deck, toward the backboard rail. Once the rail was at his feet, he looked back and saw the mast directly overhead—he was standing at right angles to it. Big Tom peered past the skimmer's rail, afraid that he would see precisely what he saw: the calm harbor stretching straight down from his toes in a wall of aquamarine.

Could he be dreaming? Big Tom thought about it. Hmph. Too real. In a dream, had he ever smelled the salt stench of the docks? Had the sun ever scorched his eyes? In a dream, had he ever felt the vile bubble of vomit pushing at his throat that he felt right now? No.

Big Tom turned around and stepped again toward center deck, his testy stomach settling as he came upright again. Standing at the bottom of the wooden bowl, he wondered if he should call to the others on the dock. Would they see what he saw? Or had the powder and bourbon finally burst some mental gasket, as the late Dr. Scaramouch had always warned him?

As he started for the gangplank, a latch rattled and the door of the aft hatch—presumably leading to the captain's quarters—fell open. Big Tom stopped and stared at the black rectangle fifty feet away, feeling fear suddenly pressing at him like an awesome weight. He wished he had borrowed a snub gun from one of the toughs on the dock.

A slender, dark-skinned figure stepped out. He wore black leather boots up to the knees, billowy trousers and a dark blouse shot through with random red and gold threads. His head was rimmed with a peach-colored turban folded so that a tail of material fanned protectively over his neck. His chin bore a closely trimmed beard, and a narrow, knotty moustache arced across his upper lip. He was adjusting the turban as he came through the hatch, as if he had just finished dressing, and upon seeing the distraught merchant at center deck, the stranger gasped in shock.

"Hoa-ye! Who are you?"

The words resounded up the curved planking, surrounding Big Tom with ghostly acoustics.

"I, uh, I might ask that of you," he replied. "You've docked in my harbor without permission."

The dark man's eyes widened. "We've docked? Landed? You mean we've made Thomas Island already?" His words were low and ringing, the way congas would sound if they could speak.

"Ya, and I am Big Tom of Thomas Exports, and owner of the island."

"Ho, then," said the thin man, growing more comfortable, pushing the turban to an angle. "Ahem. Ah, somebody here call for a doctor? He's arrived."

Big Tom's eyelids sank closed. The edge had now worn off his dose of powder and the cockeyed mania seemed to be subsiding. So that was it—the doctor. Hoo. Finally, some help for Little Tom, still strapped hand and foot in the clinic.

Big Tom opened his eyes, now a little irritated at the showy arrival. "Son, would you go below then and get him. I have an immediate task for the doctor."

The stranger blinked. He looked back at the open hatch, frowning. For a second, Big Tom thought he saw a flash of deep red in the dark man's pupils, but he dismissed it as another illusion fomented by the stark sun and the powder.

"Go get him?" the stranger asked. "But 'him' is me. I am the doctor sent by the Government."

Big Tom coughed and felt the sweat gathering in his underdrawers. "Oh, ha. Sorry. But we get rather afield of mainland ways out here. On the islands, these parts, a man such as you would be thought a Rafer."

"That would be quite natural," the stranger said. He removed his turban, and a torrent of minuscule black braids fell to his shoulders. Five of the braids were tipped in gold. "Because I am a Rafer. Name's Rutherford Cross Jr. You may call me Pec-Pec."

"I have heard of you," Big Tom said. "Some kind of Rafer ruler." He took a step backward, even though Pec-Pec had not moved far from the hatch.

The dark-skinned man giggled. "Hmm. A contradiction in terms. Rafer. Ruler. I might help out a government, but I'd nay be one."

Big Tom's panic took over. He scrambled for the gangplank on his hands and knees, mindful of the nausea that walking upright would bring him. But the gangplank was no longer in place. It had folded itself in half and clamped into storage position, becoming part of the starboard rail. Big Tom peered over the rail and saw nothing but sea. All around. Starboard, backboard, forward, aft. Thomas Island was not to be found.

The merchant's chest was heaving, sweat dripping from the tip of his beard as he clung to the rail. "You'll not kill me without taking a bang or two yourself."

Pec-Pec waved him down. "I'll not kill you at all," he said. "I'm a Healer, as was my father."

Big Tom groaned, but began to edge himself back toward center deck, sliding on his wide rear until he could stand without vomiting.

"This is an odd crate ya have here. Stands ya on a tilt and docks and sets sail again on her own."

Pec-Pec threw his hands open, saying, "You're known far as a shipbuilder, so I guess you unnerstand what it's like when a skimmer seems to take on a life of her own."

"You built this thing?"

"Oh, no. Thass part of the problem. Won her in a chess game from a Brazilian undertaker. If I could make a skimmer from my own mind, mayhap she'd be more cooperative, no?

But you see I haven't hammered out all the nickers on this one yet. Sometimes, she juss does what she thinks best."

"Brazilia?"

"Ho, Brazil. Thass a place many miles south and many years ago—where I got her." Pec-Pec tapped his foot on the deck. "Bad chess players in Brazil. Back then."

Big Tom stood weakly. "Well, I can see what ya done to your crew—made 'em sick is what. Nobody could work long on this deck."

"To a man with the right skills, this is the perfect deck," said Pec-Pec, looking hurt. He crouched and spread out on all fours, touching his chin to the wood. "Look, to a discroller the curvature of the deck works quite well." The Rafer began to spin his body against the deck like a jar lid, and abruptly he cartwheeled up the starboard side.

Big Tom gaped. In a blink, Pec-Pec had appeared sitting cross-legged on the starboard rail. This spinning business reminded him of what his house boy, Gregory, had been practicing. So it was a technique the half-wit had learned from the Rafers.

"See?" said Pec-Pec. "From one side of the deck to the other in a fraction of a second. Now, here's a more important maneuver." The Rafer dived off of the rail onto the sloping wood. He spun down the deck, up the backboard side, and catapulted himself into the sky.

Big Tom lost sight of him, then spotted him dangling from the high rigging of the main mast. The dark man released his hold and fell to the deck. He diverted the force of his fall by somersaulting onto the wood bank and sliding on his back to the spot where he had originally stood center deck.

Pec-Pec was grinning. "Guess what would have happened to me on a flat deck?"

"That fall," Big Tom asked wearily, "another Rafer technique?"

"No. The hit-and-roll. Paratroopers."

"Para..."

"Ancient sky warriors. When people could fly."

"Oh, yes. Fly. Why not? My grandpa spoke of it, crazy

poker." Big Tom looked to the sky and found not a cloud. The skimmer gave no sense of motion either, and he felt tempted to climb to the rail again to see if they might be returning.

Pec-Pec seemed to read his mind. He sat on the deck and motioned for Big Tom to do the same.

"First we talk," the Rafer said, pausing until the merchant had eased his sweaty bulk to the deck. "Forgive my toying with you—now I will tell you what I am about. It is true that I am sent by the Government and it is true that I am a Healer, and I will tend to the sick on your island. For a short time anyway.

"But the healing is coincidental to my real purpose here. The Monitor is dead, and the new leaders implement new policy—try to do it quietly, to prevent panic."

Big Tom stared at his knotty knuckles. He was nearly broke, and he could see that his little empire would never have a chance to revive itself. "Ya should have just sent word with Captain Bull," he said. "No more barge trips—no more contract on the red-leggers. Right?"

"Ya. But we did send an emissary, our own emissary, directly to you. To ask you to stop the trade, first. And second, to give you a choice: to become an undesireable, a fugitive from the new Government, or to help it with a new mission. But when the trade did not stop—well some of the less patient revolutionaries, they decide to stop the red-legger trade themselves. Start from the mainland first, then work their way out here. Hangings and hackings. Not very discrete, but I'd say your market has dried up."

"But I never saw this emissary."

"Or you killed him."

Big Tom stood quickly, even though his knee joints screamed pain. "No!"

"A blond man. Young. Named Gregory."

"Greggie!" Big Tom hesitated, but decided the truth might for once serve him well. "He showed up on the island with a head wound, talking foolishness. Nay a body could unnerstand him. I swear on it, by the bellies of my wives."

Pec-Pec frowned and waved his hand. "Sit. A man such as you could blow wind all day—such excuses. All of that is irrelevant, because the new Government wants you alive."

"For a mission, uh?"

"They want a ship, large and strong such as only you could build. For crossing the Big Ocean, months or even years. They have decided to find out what has happened to the other lands."

"Useless, wouldn't ya 'spect? Radiated?"

"It can't be all gone—look at our own mainland."

Big Tom's head began to hurt. "What proof do you have," he asked slowly, "that the Monitor is dead?"

The Rafer held up his index finger. "If you like, Mr. Flesh Merchant, you may wait on Thomas Island for the next arrival of the tug boat. Aboard it will be a dozen irascible revolutionaries who will not be as patient with you as I. And trailing from the stern will be the body of your Captain Bull as trolling bait. Other than that, I have one thing I can show you."

Pec-Pec sprang to his feet and disappeared into the hatch. He returned dragging a rubbery satchel shaped like an oriole's nest. Grinning, Pec-Pec pulled the grab-handles apart and reached in. He pulled out a handful of blond hair sopping from a briney liquid. Hanging from the hair was the pickled head of a bull-faced man.

"He was wearing sunglasses," Pec-Pec said, "but I lost 'em."

Finally, Big Tom threw up.

30

Healing

NIGRA.

Pec-Pec rarely heard the word—only among island Fungus People.

Stone-faced, Pec-Pec had gently lifted back the gauzy swath over Little Tom's crotch. Around the hospital bed were Big Tom, still looking blue-green from his voyage and clutching a fresh bourbon-on-ice, the beefy attendant Lily, and Gregory, looking a little worried but mostly vacant. Gregory had seemed to recognize Pec-Pec, but cowered when he first saw the Rafer. It was as if Gregory felt he had done something wrong—failed his mission, perhaps.

Pec-Pec had pointed out the row of festering puncture wounds along Little Tom's penis, saying, "Ah ho. That's the root of it. The bite of a Rafer tosser disk."

And Big Tom had coughed, skeptical. "A tosser disk? Not in his willie." But silently the merchant remembered the story that Bark had told—about the young Rafer woman forced into the master's cabin of the Lucia. Sampling the merchandise. And smoking ganja while on command.

And then Lily harumphed her own doubt about the dark-skinned healer and waddled toward the door of the clinic room. To no one in particular she whined loudly, "Well, I'm glad we gots a doctor again—even if he is a nigra."

Pec-Pec watched her wide churning buttocks disappear into the chipped-linoleum hallway. Nigra. He made two mental notes: Someday, make a study of isolated island lexicography; and someday, make a study of the effects of in-breeding among the Fungus People.

He unbuttoned the backpack he had placed on the wheeled surgeon's table and began to empty its contents—pouches of fan-shaped mushrooms, acrid roots, shards of dried meat, and spices. Big Tom's eyes widened: The pack seemed to hold more than physically possible.

"Please draw a warm bath, Big Man," Pec-Pec murmured, taking advantage of his authority to give the island owner a new name. "And I must have a kettle of boiling water."

Finally, Pec-Pec told Big Tom to cut the restraints, and the delerious Little Tom began to scratch feverishly at his crotch again. Big Tom and Gregory grabbed him by the wrists and ankles and dragged him naked down the hall to the tub room. The young seaman's eyes were open, but his head lolled aimlessly and he stammered his way through a droning nonsense song as they shuffled down the linoleum: "La me treeeeee...in coffee leeeees...."

It was an ancient upright tub, the kind meant for muscle therapies. But being one of only three tubs on the island that was fed by running water, it was used most often for mere bathing. The steaming water thrumbled and swirled into the tub from a pair of jets. When they sat Little Tom on the submerged bench, he relaxed immediately and his singing subsided.

Pec-Pec entered the room sloshing a bowlful of his eclectic ingredients mixed with a couple of cups of boiled water. The green-black mixture produced the odor of dank mustard, fumes that brought tears to the eyes. Unceremoniously, Pec-Pec threw the entire bowl into Little Tom's bath, and the soothing water turned the color of ink.

The Rafer studied his patient's eyes one at a time, then

grabbed him by the neck and dunked him under the water, holding him there firmly.

Big Tom sputtered, "He's not got the mind for holding his breath! He'll drown—let 'im up!"

Pec-Pec seemed surprised at the concern. "Hoo, this'll cure him though, Big Man. If it doesn't kill him."

Large dollops of air were breaking the surface of the water. Gregory wrung his hands and whimpered. Pec-Pec held his patient fast under the black water, and his eyes locked grimly onto Big Tom's.

"I been meaning to ask you," Pec-Pec said in stony politeness. "You remember a man come through these parts back a few months? Man name of Quince?"

Big Tom did remember the name—the doused red-legger—but he pretended to think, a puzzled expression on his face, his eyes never wandering from the sight of his son bubbling under the watery murk. "Ah…no. Can't recall."

"You sure? All his friends show up on the mainland, say they don't know where Quince gone to." Little Tom's head began to jerk involuntarily just under the surface. Pec-Pec continued, "I have to tell them that I found their friend Quince in a very bad way. That I have taken him to a place where I go, and they will not see him again. But he is happy, finally, and no more harm can come to him."

Big Tom felt as if the steaming bath were searing his own face. This Pec-Pec—a lunatic. Or? He pointed to his son weakly. "Ummm…."

Pec-Pec squinted darkly and pulled the young man up. Little Tom coughed, spewing the rancid liquid. "Ah," said Pec-Pec, seeming friendly again, "let him sit in there an hour—he will come around."

Big Tom gently touched his son's face. "His skin," the merchant said. "It's been stained, uh, rather dark." Little Tom slumped against the wall of the tub, mouth agog, still barely conscious.

"Oh, that. It will wear away, I think. Maybe. Few months, a year."

"A year! Wait…."

"But for now," said Pec-Pec, smiling widely, "a nigra!"

Gregory slept with his head pillowed against his two hands folded together. Pec-Pec, sitting cross-legged on the foot of the bed, marveled at the childlike face, the lips pursed, his once-worried eyes finally at ease for the evening.

Pec-Pec cradled a fish bowl in his lap. Inside, a delicate dragon fish the size of his index finger swished lazily. He dipped in and took the fish in his palms gently, murmuring, "Dragon fish, will you come with me?"

He sucked the fish into his mouth, and the coppery taste seemed to spread instantly—down his throat, out to his ears and enveloping his eyes. Pec-Pec swallowed, and his vision dimmed. He leaned out of his body and hovered over Gregory's face. The Rafer was now a spectre, just a point of consciousness in the air, no longer having any weight or size.

He felt himself buffeted by the ebb and flow of Gregory's breath. After twirling for a moment around the angelic face, Pec-Pec rode a narrow torrent of wind into his left nostril.

Inside Gregory's head, Pec-Pec's apprehension grew. He had done this only once before—into the mind of a Government inspector—and the memory images he had found there so enraged the Rafer that he tore the man's mind apart. It was not the act of a Healer.

This would be different, he hoped. Pec-Pec found a large book, a sopping wet volume made up of flimsy pages—Gregory's collective memory. Most of the pages were horribly torn, as if a machete had hacked through the book twice. Dozens of scraps of paper swirled around the chamber, and Pec-Pec would have to return them to their proper spots in the book somehow.

He caught one shred of paper in his cupped hands, the way a man might snatch a butterfly, then flipped through the hundreds of pages until he found the one torn in precisely that shape. He fitted the page together, ran his fingers along the rend, and the page was whole again. The page had been blank, but slowly a picture appeared out of Gregory's boyhood: a grassy hill topped by a spinning windmill.

Pec-Pec sighed as he surveyed the myriad scraps wafting about him. It reminded him of one of the paperweights the Fungus People make—the kind with the snow glittering about.

Hoo. This was going to take hours.

31

For History

Sunreader dotscript
Portfolio 17
Page 9
Jersey Saple

MATTERS related to the arrival of Rutherford Cross Jr., a.k.a. Pec-Pec, on Thomas Island.

Might I break form long enough to pose a thought question? How can history be preserved with any credibility when its witnesses cannot agree even on the very day of its happening?

That complaint stated, I will recede again into my preferred journalistic anonymity to record as closely as can be determined by a gossipy blind man what has transpired this week on Thomas Island. It is an account pieced together from the varied testimony of docksmen, wood whits, a jailer, and one of Big Tom's wives (whose name will not be recorded here).

Not the least of the unusual events was the actual arrival of Pec-Pec, known variously as a Rafer god, a thief, a magicman, a charlotte, a rogue, and a revolutionary. All agree that his skimmer arrived under no visible power or piloting.

Big Tom has stated to many that he boarded the ship; that it left port; and that he consulted with the lone habitant of the skimmer, Pec-Pec, for half of an hour. Numerous observers on the dock swear that the captain had stepped out of sight onto the skimmer's deck for no more than ten seconds before he returned with vomit in his beard. (Cross reference to previous observations concerning Big Tom and a substance commonly known as "the powder," as well as a rogue trader known by the name Delano and a produce man called Steinbrenner. Portfolio 3, Pages 2 and 7.)

The arrival of Pec-Pec signals a long-rumored economic upheaval for Thomas Island and the Out Islands—specifically, the announcement that the Government no longer will be requiring the round-up of red-leggers. It is a proclamation hailed by some as a new era of freedom and by others as a return to the anarchy of the Big Bang days of centuries past. Opinions on this matter reliably correlate to each observer's dependence on the red-legger trade.

Accounts of two "healings" by Pec-Pec must also be considered somewhat dubious and hysterical. Little Tom has broken his fever and his delerium is receding, although he still seems haunted by the imagined smell of captive red-leggers. Odd what hallucinations the human mind chooses to torment its owner with.

Gregory, the half-wit house boy, is the other healing getting much talk. He does seem to have recovered his mental command and a sharpness of eye. But it is reasonable to suspect that both Little Tom and Gregory were healing quite naturally on their own before Pec-Pec arrived with his medicine show.

The ramifications of the cessation of the red-legger trade are intricate and not fully known. It has been talked about the island quite heavily—among those without any position to know—that Big Tom somehow lost a great deal of wealth in the sinking of the Lucia. Among those depending on his enterprises, the hope is that Big Tom will be in a position to secure a new Government contract.

And speaking of the Government, an odd crew of

Government men arrived two days after Pec-Pec. They are a forthright but ornery lot who give Pec-Pec wide berth and explain themselves little. Except to say that they have been stationed in a temporary advisory capacity. Their only official act so far has been to search the timber supplies of the shipyard, apparently for evidence of hijacked materials.

They are grim, and it is said they are piloting Captain Bull's tug. Their leader is named Fel Guinness.

32

A Report to Headquarters

PEC-PEC sat cushioned by a bank of moss on the wooded mountainside. Far below, his panel truck was barely visible. He had parked it where the sporadic macadam road had finally surrendered to pine saplings and underbrush. Then he had hiked the rest of the way up, to where a frame of ten-by-tens formed a black square on the shaded hillside, looking like the entrance to an ancient mine shaft.

He waited patiently. Just from his seat he spotted a dozen herbs he thought he might collect—later, if there was time. That rabbit tobacco, especially. It had been a long time since he had seen rabbit tobacco.

When a metal door finally opened, down in the darkness of the tunnel, it threw out a dim oval of light that exposed the wood frame for the fake front that it was. A sturdy figure stepped through the hatch and limped down to take a seat by the Rafer. He appeared to be much older than Pec-Pec—balding, gray—although Pec-Pec was his senior by several hundred years. The man from under the mountain sat and smacked his fingerless right hand at a leg of his green camouflage jump suit.

"Humph," the grayhead said. "Ordered these from the Northlands, an' they were too piss-plum dark for our vegetation. A hunnerd pair a camouflage suits, an' I had to bleach down every one of 'em or they'd never work in these parts. Humph."

"Ah, Rosenthal Webb. I am glad to see that you still find much to complain about. Your revolutionaries have won, but there is much left that is wrong with the world, no?"

Webb stood again, uneasy, and dusted off his rear end. "So. We'll have us a ship?"

"Oh ya, Big Tom is quite convinced that the only thing that will keep him off the end of a trolling line is cooperating with this new Government. He will build you a ship to cross the big sea. I had to show him the Monitor's head, but he's a believer now. He insists on keeping the island, though, and we must ship to him advance money and the timbers."

Webb wiped at his red eyes and grunted again. "There'll not be much advance money, not till—um—not till the council is more attuned to the idea of an ocean ship. But I'll get him the cut of the entire Northland if that's what it takes. If I can keep the timber clippers from disappearing. The Monitor allowed juss seven made, and four are...." He shrugged.

Pec-Pec's eyebrows rose with a mischievous idea. "Ha! Mayhap it's revolutionaries such as yourself taking the clippers. Mayhap it's time to tell all the sectors that the Government is new. There are rumors of this already even in the Out Islands."

"Ya, rumors," Webb said wearily. "Well, our people are almost in place in New Chicago—thass what the Revolutionary Council is waiting for. We're finding some favorable manpower in the old mining prison, too. In Blue Hole. If all goes well we will announce it soon—if all of Merqua doesn't already know."

"Big Tom says he will have you a ship by spring. And one final condition he asks that I bring to you: He must make the voyage to find Europe. Captain the ship."

"Ho. Well. That's not decided yet. Ya see, I'm moving a little in advance of the council's wishes—they don' know the building's ta start. Who do you think should go on the ocean ship?"

Pec-Pec looked sullen, staring at the tips of his black boots. He did not answer.

"Ey, Pec-Pec? Who should go?"

Pec-Pec began slowly, and Webb read anger and unease in the voice. "Rosenthal Webb, I must caution you against such a clustering of your Fungus People. History shows that this might not go well—these people brought together by fear for their lives and hate and money and—" Pec-Pec's eyes seemed to flash red for a moment "—and, well, I have heard whispers of a Cantilou that has been drawn to the region. And these are conditions on which a Cantilou would thrive."

Webb pressed his lips together. "Cantilou. The myth, pre-war, older even—"

"A Cantilou would have you think of him as myth," Pec-Pec said. "That is his way. He can scratch soil into the brain to cover his tracks."

"You mean this," Webb said. "You actually would have me believe that this Cantilou beast is marauding in the islands?"

"No. It is the Cantilou that would have you not believe it."

"Ah."

"I would have you believe this, Rosenthal Webb: You know of the mountain feline which you call the wildcat. Yes?"

"Of course. Nasty animal."

"Then understand this: What the wildcat is to you, the Cantilou is to me. By now you must have gathered something of my way of being—our lives are on different planes that merely intersect at this point. But the Cantilou is on my plane as well. His world, too, intersects at this point."

"And how many of these Cantilous would there be?" Webb asked.

Pec-Pec shrugged. "Enough to meet demand. Always enough."

Webb was silent for several moments.

"So, then," Webb said. "You will not offer a suggestion as to who should cross the Big Ocean in the new vessel?"

The magic man sighed and nodded sadly, letting his beard touch his chest. "No, Rosenthal Webb. That is the last of it—I have persuaded this Big Tom to make a large ship for your new Government. But I do not want to be part of your new Government. You must decide these things, who should cross the Big Ocean."

"But you instigated much of this yourself! You directed us all out west—to the canyon where the Monitor was hiding. And, you bit his head off!"

"No. The fish. The fish bit his head off."

"Your little dragon fish. Ya."

"Ya. Only he was made big for a moment."

Webb rubbed again at his eyes, glanced at the grime on his fingertips, then thought better of the effort. "You're a Rafer. You hate governments. You hate bangers. But all the while the continent is springing haywire like a dropped clock. You're like your friend the inventor, Cred Faiging. He'll stay in his compound, behind the wire. Said he traded with the old Government; he'll trade with the new one. Juss leave 'im alone."

Pec-Pec shrugged again. He leaned forward, picked a stalk of rabbit tobacco, and sniffed at it appreciatively. As he rolled it between thumb and forefinger it glowed and began to smoulder, and he sniffed it again.

"But, hoo, we've got pirates up and down the coast," Webb continued. "Fel Guinness has hanged every Southland farm supervisor, criminal or not. And now the worst pig-pokin' slaver in the Caribbean you've hired on to build me an ocean ship."

"I directed you to him, suggested you have Gregory contact him, because he really was the only one among your people, Rosenthal. Besides, until spring—that is not too long. Do what you will with him then."

"If I promise him he'll captain the ship, I'll have ta let 'im."

Pec-Pec frowned. The day was dimming quickly, and that early evening known to the mountains was falling.

"Getting cool," Webb said. "Let's go inside."

Pec-Pec glanced back at the open hatch. He had been inside once—the stuffy tunnels and ladders, the life support systems and generators run by the mountain-top windmills, the large meeting chamber where the decisions of the Revolution had been made for decades.

"No. Ha. Canna go in there, thank you. You should close 'er down, Rose. No need to live in there anymore."

Webb scratched at his neck. He might let the old headquarters fall to rot one day, but it was a lifestyle hard to let go of.

"Well, g'night then," he said. "And thanks." Webb turned to go.

"You're forgetting...."

"Ah...Gregory? How is he?"

"Should not travel yet. But that is juss as well. Said he wanted to stay in the islands for a while. Watch the ship go together, I dunno what else. Guinness has started his duty there now, and he will protect Gregory while he stands guard over Big Tom."

Webb hawked and spat into the pine needles, then disappeared into the tunnel sadly.

Even in the dying light, Pec-Pec could see the red in the phlegm.

33

Hesitant Pursuit

BILLISTER marveled at the grand stairway that led to nowhere. They were outside of the abandoned school building that served as temporary dormitory for the freed farm workers. A playing field gone to weeds flanked the brick building, and two large nets were rotting at either end. Soccer. Billister had heard of it.

The large stairway actually was a seating arrangement, for large amounts of observers of the game. Let's see. A cow's stomach was filled with air and sewn closed. Two teams would kick the inflated stomach about the playing field until....

"Over there, please." One of the shelter staffers had tapped him on the shoulder. Billister had been in an obedient line of former farm workers filling the bleachers, but a man in a drab green shirt was directing him to the little wooden platform down front.

"Me?"

The shelter man nodded yes.

Another shelter man, this one wearing a brown tunic reaching to his feet, waved to Billister from the speaker's stand. His head was shaved, like Billister's had been until recently, except that the shelter man wore a small pony tail sprouting from his left temple. Also on the stand were a thin metal post topped with some kind of electronic instrument and a cabinet connected to the post by a wire.

As Billister stepped through the high grass to the stand, dozens of burrs attached themselves to the cuffs of his trousers. He mounted the platform and began picking them off, grumbling to the man in the tunic, "Irritating vegetation."

"My name is Ponzer," said the shelter man, ignoring the complaint. He tapped at the electronic instrument and the cabinet to his side boomed with the amplified noise. He stepped away from the microphone again. "I am told that you are the man Billister from the islands, the one what speaks both English and Rafer."

Billister finished picking the burrs, and two of his fingers were smeared with blood. "Ya," he said. "And Spanish and Latin and French." He watched the orderly crowd, half of them dark skinned, filling the bleachers. They moved so cautiously, precisely as told, as if they doubted their new freedom. Billister wiped the blood onto his newly issued trousers, a pair of Government surplus khakis given to him in the shelter. They bore the name L. Banner stenciled inside the waist, and Billister amused himself imagining a man by that name driving his delivery truck, or whatever, with no pants on. They were rather roomy, as trousers go, but still Billister preferred tunics and he felt jealous of Ponzer's.

"I need you to translate for those who do not unnerstand," Ponzer said. "Please say into the microphone, in your Rafer language, precisely what I say in English."

Billister nodded. They waited until all of the new shelter residents were seated, filling three-quarters of the bleachers. The sun was rising, a blinding ball of mist, and Billister was beginning to dread the steamy mainland day that was coming.

"My fellow Merquans, welcome," Ponzer said into the mike, and his tinny voice howled across the unused playing field and bounced back off the brick apartment building beyond. "I am Alo Ponzer, director of the Chautown Shelter.

Let me apologize first for the limited accommodations and provisions, but I can assure you that we are diligently rounding up sufficient food, clothing, cots, and other materials to make your short-term stay in our shelter comfortable."

Ponzer stepped back from the microphone and motioned Billister up to it. Billister repeated the essence of the message in Rafer, and was surprised at the feeling of power brought by his voice dashing over the stands. He stepped aside and noticed that two of the new Government men were now flanking the door to the old school, each with a semiautomatic with those curved ammo clips.

Ponzer continued: "In a moment, I will review the possibilities of new, voluntary work assignments, relocation arrangements, and options open to every one of you. But first-now, I would like to set the record straight about the inevitable rumors, as it is easy to misinterpret what is heard or seen without the proper background. The Government, for which we desire unity and power, has taken a humane turn and has decided that Ag Agency field work will be voluntary, and not punitive as it has been in recent past. This has merely involved a few personnel changes in the supervisory positions."

Ponzer motioned Billister forward again. Personnel changes? Billister glanced back at the sentries with their evil-looking bangers. He paused to compose his translation, then began, "The Fungus Person standing here asks me to make you believe that...."

In exchange for his services, Billister was allowed to be among the morning's first shift of shelter residents to use the men's shower room. They were rationed a quarter hour, and Billister showered quickly, saving most of his time to razor away the tight black curls that had sprouted on his head and face. The razor was a flimsy device, built so that the blade itself could not be removed. It was tethered by a thin chain to the wall beside the locker room mirror. He used the old razor carefully, in his methodical pattern, to avoid cuts. Then he toweled off and dressed again in the same clothes.

Back in the main school building, Billister feared that he might be asked to man one of the information tables clotted with the curious and confused. He gaped at the array of hastily scrawled signs, the milling suspicious and unshowered field workers. He found a door, marked in fading English lettering "Fire Exit Only—Alarm Will Sound" and leaned into it. It fell open and there was no bell.

The noon street of Chautown sweltered, and Billister noted how even in a mainland capital, the weather did not cooperate—just two blocks from the waterfront, there was no cooling breeze. No relief.

The street itself was a clatter of horsecarts and motor wagons, sand and potholes and dung. The dainty ladies in long dresses carried parasols; the male drivers cursed, shirtless in their seats; businessmen hurried about with leather cases. All of them were Fungus People.

Billister looked high for two landmarks and memorized their positions—a steeple here, a towering oak webbed with Spanish moss there. He set out north, feeling secure as long as he could catch a glimpse of the sea when the buildings parted at the end of each block.

Four blocks up he found a flower stand, a wall-less shelter with bins of blooms displayed in the shade. The sidewalk was wet from sprinkling to preserve them. Hah. A little outdoor store with no purpose other than to sell pretty plants that would wilt in a few days.

A particularly beautiful woman was buying a cluster of purple irises. He studied her profile under the white, wide-brimmed hat—faultless cheeks and a rounded nose poised over an open purse. She selected a few centime notes and gave them to the attendant, then walked west with her paper-wrapped stalks.

Billister stared into space, still studying the ghost she had left behind, that profile. Her hair had been the blackest possible ringlets, her nose gently flared, her skin the color of coffee with a dash of cream. Undoubtedly a Rafer. At home here in the festering coastal capital of the Fungus People. Gliding uphill into the elegant residential neighborhoods overlooking the harbor. Trailing behind her a waterfall of white skirt ruffles.

He followed. Up the easy rise to the shaded streets, where water hissed in precise spray patterns over trimmed lawns, where staunch iron fences guarded mansions, where even the wide edifices losing their whitewash looked regal in their timeworn weary.

When she turned a corner, Billister hung back, tactfully watching children torture a small park's swing sets and little steel carousels. Some of the youngsters were dark skinned, as were some of the distant parents watching from the row of benches. For the first time ever, he imagined himself a parent, watching his son dip himself upside down from a plank on two chains, swinging gaily in a public park.

He almost lost her, for she turned again at the next corner. But her form was an unmistakable beacon along the oak-shrouded walkways. With a series of rapid trots, he caught up to a respectable half-block distance. She never looked back.

There were few men on the streets—not particularly unusual for a residential neighborhood during a work day, he guessed. He did meet on the sidewalk a dark-skinned gentleman, equally elegant as the woman he was following—finely tailored linen coat and trousers, a dark brown leather case dangling from one arm.

Billister greeted him with the traditional Rafer salutation used among strangers, "Sownda say-bode, hom." It was not a taxing exchange, even for a busy man, but the manicured gentleman merely flashed him a quizzical look and walked on.

Finally, the stunning woman, the object of his hesitant pursuit, threw up the latch of an iron gate and glided up the concrete steps toward a broad, three-tiered mansion. Billister stopped at the closed gate and watched with frantic helplessness as she ascended the wide porch hung with swings and jungly potted plants.

She drew out a key, and as she fit it into the door, Billister shouted in desperation. It was an improvised plea, a rough one, for there was no tradition fitting such a situation—a Rafer man daring to follow a Rafer woman down the streets of a foul mainland metropolis.

"Woun-nuitte!" he shouted, the way one man might ask another to stop for casual conversation. "Woun-nuitte!"

The woman turned slowly and regarded the rumpled man at the gate. She propped the bundle of irises over her right shoulder, soldier-style, and swayed down the steps again. Her eyebrows rose, asking the vague question, asking for a repeat of whatever had been said that could not have been heard from such a distance.

Billister now faced her directly, and he felt that tingling privilege, that reward. The purple iris blooms shimmered over her shoulder, and Billister considered how envious all plant life must be, for there was no flora known that glowed with the deep brass of her complexion.

He said it again, almost a prayer now, "Woun-nuitte!"

Her lips pressed together and curled in unison. "You've been out ta long in the noon sun," she drawled in that rough tongue of the Fungus People. "Makes a man talk oddlike, no? You here 'bout the sign? The sign?"

Billister felt his chest collapsing, his hope dissipating at the horror of a delicate dark-skinned woman cognizant only in the Fungus People language: How could this be? And he felt his reason sliding its battered self over to that frame of mind in which one human may converse with another in the rocky tongue of English. He asked meekly, still in awe of her, "What sign do you speak of?"

She coughed into a gloved hand, a broad polite excusing of everything that had come before, and pointed her bundle of flowers at a living room window behind her. A small hand-lettered sign there read, "Live-in house servant desired."

It was as if Billister had lost control of his own mouth, for he felt it spread out into a gentle smile and he heard the throaty English words escape his lips, "Ho, ya. The sign. Of course, I came about the sign."

Her brow tightened with consternation under the white hat brim, and she asked, "But do you have any experience?"

34

Forbidden Territory

MOORI led the horsecart herself, up the steep slope of the back access drive to the mainhouse's delivery door. Gregory was there squatting on the stoop sipping a Liberty Ale and it was not even noon—looking a bit bemused, she thought. Hmph.

Her hair had sagged into sweaty bronze-red tentacles about her shoulders. She tied the horse's leader to the ring post, gave the hitch knot a yank and a piece of the leather came away in her hand. She snapped: "Pig-fuckin'-poke bastard!"

Gregory was on his feet. "Lemme help with those sacks." He grabbed a corner of burlap but Moori stopped him, a firm hand pushing his wrist away.

"Noooo," she said emphatically. Gregory read the tension in her voice, resentment. "As I explained in the kitchen lass night and in the out garden—ho—two days ago, Big Tom says you are not to even lift yer own willie ta pee. You're the recuperatin' patient, he says, though the truth is that he wants not ta be drawn and quartered by yer buddy Fel Guinness and the other new mainlanders." She muttered the last part.

Gregory had decided against looking hurt anymore. He

returned to the stoop, where he picked up his ale and tipped it back. He sniffed. "Ya, okay. But she's your house too, an' I figure this ta be part your desire as well."

Moori undid the knot, pulled more of the leather through the ring, and redid the hitch in exasperated tugs.

"Ya know what these vegetables are costing now?" she said, sweeping her hand at the cart. "And I say this not just 'cause I never had to haul the deliveries before. The produce here was never so up with the centimes. We quit sending the mainland the red-leggers to work the farms, an' the farms can't pull in the crops like they used to. And now the produce they send back to us costs twice what it did before. While we're makin' pig-poke for money!"

Gregory gulped the last of the bottle. "Thass what's bothering you? The price of beans?"

She pushed her hair away from her face defiantly, and Gregory had simultaneous thoughts: She was quite beautiful. But even with his protected, non-working status on Thomas Island, Big Tom probably would slice out his liver just for the thought.

That sexual pipe dream led him quickly to a more serious memory, as if his brain had tightened up a few notches, his mind imploded a few degrees. Tym. He saw her stretched in the shadowy hammock asleep—how many weeks ago?—the stress of a beseiged life absent for a moment from her smooth face. Lips pressed together in sleepy consternation. Small breasts, firm as fists.

The clean and vivid lust of his once-impaired mind. Ah, that was the quandary. Had it been the ignorance of a dimmed consciousness, or was it a valid, lustful memory being tempered now by the return of cautious human reason?

Gregory looked at Moori again—beautiful, yes, but pathetic somehow in her sweaty desperation over the mere hauling of vegetables. He turned through the door into the large pantry, where he hoped to find another ale.

He lifted the lid of the icebox and turned his head aside at the stale and dank odor of the warming chest. Across the metal bottom of the box little nuggets of ice were quickly shrinking and disappearing down the drain hole. Four Liberty Ales stood in the puddle at the bottom, their labels slipping down the glass. The lettuce and green bell peppers probably were okay, but the eggs in the wire rack would not last the night. He didn't know about the cheese.

He knew the routine well, although he was supposed to forget. He was houseguest now, no longer house boy. He grabbed the two buckets beside the chest, went downstairs to the ice machine at Big Tom's bar, and filled them.

The door to the downstairs bathroom was ajar, and whimpering noises came from inside. Gregory pushed at the knob, a heavy brass fixture the shape of a woman's breast. Little Tom was hunched over the round porcelain sink, a wire brush in his hand—the one Gregory had once used to clean the outdoor grill. A patch of Little Tom's brown-dyed forearm was rubbed raw.

The heir to a crumbling Caribbean kingdom turned his red eyes toward the intruder.

Gregory jabbed a finger toward the near-bleeding skin and said, "Ho. Now you black and you red."

Little Tom's nose was twitching. He took the nub of a hand-rolled cigarette from the edge of the soap dish and sucked hard. "Gregory, do you smell something?" he asked weakly.

Gregory sighed. "You're in a crapper, poo-bah. You're bound ta pick up somethin' foul. But all I smell is ganja. Why don't you give it all a rest? The ganja. The skin, hey. Give it a rest, too."

Little Tom was naked, skin an even coffee color. Although Pec-Pec had denied darkening the young seaman's skin on purpose, Gregory preferred to think of it as an intentional prank. But Little Tom's infections did seem to have subsided. Gregory pointed and asked, "So how's your willie doin'?"

"Good anuff. Works."

"All them holes, I thought we might use you for a lawn sprinkler."

Little Tom kicked the door closed in his face.

Ho. This whole house is pig-poked—no humor left, Gregory said to himself. He went back upstairs with the filled buckets, removed one of the ales from the box, then dumped the ice in. Gregory arranged the buckets where they had been before, hoping no one would notice he had performed a service for the house. He hesitated, then pulled a second ale out of the ice and shut the lid.

He took the ales up the stairway to the second tier and walked down the polished hallway past the quiet rooms. Ashtrays overflowed. In the smaller bedrooms, little used since Big Tom's other wives left him, the closet doors gaped open and abandoned bedclothes still lay in rumpled heaps. Most of the women had returned to trug work on Cell Island; a couple of others caught a tug for Chautown. They were a blur to Gregory, a half dozen sweet faces he recalled from the time before Pec-Pec had healed him. He shrugged—he found it less than sad. They had all been trugs before, and were hardly more than that in the service of Big Tom.

Change of assignments, that's all. Gregory had seen many changes of assignment in the Revolution.

Ironically, Moori seemed to miss the other wives more than Big Tom did. Gregory sucked at one of the ales as he walked. He wondered if Moori had had a lover among Big Tom's "lesser" wives. He had heard of that. Sometimes, in a house full of women....

The end of the hall opened onto the veranda, the same one that curved past Big Tom's master bedroom. Out here, the air was moving ever so slightly, like the whisk of a passing bird, but Gregory was thankful for the little breeze. He propped the two ales on the rail and watched the shipyard below. He picked out Big Tom by his squat form—strutting about, waving his arms, having to supervise the yard himself now with such a tight payroll.

If Gregory squinted his eyes, he could imagine the hull filled in the rest of the way, the ship taking form at the waterfront. It seemed absurdly huge, and Gregory thought of the mythological beasts called elephants—those cumbersome creatures Rosenthal Webb had told him about.

The old revolutionary had told him many a tale to alleviate the boredom as they had crossed the western sectors—how long ago? two years?—to kill the Monitor. Like an elephant. Gregory imagined that a ship of this size would be about that graceful.

Four of the dozen men from the new government were down in the shipyard, as always, observing the construction, making Big Tom uncomfortable. They were a surly lot—cliquish, quiet, bunked out each night up the hill in those cells that had once held the red-leggers. How odd, Gregory considered: These men had been as much a part of the Revolution as himself. Yet he had never known them, except for Fel Guinness, and felt little kinship. He wanted to tell them he had been part of the band that actually had slain the Monitor. He wanted them to know, to suddenly snap into reverence like a soldier grunt stumbling across a general. But he could not think of a modest way of bringing up the subject.

Out far beyond the harbor, two low and sleek skimmers eased their way east. Rafers, Gregory figured—the new long sailcraft they seemed to be favoring these days over their traditional catamarans. Big Tom had pulled in most of his own skimmers, and what few crews remained in his employ spent most of their time just patrolling the perimeter of Thomas Island.

Gregory watched the new Rafer skimmers until they melted into the horizon. Hmph. That new design—like some hell-bent sea swan. Where had they learned to hammer out yachts like that? They were certainly nothing that ever crossed Big Tom's drawing board—not his style at all. And where would they be getting their timbers for such craft? Pirated lumber from the mainland?

Gregory spat over the rail. Depression: Tastes like a mouthful of brackish water. He had seen many men damaged in the service of the Revolution—Rosenthal Webb himself was missing a fistful of fingers. Did it always feel this way—after? Like a lone duck hurled aside by a hurricane? Directionless, loveless.

(Webb had warned him once: "Careful not to follow that penis of yers too often. I see that it changes direction more 'n a weather vane.)

It had seemed just a few minutes, but both ale bottles were empty. Gregory thought of wandering down to Sanders's Shebeen—the pub would be fairly empty this early. A long afternoon of lazy thoughts....

No. He stepped back from the rail. Time for a walk, he decided. A project. Exercise. This boredom, this inability to contribute to the working of the island, was going to drown him in ale. He would....

His eyes darted about.

He would....

The garden below: pebbled paths, fruit trees, shrubbery growing ragged, the locked shed.

He would...open the shed.

Big Tom had specifically forbidden it. Only the old merchant himself could go in there—and he did, almost daily. One of the recently departed wives joked that he was having sex in there with Five-Finger Rose—his right hand. "Wat else 'ud it be?" she asked. "He ain't got it up no other time! Haw."

Ah. A daring idea. He turned back down the hallway to the master bedroom.

There were secrets to a house known only to the person who had spent a long time emptying its waste baskets, hanging up tunics carelessly tossed aside, sweeping up the remnants of the last night's revelry. Gregory pulled at the double oak doors of Big Tom's wardrobe, let them creak softly as they always did, and listened for reaction from anywhere in the house. There was none.

A half-dozen of Big Tom's finer tunics lay on the floor of the wardrobe, a tangle of silk. Gregory sighed and leaned in. Across the top inside panel of the cabinet was a row of keys hanging from finishing nails. Back door, front door, office, hospital supply room, Sanders's pub, garden shed. He took the last key and closed the doors again.

At Big Tom's dresser he stopped to peer at the little looking glass mounted on a lacquered driftwood base. Gregory pushed the blond curls away from his forehead and studied the pink and crooked scar. He thought through a now-very-familiar conumdrum, a recurring daytime nightmare: I can not say for sure that my mind is healed. Is that because it actually is healed? Or because it is not healed?

He touseled his hair back over the scar and turned for the door.

The shed was oddly aromatic, the lushly pleasing rot-smell familiar to plant tenders. Gregory shoved the door closed behind him, the top hinge being relaxed enough to make it drag the ground. He hadn't brought the lantern hanging outside, and it was possible he wouldn't need it. Reeds of light criss-crossed the interior—from the cracks around the door, from slipped shingles, from the paint peeling off the single window.

As he stepped down the alley between the bins and the bales his disappointment grew. It seemed to be a very normal garden shed—soils and clay pots, dozens of seed packets sorted out into the slots of an old post office letter rack.

Oh, but here was an odd thing. To his left, atop a pile of manure sacks, sat a cat-looking beast. It had been stuffed by an amateur taxidermist perhaps two decades back. Stitches showed at each shoulder joint. The lips were split and curling back into a ghastly sneer. Most of the hair had worn away from the face. The taxidermist had used large dark marbles instead of natural-looking eyes, and the effect was as mesmerizing as it was horrifying.

As he stared, the voice came out of nowhere: "Gregory," it said softly, and a chill howled up his spine.

He leapt back from the creature. The corner of his eye caught the glare where the shed door had been pushed open. He had been discovered, and his heart hammered.

The voice came again, louder, this time a question: "Gregory?" And he saw then, silhouetted by the blinding sunlight, the unmistakable form of Moori standing in the door. It was she that had spoken, not the frayed cat. Still, his veins throbbed audibly. Perhaps Moori would not tell Big

Tom he had stolen into the shed. Gregory tried to retrace his reasoning: What did he think he might find that would have been worth being de-balled by the old slaver?

Moori pushed the door closed behind her and walked hesitantly toward him, head nodded. She was mumbling, and her words were punctuated by sorrowful gasps: "...can't do it anymore...Big Tom, he'll hardly speak to me. Nothin' but powder, bourbon and that pig-pokin' boat...." She stopped just short of touching him, head still down, thick red hair brushing his chest.

"Your friends?" She looked up, chin trembling. "Can you help me get...he'd kill me...get to Chautown?"

Gregory watched his own hand rise slowly, in awe of the motion as if he were detatched from it. His fingers combed through the outermost strands of her hair, lifting them into a narrow beam of light.

"You didn't leave the vegetables out in the sun," he said, "did you?"

Moori's chin stopped quivering, and she shook her head a bemused "no." The rest was a spontaneous combustion. No tease, no parry, no hints or invitations or calculating give-and-take. Their mouths pressed together urgently. Gregory's hands slipped easily into her loose blouse and found her breasts sweat-moist. Moori pried open the military clip of his belt and tore open his fly buttons in one motion. She sighed desperately and ducked her head to give him a quick and delicate tonguing—a promise. Gregory stood helplessly in the dark, hands lightly stroking the corners of the mouth that needed no guidance—knew exactly what to do.

When Moori stood she led him to the rail of the open peat moss bin. Propped on the ancient two-by-four, she hiked her skirt and pulled him to her, a hand on each side of his buttocks. Gregory obliged, disbelieving. The danger seemed to linger only distantly—in a cobwebbed corner of the shed like some banished ghost. He ran a stroking hand under her thigh and found more moisture. Moori pulled him backward and together they fell into the earth-smell of the peat moss.

Gregory supposed he had been drowsing. The slivers of light knifing through the dusty air had dimmed. Moori seemed to be asleep, naked in the soft grime of the peat moss. The tip of her nose, one cheek, and her rump were covered in gold and brown flecks. What a mess she was. An alluring, warm, satisfying mess.

It was an odor that first stopped his heart. The sour reek of bourbon. And then Gregory heard the scritch-scratch of someone shuffling by. The shed suddenly felt very, very small. Gregory tried to remember: Had Big Tom been wearing his shin blades today? Probably—he usually did. Then he thought of the merchant's powerful red hands, and then of the garroting tree just out in the garden.

Gregory heard Big Tom's voice boom, almost a ritual chant, "Cantilou, ha, Cantilou, Cantilou, good evening."

The reply that came—from where?—was a horrifying, high-pitched keening that goaded the old merchant: "Soooo, how goes the Government work? The ship building? Now that you have no flesh to harvest? Eh, pirate? Eh, Government man?"

Moori was beginning to stir, responding to the voices, and Gregory carefully placed the palm of one hand over her mouth. Beyond that, he dared only to move his head the two inches necessary to see under the bin rail, enough to see Big Tom lifting knife-loads of powder to his nose in the dim light. Gregory's suspicion was correct, and he felt ill: Big Tom was speaking both parts—his own voice and the imagined rantings of the cat beast.

"Gumment, pah, the new Gumment," came Big Tom's natural voice. "It may a commissioned the big sea skimmer, but they'll not have her unless I'm aboard as captain. Hah."

"Or, they'll use yer ample body for trollin' bait first voyage."

Gregory watched as the slaver, weaving over by the manure sacks, paused for another snort of powder. A trail of white now streaked down his moustache and beard, and he held the knife aloft dramatically as his face brightened.

"Trolling bait! That's what we will have, Cantilou, when I find who it is that broke into the garden shed. Thank you—trolling bait. Did you see who it was Cantilou?"

"Is not for me to say," came the whine, "but a careful rapscallion would have locked the shed after he left...."

And Gregory stiffened when he heard Big Tom complete the thought in his own voice as he turned toward the peat moss bin. "...unless he has not had time to leave at all!"

At the rail, Big Tom propped each elbow and let the knife dangle casually between thumb and forefinger. His red eyes darted back and forth between his captives, and his mouth under that bush of beard fell into a somber O-shape. He smelled more of whiskey than Sanders's Shebeen itself. He whispered, "Moori."

Gregory sat forward, still naked and ready to bolt. Moori was fully awake now and pulling on her blouse and skirt—somewhat foolishly, Gregory thought, as they would be no help against a maniac's blade.

All ebullience had drained from Big Tom's face, and he suddenly looked very old. That's what it looks like to watch a man die, Gregory told himself. The merchant's lips began to quiver. Shoulders hunched, he about-faced and returned to the stuffed cat. He cradled the long-dead animal in his arms, fell to his knees on the dirt floor and wailed in a crazed mixture of adult voice and soprano Cantilou.

Gregory was over the rail, trousers in one hand and tugging Moori with the other. When he glimpsed her face, Gregory thought there was a hint of glee—could she have planned it this way? No. Maybe.

They sprinted over the white stones through the twilight garden, clothes fluttering under their arms. At the edge of the garden Gregory hesitated: Up the hill to the protection of Fel Guinness? Staying on the island would eventually mean a confrontation with Big Tom, perhaps a bloody one. Gregory wanted to live, and Big Tom had to finish the Government's ship. Better to leave the island altogether. After a moment's consideration, Gregory sprinted up the porch of the mainhouse, dragging Moori.

"He'll find us here," she said.

"Two minutes," he answered, breathless. "Grab some things. Clothes, cash, trading metal. A weapon?"

Big Tom's pitiful wailing pealed up and down Crown Mountain in the dying daylight. Moori looked sadly toward the garden shed. "Okay," she said, "but the Government boys—your boys—took all of his bangers."

When they reached the docks all that remained of the sun was a strip of crimson along the horizon, a slice of melon lying on its side. Gregory wore a small backpack; Moori lugged a stuffed satchel in each hand. The shipyard just east was quiet now, the musclers, the wood whits, Bishop, Bark and the rest of the island having retired to Sanders's for the evening. The mammoth ship-in-the-making cut a mountainous silhouette against the harbor.

But Gregory was looking for another craft, and much to his relief it was lolling, low and long and double masted, in a berth near the end of the platform. The boat was dark and the gangplank hauled in, so Gregory pulled the cord wrapped twice around the near piling. A high-pitched bell tinkled on deck, and a voice responded, thick with Southland twang: "Lay off a that son—pull yer own rope."

The tip of a fat cigar then glowed bright on deck, and Moori pointed as she made out the form: a four-foot man in a folding chair, feet propped on the backboard rail.

The little man's bare feet fell to the deck in a lazy whump-whump. He stood and sauntered, stretching, cigar clenched in his teeth. As the dwarf neared, Gregory made out a face familiar from those foggy house boy days: a wide, oversized head, a scarred and flattened nose, as if the cartilage had been whittled out by a backwoods surgeon.

"Steinbrenner," Gregory said.

The man nodded his large head. "Gregory, Moori, 'lo. Something wrong with the potatoes I brung ya?" he drawled.

"Not at all," Moori whispered. "We need your help." She glanced back down the dock. Big Tom had ceased his bawling, leaving all of Crown Mountain and its dwindling population eerily silent—save for the occasional hoo-hah emanating from Sanders's pub. God knows what Big Tom was up to now. "We need to leave the island immediately—you must take us. To the mainland, preferably Chautown."

Steinbrenner snorted. "Ah. A lady used to havin' her way."

Gregory unfolded a sheet of white paper and handed it to the produce boatman. Steinbrenner snapped it open and squinted at the writing. "Mmmm...by authority of the Revolutionary Council...please afford all courtesies necessary for the...mmm...signed Rosenthal Webb, chief of Revolutionary active forces." He stretched over the rail and handed the letter back to Gregory. "And just who's this Mr. Rosenthal of yours an' why should I give a pig poke?"

"The new Government—you been to Chautown lately, you've heard," Gregory replied.

"Rumors is what I heard, ya. A few toughs strung up some farmers—same musclers what got a strangle on Big Tom here, made 'im stop the red-legger trade." Steinbrenner shook his head. "Bad year for Big Tom. No wonder he doin' so much a the powder."

Gregory shrugged off his backpack and unbuttoned the top. "Okay," he said, tossing the boatman a drawstring bag the size of an orange, "whatcha say to this?"

Steinbrenner snatched the bag out of the air with his left hand. He broke the string in his teeth and shuffled out part of its contents—large, ornately engraved coins.

"They's fourteen of 'em there, worth close to 10,000 centimes," Gregory said.

"But this's Rafer brass."

"Man like you does all sorts of trade—would know how to make use of 'em. No? Let's pitch off now."

The produce man snorted and counted the disks twice. Then he threw his weight onto his gangplank and teetered it over the rail until it slammed onto the dock. Gregory and Moori undid the lashings and boarded.

"Moori, you're running now from Big Tom, like all his

other wives did." There was reproach in the seaman's voice. "If thass so, not a word to anyone about how ya made off."

They were center-harbor before Steinbrenner had all of his sails set. Moori approached him at the helm.

"How do you know how much a the powder Big Tom's been using?" she asked.

The captain grunted and kept his eyes straight ahead. "Young lady, you sure I shouldn't let ya off with the trugs at Cell Island?"

Gregory was leaning on the starboard rail, somberly watching Thomas Island fall away into the darkness. "Steinbrenner's a produce man," he said. "Where do ya think Big Tom gets the stuff, 'cept from the likes of him?"

35

The Debriefing

SEVEN aging, somber faces circled the conference table. These were the masterminds of the Revolution—a band of eccentrics who had spent decades of their lives under a remote mountain in the range known among the ancients as Blue Ridge. The Revolution was done. Mission accomplished, partly at the hand of this youngster summoned before them for interrogation.

Gregory stood nominally at attention at one end of the table. Feet apart, hands behind his back. He had been home for forty-five minutes.

Virginia Quale was fripping at the corner of a note pad covered in her furious scribblings. She leaned back into the chair padding and sighed. "My goodness, it is a harried life that you have been leading these past couple of years, Gregory." She was beginning slowly. "And it is well recognized by every member of this committee that your adventures and endangerment and injuries have all been in the service of the Revolution and its subsequent Government. Now...."

Winston Weet could not contain himself. He thrust his pudgy face forward: "But dammit Gregory, you had been ordered by Mr. Webb merely to contact this Big Tom, to determine his willingness to construct an ocean ship—not to begin the construction of one! And your actual orders, you may or may not know, did not even carry the weight of this council."

"My orders were to contact the old slaver about the possibility of making a ship, ya," Gregory responded rigidly. "And after my accident my instructions, as relayed by the Rafer Pec-Pec, were to recuperate on Thomas Island until travel worthy."

Quale jumped in again. "You are being elliptical, Gregory. Our concern is that there have been many other matters in Merqua to be straightened out before we can allocate resources to a mission over the Big Ocean. Just how is it, then, that this Big Tom on a remote island is constructing an expeditionary vessel for the new Government?"

Gregory gripped his hands together behind his back and felt his scalp growing sweat-moist. Webb was sitting there appearing unemotional, except for the nervous thrumming of his finger nubs against the conference table. Webb, Gregory's long-time mentor, had set the project in motion with the complicity of the Rafer magic man Pec-Pec. That would not sit well with the angry council.

Gregory surveyed the ring of dour faces and made his decision: He would employ a common Revolutionary field technique designed to alleviate vexing dilemmas among human beings. He would lie. With just enough truth to make it seem plausible.

"Forgive my, uh, 'liptical testimony," Gregory began, "but there's a sequence of events what makes my actions clearer. After my injury, the island Rafers delivered me to the home of Big Tom the tradesman and shipbuilder—the very man I had been sent to find—where they apparently thought I would receive the best medical care. By irony, it was another Rafer, Pec-Pec, who brought me around."

Quale still fripped impatiently at her pad of paper.

"When I regained my full faculties on Thomas Island, ya see, circumstances had changed since I was given my orders—juss to approach Big Tom. Boatsmen were bringing in rumors from the mainland that the Monitor was dead, that there was a new Government, and that it was hanging all enforcers of the old system of forced labor." Gregory shrugged. "I knew that much was true. It was also rumored that a crew of new Government musclers were sailing for the islands, an' that meant doom for Big Tom and his men."

Gregory paused and cast his eyes down for a humble effect. "I had feared that the loss of Big Tom would be the loss of Merqua's best shipbuilder, now and for all time. So with Pec-Pec's help, I persuaded Big Tom to start immediately the construction of the Government's ocean ship. Even yer gentleman Fel Guinness would know better than ta whack a man working on a project for the new Government, former slaver or no."

Eliot Korhn was wearily resting his forehead on his fingertips. "Now that the plans fer the ship are drawn an' the construction's begun," he said, "what's ta stop us from, uh, whacking Big Tom now and completing the craft ourselves?"

Gregory pressed his lips together. "True, any builder could follow the old bugger's blueprints, except for one thing: Big Tom says the plans are not complete. Built as the plan specifies, the ship 'ud go down in the first heavy sea. There's some structural detail he's left out, something that can be added late in the building."

"But at some time the ship must be absolutely finished," Weet put in. "And from that point any rack of sailors could take her ta sea if Big Tom were, uh, absent." While his words were diplomatic, his expression showed his distaste for the slaver.

Webb laid his hand flat on the table, his sign for an emphatic pronouncement. He spoke for the first time in the meeting: "Get your minds right, please people, that we'll not be putting Big Tom away anytime soon. He aims to captain the ship, ya see. And even as detestable a man as he may be, that would do little harm. But the good it would do us: Well, he'll not only see the ship finished, but he'll see her rigged right, and seaworthy, and across the Big Ocean. That's a seaman's pride we can count on."

"If I could be dismissed now?" Gregory interjected. He let his shoulders sag an inch to illustrate his fatigue.

"Of course, Gregory," Quale replied in that motherly tone that no one took to be genuine. "How long a rest would you say your body requires?"

"Through the night would be it," he answered. "Twelve or thirteen hours."

Quale leaned over and spoke quietly into Webb's ear, then listened to his whispered response, nodding. She drew a timepiece from the side pocket of her blouse and clapped its copper cover open and closed again. "So gentlemen, we shall meet at ten A.M.? Now that it seems inevitable that we will have an ocean craft, against the wishes of some of us, I believe it will be in order to brief Gregory on his next assignment in the morning."

Gregory felt the sickening disbelief churn his stomach. All spring and summer he had spent in a head-pounded haze. Now he would be allowed to rejuvenate just a day or so before shipping out again.

He marched silently to the opposite side of the room, pulled the exit hatch open and thrust himself through it. After being away for so long, he found the dim corridors smothering. He stooped instinctively to avoid the lacquered black piping and conduits—a lifetime of that did not dissipate so easily. Footsteps were clacking up the concrete after him. It had to be Rosenthal Webb. No one else had that limping pace, that determination in his stride.

"The Revolution," Webb began explaining, even before he had caught up. "The Revolution is done, but it means nothing unless we put the rest of it in place, Gregory. You can not stop. I'm sorry. The Government alone will take years to recreate. The ocean ship must sail—there is speculation that parts of ancient Europe might have gone untouched. Can you imagine what that would mean?"

Gregory stopped by the hatch in the corridor floor where the ladder, bolted to the wall, would take him to the sleeping quarters down on Level Five. Already, mentally, he was checking in at the desk, taking the fresh sheets and spreading them out....

"No, Mr. Webb, what would that mean? Another Government to overthrow? Eh? What are the chances that whatever form of rule we find over the Big Ocean is going to be of our liking? The rumors point the other way, don't they?"

Webb pressed his lips together and put a friendly hand on Gregory's shoulder. "You sleep now."

"Hard ta sleep when you've juss had yer butt chewed by the council of the new Government"—he jabbed a finger angrily—"while lying to protect you."

Webb smirked. "And a good lie it was. They see it was a mistake ta put Guinness into the field like they did—he killed many people unnecessarily, and could have killed Merqua's best shipbuilder. Embarrassed as they are, an' with the ship already under construction, I'm sure they'll give the rest of the expedition the go-ahead."

Gregory mounted the ladder and began to climb down. "Well, excuse me. I'd better give sleep a try if I can calm down. I'm the one what's gotta leave soon on a new mission."

"The next assignment, what Quale has in mind is not so bad," Webb said. "We want you to gather the crew and emissaries for the ocean ship, those that aren't already on Thomas Island. It should take long enough, the recruiting, that you probably wouldn't be done much before Big Tom finishes the ship—spring, hey."

"You want me to recruit the expedition?"

"Ah, within limits. Ya. An' most people of use to us, I would think, could be found in Chautown—it being such a shipping center." The old man's eyebrows rose suggestively. "You know anyone in Chautown? Any friends?"

"Ah," Gregory replied. "I did leave Moori there, didn't I?"

"One lass thing," Webb said. "That part about Big Tom's blueprints—that was part of the lie, right? That the ship would collapse?"

Gregory looked perplexed. "Not at all. He's holding something back."

As Gregory climbed down the ladder into the blackness, he thought about the word elliptical. How appropriate. Putting aside the chance to see Moori again, he still seemed to be circling farther and farther from what he really wanted for himself—but what did he really want?

36

An Innovation

BIG Tom, in a sense, had become a red-legger himself.

They had shackled him to an orange tree in his own walled garden, and he wanted to know what comedian had chosen the garroting tree with its rusted collar still in place. His wrists and ankles bore genuine circles of chapped red under the metal cuffs. At the base of the tree, between two large roots, was a worn spot where he habitually sat. A couple of feet away were two smaller holes where he propped his heels.

The manacle chains were mercifully long, not only allowing him to sit, but also to circle the tree and relieve himself on the other side. They hadn't even brought him a bucket to sit on.

For the last two weeks, his only visitor had been his son, Little Tom, meekly bearing trays of grilled fish or chicken soup. Never a vial of powder. Never a trace of bourbon. Little Tom, still dark skinned and presumably alone now in the mainhouse, was preparing the meals himself. His lack of kitchen expertise was very apparent.

He would appear on the white, pebbled path through the neglected shrubbery, eyes downcast. Wads of cotton were stuffed into his ears—the mutineer's technique. He could claim he had not heard the captain's ranted orders, and thus had disobeyed no one.

Little Tom would set the tray in the grass, and quickly retreat. For the first few days, Big Tom had screamed his throat bloody raw each time the young man appeared. Then he had tried to trick the lad—say, "Hey, Little Tom"—hoping he would hear through the cotton and instinctively lift his head. Proof that he was not deaf.

But now, his headaches and shakes had subsided, and he had taken to awkward, metal-clanking calisthenics to put his body into shape. He listened intently to the whitting and hammering wafting up from the shipyard and tried to guess at the new ship's progress. (How could it possibly be going well without him?) And when Little Tom arrived now with the food tray, Big Tom said nothing anymore—just gave him that wearing, fatherly scowl that eventually would force the captain's way through the pressure of guilt.

He could barely recall that evening two weeks ago. He'd had a faceful of powder, half a bottle of bourbon. He'd visited the garden shed and—gawd, it still wrenched his ample stomach—found Gregory and Moori bare assed in the peat moss, of all places.

The rest was a blur of violent images, and he imagined he had done quite a bit of damage to the interior of the mainhouse. Most of the veranda doors up there on the third floor were shattered and hanging at angles from their hinges. He recalled flying ashtrays and vases, smashed furniture and paintings and sculpture, and the clepsydra cartwheeling down the main stairway. Even now, Big Tom thought, his anger seemed intact and he might still be capable of the same destruction.

He recalled, too, a montage of powder-distorted faces swirling around him in the foyer: Bark scowling, and Bishop, Little Tom and that muscler from the mainland, Guinness. It took all of them to clap the cuffs on him and drag him shrieking and flailing to the garden. Chain the bastard to a tree—that was the best cure they could think of.

Big Tom heard the gate at the east wall rattle. He glanced

at the sun's position and knew that it was not yet lunch time. Then Bishop came crunching up the stone path, drawstring pants nearly falling off of his skinnier-than-ever hips.

The little guy was smiling and had a manacle key in his hand.

Big Tom had dragged his drawing table over to the telescope in his office, where he could compare the skeletal scructure down in the shipyard to the blueprint tacked out in front of him. The inner hull planking was starting to edge its way up the framework of the new ship.

"Excellent, excellent," he said, moving his gaze from the eyepiece to the diagram and back again. "Bishop, you've checked the keelson assembly yourself?"

"Oh ya, Big Tom.... She's letter perfect.... To yer blueprint, anyway. The splinting is solid." The assistant, fearing some retribution for the captain's shackling, gave his words haltingly.

"Bishop, I'm going ta call her the Nina, after a mythical ship of the ancients. This is a dream, Bishop, the building of Merqua's largest ship—probably the entire world's."

Upon his release, Big Tom had gone first for a soak in the mainhouse tub, then slipped on a fresh tunic and marched straight down the mountain to his office. His eyes glinted and he swung his long, sopping hair merrily.

"Mmmm. Ya ever seen a fantail stern like this one?" the captain asked, peering through the telescope again.

"None that big, of course. Nothing like it."

"But the knee 'n' sternpost...."

"Solid, Big Tom."

Big Tom adjusted the focus, and his face fell grim. "Interior, now, Bishop," he said. "What is this with the framing?"

"Oh."

"What is it Bishop?" Big Tom gave the telescope a small push and it swiveled away. His eyes were narrowed and his jovial nature had vanished.

"Oh. Uh, Bark said ya warn't to be bothered in the garden—no questions, total isolation. But it was clear as

Belle's Water that the framing wouldn't hold up. It's to specs, mostly, but I had it reinforced is all."

"With eight-by's, Bishop, stem ta stern? You know how much weight that would be?"

"She's got ta hold up, Big Tom. I don' get it," Bishop said, still speaking cautiously with his newly freed captain. "Five hunnerd feet. Even with the strength of those Douglas firs what the Government sent in, ya know the first storm would kick her in half. Ya going ta sprinkle fairy dust on her maybe—that'll hold her together?"

Big Tom glanced up from his work, smiling now sardonically. "Ya, Bishop. Fairy dust. You leave the fairy dust to me—and I'll sprinkle it on when we're done with tha inner planking."

Bishop wore that determined, narrow-eyed exasperation that persuaded Big Tom to relent. The trade master opened the drawer under the surface of the drafting table and selected a drawing lead. He whittled it in the sharpener four times and sketched light, erasable lines diagonally across the hull in the blueprint.

"Now's as good a time as any," Big Tom muttered, "but this must remain a trade secret—one our lives'll depend on. Look here. Between the early planking and the outer, we'll run steel strapping ta brace the structure—crosswise like this."

"Steel?"

"Ya, steel. Quarter inch thick, five inches wide—the stuff I ordered back with the quarry supplies. We can reinforce a mast with steel, why not a hull?"

"Don't seem right," Bishop huffed. "Steel in tha body of a ship."

"An' since when did I give a pig-poke about what seems right? Now, let's go down to the shipyard. Those eight-by's gotta come out. And then we gots lots more work—lots of fairy dust to sprinkle."

37

The Recruiter

GREGORY paused on the sidewalk under a large oak growing yellow and red as demanded by November. He rechecked the address he had scrawled on the edge of that morning's news sheet, found it to be correct, and opened the gate.

It was an ancient mansion, three stories of stuccoed elegance, blinding white in the clear morning. The wide porch felt cool, shaded as it was by the overhang and dozens of dangling plants. Gregory pulled the porcelain knob set into the wall and heard a muffled chime inside.

When she opened the door, Gregory felt instantly inadequate in his faded blue jump suit. Her delicate brown eyes fluttered as she took him in, her hair was a pleasing disarray of large black ringlets, and she carried about her the irresistible odor of fresh book paper.

"Yes?" she asked.

No. This was not right. "I, uh, I am sorry," Gregory stammered. "I had asked at the, uh, shelter, and they gave me this address. I was expecting a manservant. Name of Billister. I am told he is a little shorter than I. Slender?"

She smiled, and Gregory began to sweat. "My name is Glaco ," she said, pushing the screen door open. "Please follow me." Gregory wondered how she could be so trusting.

The foyer was a mosaic of large, polished clay tiles, and the high ceilings were timbered with dark-stained oak. Down the central hallway, they passed a series of niches scooped out of the wall, each of them bearing a stone statue. Nude women, mostly. Gregory blushed.

Glacoń opened a set of double doors, held up a finger indicating that he should wait, and then disappeared behind them. After a moment's conversation in the room beyond, she opened the doors wide, stepped politely around Gregory, and vanished.

Inside, a young man sat behind a heavy desk, backdropped by sentries of leather bound books. A ledger was open on the desk, and its master was holding a fountain pen aloft as if he were in mid-calculation. The man was dark skinned, head and face shaved clean. He wore a pristine, starched cotton blouse with a burgundy string tie. His forehead pressed up quizzically as he regarded his guest.

"The name is Gregory, with the new Government. I am inquiring after a man name of Billister, a Rafer house boy, in just this summer from Thomas Island."

The dark man set his pen in its holder patiently. "I am Billister. I was born a Rafer, started as house boy, but since I have taken employment here"—he cast up his hands in good-natured dismay at the study packed with books and files—"my duties quickly expanded." He motioned for his surprised guest to take the stuffed chair near the desk.

Gregory began his pitch before he had even settled into the comfortably worn leather. "I am in charge of recruiting for a Government expedition—a project for which you are especially qualified, if my sources are correct. Am I right—that you are fluent in several languages? Rafer? Spanish? French?"

"Mmm. And Latin. And don't forget English."

Gregory laughed, and he felt more at ease. "Aside from that, you also grew up among seafarers on Thomas Island and are well acquainted with Big Tom and his men...."

A shroud of ill mood fell over his host's face.

Billister spoke evenly, almost angrily: "Please get to the point. What is this"—he waved his left hand airily—"expedition?"

"Um. Well. As you know, the new Government has just formally declared itself, although it has in fact been in place and effecting its policy changes for some months. Well, in opposition to the Monitor's paranoia, it has been decided that we must see what has become of the civilizations overseas. It is quite likely that we will encounter people who can instantly advance our technology by decades. Can you imagine—having the medical knowlege amassed by the ancients, for instance? Or mechanical flight?"

Billister rolled his eyes. "Flight? Not possible."

"No. Not legal. Until now. The inventor Cred Faiging has been commissioned to study the science of aircraft."

"And you want to cross the Big Ocean somehow—flap your wings, perhaps...."

"No, in a large ship, which is being built by Big Tom."

"And Big Tom will captain?"

"Um, yes—at his insistence, as you might suspect. And also by default. Who else could captain such a vessel?"

Billister sighed. "There are tempting facets to your invitation, Mr. Gregory. But I must ask you to consider a few details that would make me a bad choice for your expedition: That it was Big Tom who killed my mother when I was an infant. That I grew up a servant in his household, and that this summer he sold me as a common red-legger to pick tobacco."

Gregory wiped his moist chin. "It is an unavoidable matter of circumstance," he said, "that with whatever crew we assemble, there will be a considerable amount of personal animosity to overcome. Whether you join us or not."

Billister stood, squinting in thought, and paced to a large map on one wall. He clasped his hands behind his back and studied the map's details—or, more accurately, the missing details.

It was hand drawn and hand colored, showing a swath of

continent 2,500 miles wide. The brown shading represented the two vertical ribs of mountain range, one east and one west. Green showed the inhabitable lands, and amber depicted the radiation fields. The land mass was flanked by two Big Oceans (perhaps the same body of water—who could know?). To the far north were the woodlands and then the wastelands of ice. To the far south the amber radiation fields, depicted with dubious accuracy, were so dominant as to make exploration there of questionable value.

Beyond the oceans, there were no details on the map, save for a Rafer inscription on the eastern edge. Billister pointed to the markings and translated for Gregory: "Here be monsters."

Gregory frowned. "Surely you have more faith that humans survived in the other lands," he said.

Billister laughed. "I suppose that I do. In a moment of idleness I penned that, but I did so in my native language because I was not sure that the casual observer would realize that it was a joke." He waved a hand vaguely at the map. "The cartographer, by the way, might be of interest to you—H. Fenstemacher Lapp, down on Zealander Street. The best. Any captain what sails outa Chautown harbor would ask for his charts first. A natural instinct, he has."

Billister returned to his desk chair, where he closed his eyes and pinched the bridge of his nose for a long, silent meditation. "Add to my previously stated reservations," Billister finally said, "the fact that my personal circumstances in Chautown are more favorable than ever before in my life. I started work here as house boy, ya, but rapidly fell into better service for the merchant who owns this premises. Oh, the linguistics help a little with any kind of trade, but he's found me invaluable now for my accounting abilities. And best of all—well, you have met his daughter, Glaco . My fiancee."

"No!"

Billister smiled. "Yes. Fiancee."

Gregory stood slowly, sensing defeat.

"And the island?" Billister asked timidly. "How are—"

"Big Tom—powder crazy, worse than ever. Last I saw him he was talking to a stuffed cat in the garden shed."

"Talking to a stuffed cat? As one would with a Cantilou?"

"Ya," Gregory replied, surprised. "He called it that—Cantilou."

"Hmph, brain rot. Big Tom used to ask me to tell him all of the Cantilou legends, the Rafer myths about the lion with the head of a boy. After that he grew maniacal about the garden shed—wouldn't let us in, went there to blow the steam off, we thought. Like the powder, the fabled Cantilou is best left alone."

Gregory turned for the door.

Billister toyed with his fountain pen. "If you have been on Thomas Island with Big Tom," he said, "uh, you might know how things are with one of his wives—Moori?"

Gregory's face sagged even more. "Moori, hmph. Ya, she's fine. I got her off the island, brought her here...."

Billister's eyebrows rose. "To Chautown?"

"Ya. But she won't see me now. Seems to have caught the attention of a wealthy clothier—Lasalle, something like that."

"Ah. Probably Lesoli." Billister cleared his throat sympathetically. "Well, if you are in need of a linguist, I have a recommendation—although he, too, has little love for your shipbuilder Big Tom. He's right there on Thomas Island, a waterfront hermit name of Saple."

Gregory's brow wrinkled at the name. "The beach hermit, Jersey Saple? He knows languages—ones what might be of use on the other side?"

"A mile west of the docks," Billister said, seeming fond of the memory, "little shack set back from the water. Even knows Rafer. Taught 'im myself."

Gregory nodded goodbye to Glaco as unlustfully as he could and turned to descend the porch steps. When he hit the yard, he felt a sharp pang as if the sunlight were a dagger thrust between his eyes. He stopped, hunched his shoulders, and pinched his brow between thumb and fingers. Sweat suddenly drenched his body like a sticky shower. As the pain subsided into a dull throb, he hoped these headaches would be a temporary malady.

38

The Mapmaker

"YES, some call it instinct," said cartographer H. Fenstemacher Lapp in his small, musty office. "But I like to think of it as science and hard work, too. Those details come only from a lifetime of interviewing sailors—and voyaging meself. Separating the beer blather from the fact, best that it can be done."

Lapp actually had no lap at all. He sat in a battered oak chair, his belly welling up in creased segments like stacked watermelons. A black string tie draped down over an oxford cloth shirt that spread wide between button holes to reveal hairy flesh.

"Mr. Lapp," Gregory said politely, still studying a wall hung with framed maps, "doubtless you heard the announcement—that the Monitor is dead, that few of his more restrictive dictates will be enforced by the new Government?"

"Hoo, ya. An' as if to demonstrate the new leniency, most of the farm camp management here is swinging from hemp."

Gregory's jaw muscles bulged rhythmically. "It can not be denied," he said. "But it was a mistake, being that harsh. Some of them should have hung, I unnerstand—with a trial, too—but not so many. But what I have to say to you is that the old restrictions connected to your profession are undone now—about cross-ocean travel, about charting those territories. Whatever is out there is not ta be feared, but explored."

Lapp patted his fingertips together in dainty but sarcastic applause. "An' what means this ta me?"

"What means this is that for weeks I have been wandering the docks and shelter houses, Customs bins and what-have-you. You are the best of the catographers, everyone agrees, and I am needing a cartographer for a new Government mission—to cross the Big Ocean. What I am needing of a cartographer is two things: one, the course-charting with the captain, of course, and to map the new lands as we find them; two, the ancient maps what the Monitor had ordered destroyed—only a man of your science would have dared to keep such things."

Lapp's eyes narrowed, and he scratched at his belly in one of the openings of stressed oxford cloth. "I am an abider of the law," the cartographer said, "an' I'll not have you implying otherwise."

Gregory turned away from the wall to look Lapp in the eyes. "I really don't care about that, and no harm can come to you now for having ancient maps. But I was noticing a mistake you made in an early map, mayhap thirty years old—it was mounted in a home here in Chautown. The map showed remarkable coastline detail around the Gulf of Texaco even along the radiation fields, where no sane captain would take his ship. Your later maps here are more cautiously vague, of course, but I was wondering where ya might have gotten such detail as a younger man unless you had for reference the maps made before the radiation fields were irradiated—ancient times."

Lapp shifted his bulky frame in the chair and pinched his whiskered chin. "I guess ya have me there," he said. He paused long in thought. "Tell me more about this expedition?"

39

The Confrontation

AS the dim lump of Crown Mountain appeared on the horizon all of Gregory's old dread returned like a virulent flu. Big Tom was waiting there for him. Whatever had become of the old slaver's mania, Gregory would know soon enough. He imagined Thomas Harbor scorched by a madman's fury—twenty skimmers bottom up in the shallows, perhaps; the blackened tips of pilings all that remains of the docks; a plume of smoke rising from the ruin of the mainhouse; worst of all, those valuable, sweeping Northland timbers of the new ship splintered about the beach—tomorrow's driftwood. Just how extensive was Big Tom's potential for self-destruction?

It could not be as bad as that. By sea courier, Gregory had received Big Tom's emotionless directive to collect his emissaries in Chautown and to haul out a final skimmer-load of provisions—even the perishables, which meant that the first overseas exploration was about to begin. Somehow through his powder fog and despair, Big Tom must have finished a reasonable ocean craft.

Gregory crossed his sweatered arms over his chest against the early chill. He shared the seventy feet of deck only with the pimply young captain and two grizzled crewmen. Still dozing in the cabins below were Gregory's newly recruited explorers—the mapmaker-navigator named Lapp, an inventive cook who was also familiar with photographic equipment, and four sea hands proven loyal to the new Government.

The youthful skimmer captain had been eager to make this charter run to Thomas Island—he let on that he considered the Blue Islands to be an opening frontier for trade, now that the new Government was extending its influence and protection.

"The Rafers, them on the islands, they're amenable would you think to an influx of mainlanders—the trade good for all of us?" he had asked. Gregory had nodded affirmatively, although he was certain the Rafers had not been consulted. Those negotiations would be among a long list of fine points to iron out over the years.

By the time Gregory's chartered skimmer rounded the southwest corner of the island, the morning mist had burned off. This inner crescent of Thomas Island shimmered in the early light, docile and intact, perfect as a fresh pastry. And there on the west side of the harbor lolled a wooden behemoth dubbed the Nina. Her broad siding cut such a swath in the water that Gregory's eye muscles contorted, doubting that their focus could be proper. She was military neat, too: rigging taut, spotless, sails precisely folded, sheets coiled.

Big Tom, Gregory told himself, is alive and well and in control.

"Gregory, I want ta tell ya a story on myself, boy. An' I want ya to consider it the next time ya decide to poke me in the arse like ya did when ya took Moori to the mainland."

Big Tom had perched himself regally on a stool in his open-air office, commanding the room. His beard bobbed hyperly as he spoke, and Gregory found himself thinking: Maybe Bishop is telling the truth. Maybe Big Tom did quit the powder once his final-last wife had abandoned him. As soused as Big Tom might get on land, Bishop insisted, he never failed to hang straight when it came to captaining a ship. And his massive new skimmer, the Government-commissioned Nina, was now fully rigged.

Bishop had helped himself to Big Tom's stuffed chair and Bark towered behind him sullenly. Two of the Government toughs, the quiet one named Widekilter and the baudy one named Guinness, carried ugly pistols in unsnapped hip holsters. Pec-Pec's eyes danced around the room merrily, as if the proceedings were no more explosive than a picnic's.

Attention duly garnered, Big Tom began his story: "What ey Bark? A score of years ago, me and Bark comes up with a near mutiny as we was picking between the radiation fields looking for a particular ganja farm." Bark gave an obedient nod, and Gregory wondered if this was the same dubious mutiny story he had heard a dozen versions of in Sanders's pub.

"Once we found the farm," Big Tom said, "the crew dropped the sheets and swore we were pickin' up nay bales until I agreed to split the proceeds evenly among all—ta compensate for the dancy-dance around the radiation. Hmph.

"Well I say, now, that a man ain't bound by promise made under extortion like that. Once we entered the Out Islands up these parts, Bark and I decided we could handle the skimmer ourselves and thought to teach the crew a lesson. We put 'em off on that bare rock called Dead Man's Chest. Ya know? A hunk of harddick twenty miles from nothing.

"Told 'em we might be back in a few days—ta take the survivors home. And we left 'em plenty to drink. A case of rum. Hah. Stranded for days, and nothing but alcohol.

"What would you choose, Gregory? One of four men, ya don't know when rescue will come, and the only drink to be had will dehydrate you quicker than drinking nothing at all. What would you choose? Better to drink—and die quickly but stoned? Or better to thirst and wait, trust in the rescue? What do you think we found when we returned, Gregory?"

Gregory was in no mood for guessing. His forehead felt

tight, as if a migraine might be returning. "I...don't...know," he said.

"You're right!" Big Tom cried, laughing. "No one knows. These twenty years, Bark an' I haven't bothered to go back yet!" The reaction in the room ranged from Bishop's dutiful chuckle to Pec-Pec's grim silence.

Gregory threw his hands open, pleading innocence. "I can assure you, Big Tom, as a representative of the new Government, that I have no intention of letting personal feelings interfere with our voyage," he said.

Big Tom sneered. He stood and marched to his drafting table, where he pulled open a drawer and extracted a small bundle of letters. His beard of gray speckles quivered. "These," he said, shaking the stack of papers at Gregory, "are letters from Moori. Says she wants to come back when things settle down, that she regrets her mistake with the half-wit—thass what she calls you, Gregory. The night in the shed with her—know what she thought of it, ey? She thinks it was yer first time, Gregory. Mmmm? First time? Heheee! What are you—thirty-five?"

"Well there's a man name of Lesoli...." Gregory desperately wanted to blurt the details of Moori's new lover, but he instantly regretted that his sheet could be yanked so easily.

Big Tom threw the letters onto the drafting table, eyes cold. "Who...is...Lesoli?"

The tension in the room began to harden like concrete. Silent seconds ticked by. "Ah, Big Tom, I was changing us from a painful subject," Gregory finally said. He lifted his leather case from the floor, unknotted the center tie, and drew out several sheets of yellowed, delicate paper. "Um, Lesoli is a merchant in Chautown, a trader of ancient items gleaned from the salvagers. Some he sells to the science waggos—Cred Faiging and the like. Piddling knacks he sells out of a retail shop in Chautown. But these"—Gregory tapped his finger theatrically on the worn papers—"I had to harangue for, threaten for. They's maps. Ancient maps, not just of the north continent, but over the Big Ocean, too. It's what we need, Big Tom—to find what's left of what once was."

"An' ain't no more," Bishop threw in sarcastically.

All of the ill tension drained from Big Tom's face, and his eyebrows spread with childlike wonder.

"Maps!" the aging mariner shouted. "No! They're all destroyed—orders of the Monitor, hunnerds of years. Can't be real maps."

"Real maps," Gregory answered. The lie he had told about Lesoli prevented him from explaining their real source, however. He would have to warn the cartographer Lapp about the story.

Big Tom took the delicate papers reverently, cradling them as carefully as one would a baby, and laid them one by one onto his drawing table. "Ooohh," he said lustfully, "they got to be real. Lookit the paper." He pointed. "England! Pig...poke. England. It's where Eng-glish comes from, ya know?"

The others were standing now around the table, in awe of the impossible documents, but Big Tom was already a step beyond. The former slaver turned to Gregory again, face empty of animosity: "This ain't a wild poke into the unknown, then—an' you knew it, dint ya?"

Gregory nodded modestly.

Big Tom stared up at the ceiling, calculating new possibilities. "An' ya say ya brought a cartographer? Ah! I knew the mission would sail, but..." His face beamed. "Maps!"

40

At Sea

THE same tug that old Captain Bull had once flogged into slaving duty was in port—brought this time by the new Government toughs. So they cabled it up, ready to tow the Nina out of Thomas Harbor once preparations were done. The Nina's maneuverability was yet untested, so it was better to have a graceless exit than a founder in the shallows.

Gregory observed from the aft deck, by the hatch to the officers' quarters, dazed as he watched the deck and rigging aswarm with sailors. At starboard, the blind chronicler Jersey Saple teetered on the gangplank with his sun reader balanced on his right shoulder. Little Tom stood on the docks, arms akimbo—he would stay behind, watch after the old man's interests. The younger's skin still was quite dark, but at least he did not mind so much showing himself in public anymore.

Gregory was still awed by the Nina's size. Five hunnerd feet of wooden craft went against all human instincts—by proportion, he mused, the ship must have all of the stability of a child's boat, one made of folded paper. Big Tom had explained the science of it to him patiently—for it was Gregory that had to certify that the captain had met his obligations to the new Government. But it was hard to trust that mere steel banding looped around the hull would keep this monstrosity together.

Center deck, Big Tom was in a full-lung shouting match with the decksman Verrengia, an independent shrimper by trade—not so submissive as the old merchant's regular sheet winders.

Gregory could hear only bits of the conversation, but it appeared the deck salt was balking at an order to clear a last few sacks of mangoes out of the way and into the holds. Big Tom had angrily thrown his walking stick aside, and through the intermittent cracks of rising sail Gregory heard him bellow the foulest of possible obscenities. But just when Gregory thought the scene would get violent, the old seaman's shoulders sagged sadly inside his crisp white blouse. From a distance, Big Tom appeared to have surrendered the argument amicably, and he threw a fat arm around back of Verrengia's neck.

The two stood awkwardly locked centerdeck as the captain drew from his thigh pocket a fat bone flute and blew four long and mournful notes. The scurrying sailors halted, and especially grim were those who had long crewed on Big Tom's skimmers.

"Men!" Big Tom shouted, and the word disappeared into the morning gusts now clean of other human sound. "We go asail today under the flag of the new Government and under the command of Big Tom. An' them what know me best know how an argument with the commander will be ended."

With one arm still crooked around Verrengia's neck, Big Tom gave the bone flute a shake. The shaft clattered to the deck, leaving a narrow steel blade in the captain's hand. With a quick lunge, Big Tom thrust the steel through the sailor's neck and severed the top of his spinal cord. Verrengia's head nodded, and the body fell away, leaving a splatter of crimson across Big Tom's fresh blouse. Big Tom was casually wiping the blade on his ruined blouse when Gregory marched up.

"You pushed that boy to an argument," Gregory accused.

Big Tom patiently reassembled the bone flute and jammed it into his thigh pocket. "Ya. Hmph. Ya. But he warn't a regular, y'unnerstand. I juss brought 'im on for something like this—will keep the rest of 'em scared for their dicks most of the voyage."

Gregory bit the edge of his tongue until he tasted blood. He recalled Billister, pen poised behind a large desk in Chautown, politely declining to join the expedition. Gregory wished it had been that simple for himself. He about-faced, walked as calmly as he could to the officers' hatch, and went below.

Pec-Pec sat alone at the grand table in the center cabin, poking delicately at a dozen oddly shaped pieces of ebony the size of horse teeth. The magic man's eyes flitted up at the intruder and down again.

"Gregory...."

There came no reply. Pec-Pec's guest paced about the small room fitfully, his face turning redder and redder.

"Gregory, have you ever played chess like this?" He nudged another shard of ebony a few inches across the polished top of the grandtable. "Chess, I mean, without a chess board? Hmm?"

Gregory sputtered his lips impatiently. "Ho, it's not so hard I imagine if you're the only player. Who needs a board? Who needs pieces what look like chessmen? Who needs rules?"

Pec-Pec's expression hardened into exasperation. The dark man removed a piece from the grand table and tucked it between the strands of hair at the tip of one of his braids. Quietly and methodically he played through his game, removing every piece the same way. Then he stood.

"You can't leave," Gregory said. "The man—Big Tom, I'm sayin'—is gullybonkers. We'll not have any crew left by mid-ocean."

Pec-Pec's nostrils flared. He shrugged. "I can advise. I can not do for you or your Government. I must go."

"But you killed the Monitor!" Gregory said. "How

could this be so much more than that—to escort the first expedition overseas?"

Pec-Pec's eyelids closed and seemed to quiver. "The dragon fish and I—we killed the Monitor, ya. An' that was much much too much. Not again will I slay monsters for the Government of the Fungus People." He placed a long booted foot on the ladder up to the main deck.

"Final advice then, Pec-Pec?"

Slowly, the magic man pointed a bony finger toward the empty grand table. "Ya," he said. "Learn it quickly—how to play chess without a chess board."

The Nina had been towed mid-harbor by the time Pec-Pec arrived on deck. He strode to the starboard rail, his black silks snapping in the wind. Then he turned a quick back flip and disappeared into the brine below. There was a great hissing and thrumbling under the water, and a black figure in the shape of a giant manta ray darted off toward Pec-Pec's anchored craft, the odd skimmer with the deck shaped like half a barrel. All of this was witnessed by no one.

Outside the captain's quarters, Gregory twisted his toe against the planking. The ship was groaning with the unnatural stresses of being towed out to sea, and Gregory strained to make out the voices inside—Big Tom and someone. Courtesy had to be suspended, however, in the face of the deliberate murder of a crewman. The new Government's mission to Europe was embarking under untenable circumstances, in Gregory's judgment, and the voyage had to be stopped to regroup. He would have to interrupt Big Tom.

He lifted a fist to rap the door, hesitated, and just threw the oak panel open. In such an act of bravado, one is not surprised to catch lovers embracing, perhaps, or an occupant attending to personal hygiene. But never could Gregory have been prepared for the shock he felt now, the horror that clenched its sickening tendrils around his gut: He had interrupted a conversation between Big Tom and a vile-looking cat-boy, the Cantilou, a living, pulsing version of the sadly stuffed creature he had seen in the garden shed on Thomas Island.

Big Tom jutted his beard toward the door. "Ah," he drawled casually, "wang it shut, would ya?"

Gregory reluctantly obeyed, then stepped into the room with the anguished feeling that he had blundered into another man's nightmare. Big Tom stood near a massive desk gleaming of polish. The Cantilou lay on the captain's bunk, forward paws flat against the blanket and rear legs relaxed into two muscular discs on either side of its buttocks.

Gregory spoke to Big Tom: "In the shed, it was an old stuffed cat what you had, no?"

Although its lips did not move, Gregory heard the voice of the Cantilou, and clearly Big Tom did as well. "You see what I wish you to see," the beast told him, "in the same way that you are hearing the words that I wish you to hear."

Big Tom was looking puzzled, and the aging captain huffed his fat frame down into the desk chair. "Ho up here," he said.

"Ho up your own," the Cantilou's voice replied gruffly, although the boy's face on the feline body still showed no emotion. Its wide black eyes stared indiscriminately. "You, Big Tom, with an ego larger even than yer belly, wishes to be the first captain across the Big Ocean. An' you, Greggie, the blind soldier of this new Government—well, for both a ya, this is a day for a change of expectations."

Big Tom stroked one set of fingers through his beard and turned his puzzled eyes on Gregory. It began to dawn on Gregory that the rotund captain was nearly as baffled as he.

The cabin had grown unnaturally warm, and Gregory was aware now of a gut-turning odor, as if the stench of the darkening blood splashed across Big Tom's blouse were amplified forty times.

They heard the Cantilou sigh, and the beast delicately crossed its paws. "Hoo, well," it said, "wouldn't ya think it time to go up on deck?"

It was then that Gregory noticed the muffled shouts

and foot-poundings coming from above, signs of a crew in panic. The two men stood simultaneously and bolted out the door, down the corridor, through the center cabin to the hatch ladder. There they had to wait as six of the new Government's toughs clamored down. Gregory caught Widekilter's elbow—Gregory liked him best—and said, "What is it?"

Widekilter slapped the butt of his holstered pistol. "Prolly we'll be needin' something bigger. Going down to tear into the lockers."

The Cantilou, alone in Big Tom's cabin, uncrossed its forepaws and sighed again: "Hoo." Heard by no one.

Just minutes before, the crew had cast off the tow line and the tug that had pulled them to open water was circling its thrumping and labored way back toward Thomas Harbor while a deckhand astern reeled in the cable. Out of the harbor's protection, the spring sea had come to life, darkened, glistening, like a lolling plain of liquid obsidian. The Nina was now at half-sail, as she was expected to be until they cleared the Out Islands.

But it was the horizon that had inspired the howls and panic. Evenly spaced, in all directions of open sea, were nine dark skimmers of unmistakable design: the sleek new vessels that the Rafers had somehow come to possess.

Nine. Who'd a thought the savages could have built so many in just a few seasons? Or crewed them competently?

Bark was apoplectic up on the pilot's deck, shouting his orders. Sailors scrambled like monkeys through the rigging to set the Nina full sail, with the thought of ramming past the Rafers if they intended any harm. Two decksmen were setting the gunpowder and shot in each of the ship's six cannons—three starboard and three backboard.

Big Tom turned to Gregory and grumbled, "Ho, it's a pig's arse of a morning," then limped off toward his first mate.

"I've headed 'er due east," Bark shouted as his captain approached. "Hang 'er like so an' pray ta god we juss have to meet one Rafer skimmer head-on. Two more, most, might catch us broadside. But it'd take six er more of those little things ta do us much harm."

The Rafer skimmers were still quite distant, and Big Tom had not had a chance to draw out a telescope from the servator on the backboard rail. "Those back six, then, can we outrun them?" he asked.

Bark squinted into the unfamiliar rigging of the new ship and glanced astern. He shrugged—who could really know? "We get full sail boogerin' fast, I'd say ya," he replied.

Big Tom dug the fingers of his right hand into his beard. He glanced back at the diminishing Thomas Island, the spits of land forming the harbor like a protective embrace. The wind pushed his hair up into a demented, graying halo. "Would not it be better to come about? Take 'er back in?"

"Time we come full 'round, I gully they'd be on us," Bark hollered impatiently—he had considered all of the options, of course.

"I 'spect they'd go after the sails with fire arrows—put us to a stop," the captain said. "Have the hands haul up buckets of water in case."

Bark's black eyes shifted away. "Ya, Big Tom, soon's we're full sail."

"And have all starboard cannon draw bead on that one skimmer," Big Tom ordered, wagging a finger eastward.

Gregory found Jersey Saple clinging unsteadily to his sun reader as the deck surged and then fell away with increasing urgency. A portfolio of dot scriptings fell from its storage slot on the apparatus, and the pin-pricked papers scattered on the decking. "I'd meant to lash the reader down, but we've made such a rough start," the scribe told Gregory, his sightless eyes rolling wildly. "Help me, hey, or it'll be dashed ta kindling."

Gregory dragged the sun reader to the wall below the pilot's deck and tied it securely. He placed Saple's hand on a rail post. "Hold 'er there till we're out of this."

"What's all the poking fuss?" Saple asked.

"Oh, Rafer skimmers. All over—gawd. They's closing in,

but I'm not sure thass such a danger," Gregory said. "You know a crew like this, what been hauling red-leggers up until now. Sets 'em on edge."

"Ya, sets 'em on edge," Saple repeated, as if trying to reassure himself.

The Nina plunged ahead ever more forcefully as each square of canvas pulled taut and billowed. Her bow pounded through the gentle waves effortlessly, dolphinlike. But still the Rafer outriggers sliced closer. They were visible now in precise detail: long and elegant shafts lilting over the emerald water. Intricately carved aplustres bobbed from their sterns like the tailfeathers of demon swans.

The one Rafer skimmer straight ahead had turned east as well, and was matching the Nina's speed and direction closely enough to come alongside. Bark ordered the helmsman to veer a few degrees south to evade, but the smaller skimmer did the same easily, and it became clear that such maneuvering would slow the expeditioners fatally.

Finally, a flower of black smoke burst silently over the near skimmer, and seconds later the ominous sound—the crack of gunpowder—reached the Nina. Then a cabled lance crashed into the Nina's starboard side.

Big Tom sprinted forward and leaned over the rail to look. It was a multipronged harpoon. The point had burst through the hull just below the forward cannon, and four anterior barbs had sunk themselves securely into the wood. The harpoon's thick hemp cable sagged into the sea in the direction of the Rafer skimmer.

The fat captain spat, turned back, and grabbed a passing sheetsman by the sleeve. "Where's yer blade, Fenton?" he demanded, and the frightened seaman produced a ten-incher from his thigh strap. "Over!" Big Tom demanded. "Whack the line, son."

Big Tom grabbed the sailor by the collar and slung him overboard, dangling him carefully until his toes touched the shaft of the harpoon. Stitches along the shoulders of the young man's shirt began to burst—phitt, phitt, phitt—until he put his full weight on the protruding Rafer missile.

"Slash it, boy!" Big Tom howled. "Cut the poker now!"

Two more blooms of smoke appeared over the Rafer attack vessel. Two more explosions. And two more many-barbed missiles struck the Nina—one biting into the bow and the other slamming the young sailor Fenton square in the chest. The barbed tip exploded through the wood wall and forced a small gusher of blood and flesh between Big Tom's legs. Pinned to the ship's hull, Fenton's body went limp, and Big Tom slowly released his collar.

The black fin of a feeder beast sliced through the rush of water several feet below the dead sailor. Teased by the torrent of human blood.

At 100 yards, the dark sailors aboard the Rafer skimmer were easily visible now, teams of two cranking at either side of large cable spools, others somersaulting and spinning about the curved decking like crazed crickets.

When the three dripping hemplines rose from the water and grew taut, Big Tom's belly tightened too. Over each hempline he witnessed a whirling blur of motion, and instantly three Rafers were clinging to the starboard rail of the Nina—two men, one woman, all slender and naked but for the weapons strapped to their limbs and torsos. Oddly, through his horror, Big Tom found himself admiring the arrangement of blades and tosser disks about their bodies—how they formed a kind of patchwork armor.

An explosion on deck shattered the momentary standoff. A half-moon-shaped piece of the starboard rail vanished into splinters, and the Rafer who had perched there fell overboard in a shower of red mist. Fel Guinness stood at the aft hatch, both barrels of his snubgun smoking. The remaining Rafers whirled their arms, and tosser disks caught Guinness in the throat and forehead. He gurgled and keeled over.

"No!" screamed Gregory, springing to the starboard side. Teasing the edges of his memory were images of a nurturing people who had pulled him from the sinking Lucia. "We don't know what the Rafers want!"

The tense silence lasted barely two seconds before three more Rafers—a total of five now—appeared on the rail as if by magic. As the decksmen backed away, two Rafers set about dismantling the cannons.

"We knows wat they want," growled Bark from the pilot's deck. "They wants our willies dangling from their necks!"

The towering first mate drew his thigh blade. Before he could throw, a disk splashed into his hand.

From below, Gregory saw three fingertips thump to the deck at Bark's feet, and his hope of averting a bloodbath evaporated. The first mate's throaty howl seemed to be the starting gun that set in motion a surreal circus of terror.

Hemp lines from two more Rafer skimmers slammed into the Nina, and the lithe little warriors whirled aboard by the dozens. The large ship's timbers were groaning now from the unnatural pull of the cables. The Rafers wheeled invisibly about the new decking and swarmed through the rigging above. All around Gregory, the new Government's panicking seamen were collapsing, felled by an enemy they could barely see. A few more banger blasts were fired, but those weapons quickly clattered to the deck.

Gregory thought to bolt into a Rafer spin himself, but he knew such a defense would be a laughable effort. Besides, where could he dart off to—where was there to hide? He longed for open land, or the protection of a forest. If he was to die amid this flailing carnage, well, he must die. He was trapped.

Gregory straightened his spine and walked soberly back to Jersey Saple, who was cowering in the shadow of his beloved sun reader. When he touched the old man's shoulder, the journalist squealed.

"It's juss me, Jersey," Gregory said, pulling him to a stand.

Saple's sightless eyes darted about maniacally. He shuddered. "It sounds like…a slaughter."

"But you know Rafer. Say something to them." Gregory squeezed his arm. "You know the pig-pokin' tongue. Say something! Stop it!"

Saple seemed to collect himself. He thrust both thumbs into the front of his trousers and lifted his scraggly chin to sing. His words were incomprehensible to Gregory, but they were cool and high-pitched, slicing easily through the clatter of battle and the blood-splashed sails. Gregory had heard the Rafer tongue many times, but never had it sounded like this.

"It's a nursery rhyme, taught ta me by Billister," the journalist said when he was finished. "About Big Bang Day—the Fungus People bringing destruction upon themselves."

"Great selection."

"It's the only song I know. In Rafer."

"Sing it again," Gregory demanded. "Look, they're listening."

"Hmmph. Ya. So I see," he replied sarcastically. But he sang again anyway.

The whirling dark soldiers did slowly come to a stop—some agrip in the high rigging, others busy hauling lifeless bodies up from below decks. They gawked at the spectacle of an old Fungus Person singing a song of their children. Gregory's vision began to tear up as he gazed in shock around the deck, for clearly the battle was already over. There were few lives left to save. The new Government's expedition was a disaster, although it had scarcely begun.

The Rafers had collapsed all of the Nina's sails to reduce her speed, but oddly they had left all of the rigging intact and did not seem intent on scuttling the massive vessel. Fore and aft, Gregory heard the metallic whump-and-rattle of the anchors being released, and soon all nine of the Rafer skimmers were lashed alongside.

Saple stopped singing when there came a commotion from the aft hatch. Gregory, not daring to move, watched as a trio of Rafers hauled Big Tom up out of the darkness. He was growling nonsensically and drooling into his beard, hands tied behind him and feet bound as well.

The Cantilou climbed up the hatch ladder, squinting in the bright light, and stepped haughtily over the writhing captain. The feline's boy-face fixed immediately on Gregory and Saple, and he sauntered across the deck, tail flipping.

The Rafers were gaping at the fabled beast with awe and respect.

"Oh, hell, Gregory," came the Cantilou's voice, although the dainty lips never moved, "they all know me—or my ancestors anyway—through their legends."

"Who...who is that?" stammered Saple. He was hearing the voice too.

"A booger the likes of which you wouldn't believe," Gregory mumbled to him. "I think it's a beast what's had its claws sunk into Big Tom's mind for some time."

"And you would be Jersey Saple," came the Cantilou's keening voice again. "Is it true that you know languages? Several of them, including Rafer?"

The old man tugged at the canvas of his sun reader. "Ya," he said uncomfortably. "That is so."

"Then you will be of much use to me. And you, Gregory—you as well. You will be put to good work. It was not coincidence that you escaped the blades and disks during the Rafer attack. But for the moment, you will excuse me while I attend to a detail of cleanup before we embark."

"Cantilou," Gregory said after him sternly. The cat-boy craned its supple neck around to look at him. "Did they all have to die?" Gregory asked.

The Cantilou's eyes glowed red for a moment, and the telepathic reply came, measured and menacing: "They did not all die, Gregory, but that can be corrected."

The cat-boy swaggered toward the stern. When Gregory turned to ask, "What possible use..."—there she was. More muscled that he remembered. Handsomely strapped, arm and leg, in the deadly brass disks she had once had little use for—a few of them missing, flung in battle.

Tym. So she had ordered that he be spared. It would not be that difficult—do not whack the yellow-haired man with the Rafer tattoo.

She broke into the wide smile that had been haunting him for months. An animal lust welled up in him that he knew to be the dangerous, unquestioning devotion of the half-wit that he no longer was. She approached, placed a gentle fingertip on his quivering lip, and then let it slide down to toy with his neck and the tattoo work that had been carefully needled into his skin by one of her tribesmen.

"Gragi," she said.

She pulled at his arm and led him to the aft hatch, stepping carefully around the snarling captain hamstrung there.

Gregory stepped onto the hatch ladder and turned, shock-numb, still feeling knee-deep in the fresh slaughter, the crumpled bodies of Bark, Widekilter, Guinness, Bishop and—oh, gawd—poor H. Fenstemacher Lapp. The Rafers were already swabbing the deck to sparkling again. Bodies were being hefted overboard, Rafer and Fungus Person alike, to the delight of a growing pool of feeder beasts.

Big Tom, tied there amid the thickening dashes of blood, was bug-eyed with red fury as he struggled against the leather bindings. Gregory knew he would not see the old slaver again.

"If it makes you feel any better, Big Tom...Moori, she warn't coming back. Shacked up with some clothier in Chautown—underwear salesman, or some such." Gregory continued down the hatch ladder, waiting for his eyes to adjust to the darkness, waiting for his soul to adjust to the sickening mixture of horror and joy, and wondering which cabin they would use.

When the Nina got underway again, she was set at half sail, with a new crew. At the stern, a Rafer crewman fastened a twenty-five-yard hempline to the rail and its other end he wound around Big Tom's ankles.

"I'd de-ball ya, ugly li'l red-legger, if I was juss to get a pinkie free," Big Tom told the uncomprehending sailor.

The Cantilou and Jersey Saple had heard enough of the insults and now managed to ignore them. "Pec-Pec?" asked the Cantilou. His tail switched left and right. "Well, no, Mr. Saple. On the one hand, you could say he was quite aware of what would happen—or should happen. Near omniscience such as his does have its drawbacks. But on the other hand, it could not be said that he arranged any of this—the loss of the

Government ship. No. You see, he's already quite mortified at the degree of involvement he's had with the matters of Fungus People. He finds very little pleasure now in helping or hindering them. As you know, he's done both...."

Saple held a large pad of paper in one hand and pecked notes onto it with a sharp stylus. "Ah. So. Then perhaps you could explain...uh, that splash overboard juss now—would that have been Big Tom?"

"Quite right."

"Ah." There was a short pause in which the blind writer tried to imagine a portly form bobbing through the waves. "Looking to the voyage ahead, then, perhaps you could explain why a few dozen Rafers and their little escort ships would care to sail to Europe."

Saple heard a soft laugh. "Oh, we will simply be the new emissaries. The Rafers will be the ones to find what's left of the old civilizations across the Big Ocean. But Europe? If there's time, if there's little enough radiation. But I thought we would begin with what you call 'the country of Africa.'"

"Ah. I am told now that our maps show it to be quite a large continent."

"A gigantic one. And we should start in the north, I think." Saple heard the cat-boy's tail whapping the deck. "Wouldn't it be nice to stop and see the Sphinx?"

Epilogue

Sunreader dotscript
Portfolio 23
Page 13
Jersey Saple

ON we sail into gawd knows what.

This matter of the Cantilou is a knot of bollworms. Being a Fungus Person, as the Rafers call men of my kind, I suppose that I am not meant to gully this to the bottom. But it dawns on me now that the Rafers are not the first civilization to have hybrid human-cats slinking a crooked path through their histories. They were known even to those people what the ancients called ancient.

But the Rafers take ownership of the Cantilou, for better or for worse. They do not seem to regard him as the most joyous of beasts to have in their midst—most written references in the Rafer histories portray him, at best, as a sort of troublesome satyr. At worst, a horror. But still they hailed his appearance at their sea attack with a sort of morbid glee.

Tym, the new mate of Gregory, offered an oblique explanation. She described for me the sea roiling with the fins of feeder beasts, where once there had been the wriggling body of Big Tom. "They may be feeder beasts," she said in the Rafer tongue, "but at this moment they do our work.

Fear only the beast that has come for you—the one that smells your blood."

We are a week at sail now, and the Rafer crew is as comfortable with the Nina as a wine sluggard is with his bed of old blankets. The feeder beasts have fallen away. All crew are anxious for sight of new land.

I saw a whale today—not by actual sight, as you would know, but by the sensory gift that I am blessed with. It came alongside the Nina, a breathing behemoth a quarter the length of the ship itself. And then came another and another crashing to the surface, an entire herd snorting and lolling in the waves. They are virtually unknown in the waters of the Out Islands, more storied than encountered.

Today it seemed that my blindsight developed to a new level. Or perhaps there is just more now to be seen than ever before. For I sensed in a rush all of the new waters around us quaking with life, a vibrance unknown to the seas of Merqua. And I came to the belief, haltingly, that we had entered a new land and a life system distinct from our own.

There is a continent beyond. I know this. I can feel it as surely as I feel the stylus between my old fingers. Centuries back, it was seared and blistered and scarred in the terrible war as we thought it must have been, and now it has healed over in ways strange to all of us.

Herewith I close out a tale scripted in a dot writing that mayhap no man will ever read. With my next clean parchment I begin Portfolio 24. I will take it up on a new land, at the beginning of a new history.

I and all aboard are in reasonable physical health. The Cantilou has occupied the captain's quarters, which reeks these days of the acrid odor of manure. The Rafer food is foreign but palatable—heavy with spicy vegetables and meats stewed in preserving brine.

A final note: It is for Gregory's health of mind that I fear most. What time he does not spend below decks with his beloved Tym he passes clinging to the battle-splintered section of the starboard rail. He is drawn to the gray-green waters by visions to which no others are privileged, sighted or otherwise. He stares blankly into the waves, nodding and chuckling to himself over and over a madman's punchline:

"Here be monsters."

About the Author

JEFF BREDENBERG spent the first two decades of his publishing career working for newspapers, primarily writing and editing in Chicago, Denver, St. Louis, and four other cities. He published three science fiction novels—*The Dream Compass*, *The Dream Vessel*, and *The Man in the Moon Must Die*—plus several short stories in magazines and anthologies.

In his "day job," Bredenberg was an independent writer and editor specializing in how-to and health topics. He wrote, edited, or contributed to more than twenty-five books. He was a frequent contributor to home-oriented magazines, as well. Bredenberg made frequent media appearances, including spots on *The Late Show With David Letterman*, *The Rachael Ray Show*, and the *CBS Early Show*. Bredenberg lived in the suburbs of Philadelphia with his wife and two sons.

Jeff Bredenberg died on March 2, 2010, of glioblastoma, a brain tumor. He was fifty-six. Learn more about Jeff at jeffbredenberg.com and howtocheatbooks.com.

www.ingramcontent.com/pod-product-compliance
Lightning Source LLC
LaVergne TN
LVHW091052080826
845145LV00002B/720
* 9 7 8 1 4 9 7 6 3 7 2 6 9 *